To
And

CW00421634

Things They'll Never See

Keep rockin'

MARTIN TRACEY

Martin

For Brian Upton
and
Gary Roberts.
Keep a few of those beers on ice
lads until we meet again…

Also by Martin Tracey

BENEATH THE FLOODLIGHTS
MIND GUERRILLA

ACKNOWLEDGEMENTS

Thanks once again to Ares Jun for another top-quality cover.
Thanks as always to my family for allowing me the space to keep playing with words.
Thanks to my social media family and author networks.
Your support is invaluable.
And of course…
Dear reader, I thank you for engaging with my work.
Without a reader, there is no story to tell.

PROLOGUE

Alannah looked at herself in the mirror. It was a familiar ritual which she executed every morning before the uphill task of attempting to face the day. As always she failed to notice her natural and stunning beauty. Today, more than any other day, she had a particularly dreadful feeling deep within her being. She didn't know why? Depression doesn't always come with a rationale, but she felt as though today could well be one of her *bad* days.

Alannah felt guilty about her bouts of depression and she hated how much they yanked at the heartstrings of her fiancé Jake. Jake was the man who always tried to offer her words of assurance, the man who always wiped away her tears and the man who dutifully put in so much effort to try and lift her spirits. Jake was the only constant and devoted shining light in an otherwise dark and depressive world fashioned by the ghosts and shadows that she witnessed in her mind's eye.

Alannah hated the way that her depression took hold of her, but she was helpless to the waves of darkness that engulfed her. She hated the way it seemed to take her prisoner on the days where she felt unable to even venture outdoors. Even her understanding of the irony of it all did little to motivate Alannah, knowing that so many people on the outside envied the life that she had. She was successful in her own right, she had the man she wanted and she was financially secure for as long as she needed to be.

But Alannah Ashe had a secret. A secret that shamed her and tortured her. She had no need to feel shame but that's how it festers in the minds of victims. Nothing has to be their fault for them to feel the shame. It was a secret that cruelly compromised the otherwise envious life that she had. A life that should be so fulfilled and happy but which her hidden demons never allowed her to properly enjoy.

She moved from the mirror and walked over to the window. As she looked out onto the street she could see that there was a fierce frost on the ground outside and she hoped that Jake would be safe whilst driving on the icy roads. He was due home today following a trip to the USA for some much-needed self-promotion. He had been worried about leaving her for the six-day trip, but she had assured him that she would be fine. After all, her depression was currently assessed by the medical experts to be at a fairly reasonable state in comparison to some of her episodes, with no immediate danger of any suicidal tendencies.

Alannah heard the quiet thud of the day's mail drop through the letterbox and then looked downwards to witness the postman swagger away from the house with his fluorescent mailbag draped over his shoulder. Alannah enjoyed receiving mail. It pleased her to see her name on the envelope. Glad that someone had taken the time to write to her, even when the correspondence only turned out to be a piece of junk mail. Little things like this could mean the world to Alannah and momentarily lift her mood, yet other relatively trivial matters could leave her upset and anxious for days at a time.

Alannah ventured downstairs, collected the mail and took it with her to the kitchen area so that she could read it while the kettle boiled. Like most natives of England, Alannah was unable to face the day without having a cup of tea first - nothing to do with depression; it was purely an English thing. Alannah was also required to take anti-depressants at the start of the day. She was allowed to administer her drugs herself these days.

Alannah placed the letters on the table and filled the chrome kettle with water. She then replaced the kettle and flicked the electric switch in order to heat the liquid content.

She counted a number of letters; six in total, three for her and three for Jake. She placed Jake's in a neat pile so that he could open them later on his return. She opened her first letter, which was inviting her to subscribe to a mail-order catalogue in return for a twenty-five percent discount off her first order. She smiled at the irony. Where did these companies get their information from? Alannah Ashe was a top fashion model and hardly ever needed to spend a penny on clothing as top designers fell over themselves to donate their work to her, thrilled at the prospect of Alannah Ashe wearing their designs. Alannah had never posed for any sort of nude modelling, even though she possessed a body to die for, preferring instead to concentrate purely and strictly on modelling fashion products. It was strange, but when she was on the catwalk her depression became a stranger as she escaped into the world where people loved and adored her. Jake had told her that when he takes to the stage to play his music, any issues in his mind would leave him as he was king when on that stage and could not be challenged by anyone or anything. She equated her feeling on the catwalk as a similar experience, but spending 24/7 on the catwalk was sadly not practical to keep the black dog from scratching at the door.

The writing on the second envelope was typed, again giving the indication that it was from a company making contact in the hope of selling something. When Alannah pulled out the letter she could see that it was actually from the administrative department of the private clinic that she was registered with, informing her how they regretfully needed to reschedule her appointment with her psychiatrist. She would now need to visit a week later at 11.15 am. *No sweat*, she thought.

The writing on the third envelope was written by hand. This excited Alannah, as this was her favourite type of letter knowing that it was from someone who had taken the time to physically write to her. If Jake was working away, like the last six days, he would often write to her knowing how much it pleased her regardless of how many phone call conversations that they had also indulged in. When Jake had been wooing Alannah at the beginning of their relationship she had loved receiving his love letters of flowery and romantic content. But Alannah recognised that this handwriting didn't belong to Jake.

It could be a letter from a fan, she guessed, who had been dedicated enough to track her down and send it direct to her home address in St John's Wood, by-passing the PO Box number of her Fan Club. It wouldn't be the first time. She was one of the few celebrities who would always try and personally reply to fan mail.

There was only one way to find out.

Alannah's heart sank as she digested the contents of the letter.

This can't be true. This can't be real.

The timing of the kettle automatically switching off to indicate the water had boiled seemed to underline the stark reality of the words before her.

She began to shake profoundly and quickly became petrified as the writing unveiled something that surpassed even her worst possible nightmare.

No, this can't be possible. This can't be happening. Please, help me. "Somebody, please help me!" The terror was enough for Alannah to find herself calling out to an empty house.

But unfortunately, Alannah realised that against all hope the contents of the letter were real. The presence of evil in the words was the same from a distant echo that had plagued her mind and tortured her life for so many years.

She glanced over to the shelf and spotted her anti-depressants. In a state of controlled hysteria, she ran over to the bottle and opened it. She was meant to take two in the morning. She didn't take the time to count how many was in the bottle but she spilt its entire contents into her palm, discarded the pill bottle to free her one hand and then managed to grab a glass of water from the tap. It took four attempts with mammoth gulps of water to swallow the twenty or so tablets.

Then she noticed on the shelf Jake's painkillers and anti-inflammatory tablets that he took for a knee problem. She tipped the remainder of water down the sink and went to the cupboard under the microwave. Bingo! She knew that Jake would have a bottle of scotch whisky in the near vicinity.

Alannah grabbed the bottle of whisky, which was more than half full and then grabbed the packets of Jake's tablets from the shelf and shoved them in the pocket of her dressing gown. She then grabbed the letter that had provoked her desperate actions and made her way back upstairs to the bedroom. She was already becoming dizzy and nauseous with the effect of the anti-depressants but she managed to flop onto her bed. She lay on the bed and took the pen and notebook that sat by the phone on the bedside cabinet. Tears streamed down her face as she began to write her suicide note. It simply began "To Jake. I'm sorry…"

After finishing her final statement, she placed the note inadvertently next to the letter that she had received and then finished off the entire contents of painkillers and anti-inflammatory tablets using the remainder of whisky in the bottle. Usually, she would grimace at the bitterness of neat whisky, but on this occasion, she was practically oblivious to the taste.

Alannah then closed her tearful eyes for the final time and gradually slipped into a slumber of tragic and untimely death.

"Hi honey, I'm home."

Jake thought it strange that Alannah hadn't answered as he closed the front door behind him.

She must be out of earshot, he concluded.

He went straight upstairs and into the bedroom to find Alannah with her eyes closed on the bed.

Bless her she's asleep, he thought. Just for a moment.

But then he sensed something was wrong. The way her head was hanging to the side didn't look right and her skin was ghostly white in colour.

Then he noticed her left hand holding the empty whisky bottle. *His* whisky bottle. He wouldn't mind of course, but he knew that Alannah barely drank alcohol, especially whisky.

Then he noticed the empty packets of tablets on the bed. Like the whisky they had been *his* tablets.

His whisky and *his* tablets. He knew instantly that the guilt would haunt him forever.

Jake ran over to Alannah and shook her to no response.

"Alannah wake up, wake up. Come on baby, please wake up."

He reached down to her wrist and checked for her pulse. Nothing.

He moved his ear to her chest in a desperate attempt to detect her heartbeat but it was hopeless, he knew she was dead.

Jake lifted his fiancée's lifeless body in his arms and her head flopped backwards causing her stunning hair to stream down behind her. Even in death, she was beautiful.

Jake held her close to him as he sobbed uncontrollably.

Meanwhile in an old house situated much further north of England something was stirring. Something had been awakened with its own essence of desperation and tragedy. And within this old house sat an old piano that had not been used for many years, but the strings within its casing began to tighten with anticipation.

Just like the events of today something else was going to have an overwhelming effect on Jake's life - and even his sanity.

CHAPTER 1

Jake sank his tall, well-toned frame into the inviting chocolate-coloured chair situated in the hotel foyer. At thirty-five years of age his physique and accompanying good looks left little room for improvement, but then again isn't that what pop stars are meant to look like? His suntan complemented the background of the chocolate-coloured leather as he manoeuvred to gain comfort.

Jake was a charismatic individual and possessed that certain magnetic and alluring quality that made heads turn when entering a room. Jake had broken onto the music scene well before the popular talent and reality TV shows that were yet to flood the music industry of the noughties and beyond, but if he had ever needed to audition for such a contest there was nobody on Earth who could have denied that Jake Zennor indeed ticked all the boxes and more. Fortunately for Jake, his athletic build was based mainly on genetics rather than any serious effort on his part, preferring to utilise his leisure time indulging in his favourite activity of drinking alcohol rather than participating in any serious exercise. He did manage to discipline himself to attend a gymnasium twice a week and was more than happy to participate in the odd celebrity football match in order to raise proceeds for charity – where he often impressed with his footballing ability. Often embarrassed and humbled by his fame, Jake felt a sense of obligation to give something back to society and he constantly donated to good causes. He also struggled with the trend that a personal fitness trainer was required just because you happened to belong to the world of showbiz. Like many characteristics of his peers, he found the whole concept self-indulgent and annoyingly unnecessary.

Regardless of his own musical talent, smouldering good looks and natural charisma, Jake often felt that he did not belong amongst the rich and famous as his own principles often compromised the expectations that came with the job. The problem was he had still played the game to a certain extent and carved out an image that was once the order of the day – the good-looking pop star that was massively in the public eye yet ironically so out of reach to the millions who adored him. Jake Zennor was a man of intellectual conversation, a pleasure to have on talk shows – once upon a time at least, and he was well capable of carving out meaningful lyrics in his songs. Jake's band, Blossom of Eden, had been somewhere between Black Sabbath and The Bee Gees. They could rock with the best of them, but catchy tunes and commerciality were at the core of their product. As a performer, Jake had been somewhere between Jim Morrison and Robert Plant – but unlike those two charismatic frontmen, he often had a guitar strapped across him on stage. His vocal range could take him high or it could take him low. As a songwriter, he was second only to John Lennon and Paul McCartney. Jake was a product of the 1980s music scene - big hair, chiselled features and a great deal of posing. He was no doubt rich with talent, but a far cry from the type of musician currently stepping forward in the explosion of Britpop and Grunge.

The Britpop scene was an evolution of the sixties taking inspiration from bands such as The Beatles, Dave Clark 5 and The Animals, but the current chart toppers' ill conduct and manners were generally more exaggerated than those ground-breaking acts of yesteryear, and their singing was delivered in much stronger regional accents – most notably from Manchester or 'Madchester' as it was increasingly becoming known. Blossom of Eden's music had clearly been inspired by The Beatles, what band hasn't been inspired at some point by the Fab Four? But they were a far cry from sounding like the Britpop bands. After all, it was impossible for anyone to ever suggest that ELO and Oasis sounded alike – two of the most notorious Beatles' inspired bands that have ever made music. Such was the power of The Beatles that they could inspire musicians in so many different ways.

The Grunge bands didn't sound or look like the Britpop acts and mainly originated from the US, their main source being the city of Seattle with Nirvana being the most successful. The Grunge acts appeared even more disconnected from society and unlike the smart-but-casually presented Britpoppers, their clothes and hair were scruffy-looking. But both musical genres used guitars in a big way, both were explicit with their drug use and neither necessarily sounded or looked like a rock star – something that was completely alien to the stylish and velvet-voiced Jake Zennor. Jake didn't quite know how to dovetail himself into this new era of music and he was terrified of being left behind.

Jake would appear foolish to simply convert to being a Britpop or Grunge artist, it would look too contrived, but how was he going to compete with any of his current musical nemeses?

The decade had started with the shock death of one of the all-time greats in Freddie Mercury, the charismatic frontman of Queen. And that's what Jake had to try and achieve – to become an all-time great. To become a legend. That way he would become a timeless artist but his solo career just wasn't delivering half as well as it should. One of his fellow 80s artists had seamlessly stepped from being one-half of the energetic pop duo of Wham! into a credible solo performer, his debut album *Faith* winning numerous awards and delivering no less than six top 5 singles, whilst his 1990 follow-up album *Listen Without Prejudice Volume 1* continued to cement his songwriting ability and a foot well in the camp of the current dance scene. And ironically it was at Freddie Mercury's tribute concert of 1992 which gave George Michael the platform to show the world just how good he really was, stealing the show with an amazing rendition of Queen's "Somebody To Love". This was some achievement as musical competition at the event had been extremely substantial. If his performance at that concert had signified that George Michael had become the benchmark of transition from top selling band member to timeless solo artist, then Jake Zennor had a long way to go. And he knew it. Jake Zennor had never even been asked to perform at the Freddie Mercury Tribute Concert.

Jake's reason for being at the hotel today was considered to be another uncomfortable price of fame in his eyes. His manager, Abe, had arranged for an interview to take place with Lucy Ives of Lynx Magazine. Lucy had appeared very keen to interview Jake and her persistence had seemingly paid off. These days, Jake resented talking to the press, realising very early on in his career how they liked to manipulate the truth for their own gain, so his own rule if he could help it was not to participate in their games. He was even more reluctant to talk to any third party at present due to the speculation surrounding the suicide of Alannah in mysterious circumstances. Jake was determined to protect her memory. Abe, however, had felt it necessary for the interview to go ahead as he was concerned that Jake's solo career was not functioning as either would have liked since the break-up of the band.

Abe believed that the magazine interview was necessary, and frankly long overdue, to maintain Jake's profile in the public domain. Jake, on the other hand, was simply suspicious that the interview could only be an attempt to unearth some information about Alannah, his departed fiancée.

The glass that secured Jake's familiar tipple of scotch and Coke had hardly touched his lips when a soft well-spoken voice pleasantly grabbed his attention.

"Mr Zennor?" Jake was fortunate enough to naturally possess a surname that could have matched the most imaginative of stage names.

"Please, call me Jake." As Jake raised his head in acknowledgement he saw a face that beautifully complemented the pleasant voice that he had heard. A smile greeted him, as did an open hand reaching out to the rock star. Before taking the lady's hand, Jake couldn't help but pause for a second to admire the immaculately manicured nails that were coated in a smooth lavender coloured shell.

"Miss. Ives, I presume?"

"Please, call me Lucy," came the friendly reply as the attractive woman proceeded to sit down. She noted Jake's deep suntan and felt it suited him.

"Can I get you a drink?" offered Jake, giving the cheeky grin that had so often melted hearts.

"Thanks, a white wine and soda please," replied Lucy gratefully.

Jake called a fresh-faced waiter over and gave him the order, which naturally included another scotch and Coke for himself and whatever the youngster cared for.

"Have you worked for the magazine long?" Jake inquired. "Forgive my ignorance but I don't read a lot of press these days. In fact, I try not to read it at all if I can help it. No offence intended."

"None taken. About three years in answer to your question, although I have been involved in serious journalism for almost twice that long. Actually, I remember when I first started out and I was doing some freelance work for the nationals; you and the other guys were number one in the album charts with *Pride Before a Fall.* Then again that album did seem to be at the top of the tree for an absolute eternity. I actually gave it a review, and yes, I was kind before you ask."

"Oh, happy days," replied Jake, rolling his eyes as he spoke. Like most bands that had split, the memories could be bittersweet. It was actually the first time that Jake's eyes had broken contact from Lucy's intriguing face. Indeed, Lucy herself possessed a certain look that would warrant her own fair share of basking in the public eye. Both she and Jake sitting together actually gave a persona of being a very handsome couple, and oblivious to their own surroundings; they were certainly getting noticed. Lucy continued with the conversation. "I believe that my work for Lynx magazine is much more sophisticated and better received than writing for the tabloids. I feel I'm serving a more, shall we say, select readership."

"Lucy, believe me. I would never have agreed to the interview if this was a tabloid piece," said Jake firmly.

"So you have done some homework?" joked Lucy.

"Not really", replied Jake. "I told you I stay away from reporters these days. My manager, Abe, did the homework. Now, more's to the point, have you done yours, Lucy?"

"Exactly who is meant to be interviewing who here?" joked Lucy again.

"I'm sorry," replied Jake, giving the same trademark cheeky grin as earlier. "Please continue."

Lucy returned the smile as she reached into her designer handbag.

"What's that?" enquired Jake concerned.

"You really are out of touch with this line of work aren't you, Jake? In layman's terms, it's a mini tape recorder. It is okay if I tape the interview?"

Jake thought hard before his reply. "Okay, but don't ask me to sing into it. I have to charge extra for that," Jake managed a smile to disguise his discomfort.

Lucy returned the smile once more. "Don't worry, I won't. How long is it since your last interview anyway?"

"My last *official* dealing with the press was roughly two years ago."

"About the same time that Alannah died?"

And there it was. She had done it, and before the interview had barely got started. Lucy's words were like a bomb going off inside Jake. He felt his heart sink like a lead weight and his stomach turn over like a gravedigger's shovel. He stared hard as his biggest fear about the interview was realised so soon. Had Lucy's self-pronounced experience not taught her to be tactful, or was this approach a testament to her professionalism?

"Can we leave Alannah out of this?"

"Why? It's what everyone wants to know, Jake. Why did she feel that she had to take her own life?"

"I thought you said that you had moved on from the gutter," said Jake sternly. His relaxed mood had become visibly eclipsed and the once pleasant atmosphere was becoming increasingly awkward.

"Hey, I never meant to cause offence," quipped Lucy struggling to appear sincere. "Do you find it hard to talk about Alannah then Jake?" Lucy approached the delicate subject with the same tone as if she might be discussing with Jake what he liked to eat for lunch.

"Ask me about my plans for the future or my forthcoming album," demanded Jake, still staring hard. Despite his attractiveness, Jake had a naturally intense stare that could cut through ice. They were certainly windows to a tormented soul and Lucy sensed it. With that soul exposed she felt that she could really go to town on the interview.

"Why not discuss recent history, Jake? Please enlighten me. Is it just the memory of Alannah or is it the embarrassment of your previous album flopping? After all, anything outside of the top 20 has to be recognised as failure doesn't it Jake? It was certainly no *Pride Before a Fall*." Lucy let out an exaggerated giggle. "Oh, I've only just realised the irony of that title." Lucy could be quick off the draw if necessary and unlike a lot of people she certainly wasn't daunted by Jake's presence. Although Jake's previous album wasn't a massive seller, Jake's standards of success had been set by his very impressive musical achievements and prolific songwriting ability prior to launching his career as a solo artist.

"You're all the fucking same," said Jake, his staring becoming more intense.

Lucy being the true professional she was, ignored the remark and was not unnerved by Jake's manner. She had been punched at, spat at, and definitely sworn at before during her journalistic career. Recent interviews with some of the Britpop acts had augmented those particular experiences too. Intense staring from a fading rock star was certainly not going to compromise her mission. Besides, in spite of their intensity, she couldn't help but notice the magnetism that Jake's blue eyes radiated. It was obvious to her that Jake was even more attractive in real life, now that she had had the opportunity to meet him in the flesh, in spite of the circumstances. She was determined, however, that his good looks were not going to hinder her in her quest.

"Do you blame yourself for Alannah's death, Jake? I mean you were engaged to be married yet that never seemed to have an effect on your endless womanising and 'lost weekends'. That poor girl must have seen the bottle of pills as the only possible escape from the miserable, tortured life she was leading with you. The irony is she really loved you, didn't she?"

"Obviously, you believe everything *you* read, dear Lucy. People like you are so mixed up in your own little fantasy world that you actually begin to believe the crap you write. You were correct about her loving me, though. I'll give you that."

"If you say so Dr Sigmund Zennor, but the camera doesn't lie, Jake. I've lost count of the number of pictures I've seen of you with different tarts hanging off your arm, not one of them worth an ounce of Alannah I should imagine." Lucy couldn't help herself as her strong feminist principles kicked in. She was beginning to behave unprofessionally but this is what she really wanted to quiz Jake about. However, she really needed to be careful that her quizzing didn't become an interrogation as the interview could collapse without her gaining any productive information. She didn't want to leave empty handed now that she had got this close, and Lucy had drawn her own conclusions that Jake was responsible for driving his fiancée to suicide.

Fuck it, she thought. *Let the bastard have it with both barrels.*

With increased sarcasm in her voice and verging on spitting venom she unleashed a verbal assault on Jake. "Well come on Jake, let's hear your side of the story. The world is dying to know what pathetic excuses you've got swimming in your head, trying to convince yourself that if Alannah had never met you she would still not be alive today." Lucy realised that her approach to the interview could have been a lot more diplomatic, her experience and common sense begged her to gently offer Jake a way to help his cause with the public, to give his side of the story, if indeed there was one, but she wasn't willing to pussy foot around. Her characteristic impulsive behaviour, which had so often been the difference between grabbing a great scoop ahead of her contemporaries, tempted her into being dangerously direct with Jake. It was, however, an ill-advised tactic to use on Jake Zennor.

"You haven't got a clue you dumb bitch. You don't know the first thing about me or my relationship with Alannah." Jake was close to eruption.

"So enlighten me, Jake, if I'm so far off the mark."

Jake didn't answer.

"What's wrong Jake, have I hit a nerve?" mocked Lucy.

"No, you have not hit a nerve but for the first time in my life I'm very close to hitting a woman."

"Do it if it makes you feel better."

With that remark, Jake stood up. Jake moved closer to Lucy causing her to flinch and momentarily turn away closing her eyes. Even under these provocative circumstances, Jake had the restraint not to strike out. He had never raised his hand to a woman, and he wasn't going to let some ego-maniac journalist force him to compromise his principles now. Instead, he grabbed Lucy's Dictaphone, threw it to the floor and stamped on it smashing it to tiny pieces.

"Interview terminated," he firmly announced.

With Jake towering over her and looking harshly down towards his new-found enemy, Lucy realised for the first time that she may have overstepped the mark. Jake obviously had an uncanny physical presence and could pose a substantial threat to her if he so wished. She realised that her persistent badgering towards Jake had proved an unwise method. Some fear began to creep into her soul and her stomach began to butterfly. Not easily silenced herself, she now felt it unwise to challenge Jake's actions.

"Print one word of this and my lawyer will ensure that you have to live and breathe in the gutter, let alone work from it. Keep out of my face and my business from now on." With this warning, Jake stormed off, knocking a tray of drinks from the young waiter's hand on his way out.

Lucy sensed that Jake's words were not an idle threat.

CHAPTER 2

"Abe, I'm going to fucking kill you," announced a raging Jake as he burst into his manager's office. His anger had obviously not decreased since exiting the hotel foyer some forty minutes earlier to head across central London.

"Jake, whatever could be wrong? Sit down; let me fix you a scotch." Abe showed remarkable resilience considering Jake's approach, but then again he had years of experience handling his star client's flights of temper.

"I'll tell you what's wrong you prick, I've just had the displeasure of meeting some hard-faced bitch by the name of Lucy Ives who couldn't conduct an interview if her life depended on it, and the biggest joke is, my manager, who happens to be you, set the whole thing up! I knew it would be a bad idea to talk to the press, but no, Abe Hunter always claims to know what's best, doesn't he? You've let me down big time on this occasion, *mate*." Jake didn't take up Abe's offer to sit down or to have a scotch.

"Did she talk about, Alannah?" asked Abe in a genuine sympathetic tone.

"Yes, she did. I thought you were meant to be vetting these people so that I only had to promote the new album."

"But Jake, while the public sees a question mark over Alannah's death, God rest her soul, there isn't a journalist alive from London to New York who wouldn't ask something about you and her, it's only natural."

"Well fuck the lot of them then. No more interviews and that's final, Abe."

"But Jake, we need to promote the new album. I'm convinced that by giving your side of the story you can win back the fans that blame you for Alannah's death. Damn it, they need to know, it's not fair that a great bloke like you should have the finger pointing at him. You loved that poor girl. I knew it and everybody else should know it too. And, Jake, you can't ignore the fact that since the tragedy your record sales have dropped, including all the classics with Blossom of Eden. Even radio play has suffered. There is some good stuff on this new album, Jake. I can see the headlines now: Zennor's back to his brilliant best! We just need to get into people's faces and sort out this, err, misunderstanding regarding Alannah. You are the greatest songwriter alive today, Jake. It would be a crime to deprive the world of your talent mate, come on, let's get the ears listening again."

Jake finally calmed himself and sat down. He knew Abe wouldn't lie to him, even if he did have a one-tracked mind for business most of the time. Abe had stuck with Jake through good and bad times, and Jake was the only member of Blossom of Eden that Abe continued to manage. There was a lot of mutual loyalty and respect between both parties.

Jake now feeling calmer briefly reflected on things and accepted a scotch on the rocks. He hung his head slightly as he confided to Abe. It was a scenario that had taken place many times before.

"The album, the music, it all seems so insignificant without Alannah," Jake said in a very subdued tone.

"Alannah loved you, Jake. She was proud of your music and she was certainly proud of you. She wouldn't want you to give up, mate."

Jake wiped a tear from his cheek.

Abe phoned through to his personal assistant to hold all incoming telephone calls. He was going to devote some time to a friend in need; even Abe knew when to put business on the back shelf. He put his arm around Jake to comfort him.

"No more interviews Abe, I mean it."

"Whatever you say, buddy, you know I only want what's best for you."

"I know what I need Abe, I need to move out of London."

Abe wasn't expecting this and the expression on his rotund face couldn't hide the shock from Jake's announcement.

"But Jake, you know how it is. The industry dictates the need to live and work in London unless you're thinking of moving to L.A of course?"

"No mate, I need to go home. I still need time and space to grieve properly for Alannah, away from the distractions London throws at you. Anyway, I don't need to work flat out anymore; I am a multi-millionaire for heaven's sake. Besides, you live and work in London, Abe. I know you'll keep your ear to the ground and see me right. You're the one who always has his finger on the pulse; I just need some time to chill out. I need time to rediscover myself. I need to get spiritual. Yeah, I've decided. I need to go home. Sort me out some property in the Peak District, Abe. Right in the heart of the countryside, away from all this crap."

Abe was concerned for his friend but smiled as he replied, "I'll see what I can do buddy."

CHAPTER 3

As usual, Abe delivered the goods. Jake's new home was a 17th-century mansion set amongst acres of roaming, beautiful green English countryside, yet the house was positioned close enough to the villages of the southern peaks so that Jake could easily obtain any necessary supplies. Of course, Abe had also ensured that Jake was within easy reach of the quaint public houses that complemented the peak stone buildings elegantly scattered around the area. Jake had always liked a drink and usually could handle it too. He fitted perfectly into the cliché of being a rock and roll hell-raiser, way before it became a contrived addition to a musician's persona, but since Alannah's death, he had dangerously begun to drink a lot more heavily as an attempt to block out the pain.

"So, what do you think of Abba Manor?" asked Abe puffing on a fat cigar.

"Is that what it's called? Abba Manor? You're kidding."

"I doubt it's the original name of the house because as you can see this place was built long before the Swedish pop band dominated the charts. I assume a fan lived here in the seventies or eighties. I was drawn to the musical connection on your behalf."

"It's perfect," replied Jake. "Although it's in need of a spot of restoration work."

It was clear that the property had been vacant for a number of years. Thick layers of dust and cobwebs were evident in each of its fourteen rooms. There were pockets of crumbling plaster on the walls and ceilings, but crucially all the timber was free from rot or woodworm and the building was structurally sound. All Jake needed to do was to stamp his own identity on the property with some tasteful décor, although great care needed to be taken in order for the house not to lose any of its rich original character. It was naturally a Grade II listed building.

"What I can't understand Jake, is why you wanted such a big place if you are to live here alone. It's certainly a far cry from the mid-terraced cottage I found you sharing with your folks in Bonsall all those years ago, God rest their souls. To be honest, Jake, this place gives me the creeps a bit."

Jake laughed at Abe's uncertainty. "I've still come home Abe, whether I'm back in my old boyhood cottage or in a larger than life country manor house like this." There was an excitement in Jake's voice that Abe hadn't recognised for several months and it pleased him to see a spark of Jake's former twinkle again.

"You can almost taste the Peak District air Abe, it's so clean and pure. I needed to rescue my lungs from the London city smog. It's important to protect the old vocal chords, delicate tools for the trade you know."

"Does that protection stretch to giving up the booze and fags then?" asked Abe, hypocritically still puffing at his cigar.

Jake chose to ignore Abe's question, which was what Abe fully expected, and instead made his way over to an impressive looking piano. It was made of solid oak, yet was curiously jet black in colour. It also had twin candelabras affixed either side of the sheet music stand. The candelabras still held partly used candles with melted wax now shaped in a solid form down the sides, a depiction of a moment frozen in time.

"This was a bonus, Abe," said Jake referring to the piano as he played the opening phrase of Beethoven's "Für Elise" with his right hand. "It strangely doesn't seem to need tuning either, as if it is still played regularly."

"The Estate Agent stated that the piano is probably as old as the house itself and has remained here in spite of various proprietors coming and going over the centuries. Come to think of it the Estate Agent looked as old as the house himself. He was a weird, very cagey sort of fellow. He didn't reveal much history about the house despite its age. He had an extraordinary knack of avoiding certain questions, especially about previous residents. It wouldn't surprise me if there has been some foul play here in the past; I mean it wouldn't be in his best interest to tell me anything that would jeopardise a sale now, would it? I thought the price was too good to be true. This place definitely gives me the creeps; can't you feel how cold it is?" Abe gave an exaggerated shiver to highlight his point.

"Abe, it's cold because we are in a house that hasn't been heated or even occupied in donkey's years, that is set in rural England, approaching the month of October. You've been watching too many late-night movies, Abe. Relax, you've done me proud with this place mate, and if you got it for a song then all's the better."

"For a *song*. No pun intended I presume."

Jake proceeded to play the opening phrase of "Für Elise" again, but on the final note, he slipped onto a wrong key in error. He hadn't had time to remove his hand from the ebony and ivory keyboard when a door slammed upstairs; almost it seemed in disapproval of the wrong note being played.

A short, stunned silence followed as Jake and Abe looked at one another.

"And I suppose that was just the wind," said Abe. "Except there isn't a single window open in this godforsaken place."

"It must have been," replied Jake unconvincingly.

Neither man spoke for a short while as they each searched their brains for their own personal theory of what had actually happened. It was Abe who finally broke the silence.

"Is that the time?" he said looking at his watch. "I really should be heading back to London; I've a million things to do. I've arranged for your phone lines to be fitted in the morning so give me a call tomorrow Jake, should you last the night that is."

"With your imagination Abe, it is you who should have been the songwriter. Have a safe journey and I'll talk to you tomorrow."

The two friends said their goodbyes for now and Abe took an uneasy look up the old stairway before leaving the creepy premises.

As much as he loved the place, Jake couldn't help but observe all the hallmarks that the property possessed in line with the traditional haunted house. He recognised the cobwebs in every corner and on the chandeliers that hung from the ceiling. He recognised the sound of the creaking floorboards as he moved slowly through the house, as dark shadows naturally formed in the dim light giving the impression that he was never alone.

Although actually, he soon realised that he was very much alone is this creepy old house!

Worst of all he realised that he was truly stuck in the middle of nowhere. He had no phone (these were the days before the wide usage of mobile phones) and Jake didn't have any immediate neighbouring houses nearby.

No one would hear him scream that's for sure.

And then he wondered just what had caused that door to slam shut upstairs?

Shit, it is a big place to be on my own, he thought.

Just then a knock came at the front door to break his trail of thought and Jake was surprised at how something usually so innocent had caused him to jump. But then Jake noticed that Abe had left his mobile phone behind on a nearby sideboard which like the piano had been inherited with the house. Abe was one of the few people in the UK who did possess a mobile phone.

Thank God, it must be Abe.

Jake opened the door but he was astonished to discover that there was nobody there. Instead, he could just see the rear of Abe's car disappearing from view onto the road at the opening of the long driveway.

Double Shit!

CHAPTER 4

As he had no landline to use at present, Jake called a cab using Abe's mobile phone, surprised that he could acquire a signal. He had decided that he needed a drink and wanted to check out the local pubs. More importantly, he felt that he needed to be in the company of other people until he could get his head around the idea that he hadn't really spent close to 3 million pounds on a haunted house! Jake didn't like to admit it to himself, but he definitely did not feel like being alone for the foreseeable future. Besides, at present, he realised that he had no booze in the house.

The taxi quickly arrived and waited at the exact spot that Jake had witnessed Abe's car pull away at the end of the driveway. The driver sounded the horn and it was clear that Jake was going to have to walk the 150 yards or so if he wanted this taxi to chauffeur him about. Jake was even less impressed when he realised that it was raining heavily. *Cheeky bastard* thought Jake to himself; nevertheless, he grabbed his coat and walked speedily up the driveway.

"I wouldn't have minded you picking me up at the front door," said Jake as he closed the car door behind him.

"Sorry mate, but we taxi drivers can't be too careful these days. You never know who you're picking up if you're not familiar with the name given. I've not had much call to come this way before, and your house seems a bit isolated, to be honest with you. No offence intended, squire. Have you lived here long?"

Jake was a little taken aback that the taxi driver had not recognised him, but it would have taken a lot more than that to bruise Jake's ego. In fact, a bit more anonymity was what he had hoped for by moving into the countryside. "Actually, I've moved in today believe it or not," replied Jake.

"Oh, I see," said the driver in a curious *oh dear* kind of tone.

Jake picked up on the driver's vibe. "Is there something you want to tell me?" prompted Jake.

"No, no son," said the driver, "except…"

"Except what?" said Jake, becoming slightly anxious.

"Where are we going?"

"A decent boozer, I'm sure that you can recommend one."

"Ok," and with that, the driver started the engine and pulled away in the driving rain.

"And while you drive you can tell me what it is I obviously need to know."

The driver hesitated to answer as the wipers battled furiously with the rain at the windscreen. "Well, I'm not sure that it's my place to say, but you look a nice chap so I think you should perhaps have your eyes opened."

"Go on," prompted Jake again.

"Well, it could just be old wives' tales, you know how country folk and their legends can be, but local talk has it that on every Hallow's eve, witches or such like can be seen dancing around a roaring fire up on the hill just at the rear of your place. Farmers have many of their sheep go missing too. It's believed the animals are used for sacrifices in the name of Lucifer, you see."

Jake wasn't sure how to react to the unexpected information he was hearing so his underlying fear prompted him to make light of the situation. "Bollocks! What a pile of crap. Oh well, I'll look forward to that as Halloween is just around the corner".

"You see mate," continued the driver. "Legend also states that your place is built on some sort of ancient burial ground, but not belonging to any recognised decent religion that is known of. The worshipping of Satan is like a virus in the countryside, always has been, always will be. Unfortunately, whoever lives at the house that you now own never seems to experience any form of decent luck. There's been many a tragedy associated with that place. Look, I'm sorry. I don't mean to scare you. Just be careful, son."

Jake paused struggling to take in the taxi driver's words. This information was not helping his state of mind after what had happened with the slamming of doors at his apparently now confirmed haunted house.

"I'll thank you to stop trying to scare the shit out of me and instead take me to a decent public house."

"Sorry mate, no offence meant. Here you are then; I'll drop you off here."

The taxi had stopped at a pub called The World's End.

"I hope that's not an omen," said Jake pointing at the creaking sign swaying in the night's chill. The World's End. It looks a bit different to its namesake in Camden Town that's for sure. How much do I owe you?"

"Have this one on me mate. I feel a bit guilty about putting the wind up you like that. Anyway, like I said, legend and superstition are always on country folk's tongues. Take no notice of me. Give me a call later should you want to move on or need a lift home. Archie's the name."

"Thanks very much, Archie. I'll see you later then." The two men shook hands and parted company. Jake couldn't help but notice how icy cold the taxi driver's grip had been, but Archie's cheerful disposition prevented Jake from being unnerved by him, despite the spooky yarn that he had just spun him about his new home.

Jake braved the rain once more and a streak of lighting appeared overhead as he made his way into the pub. The old wooden door did not open easily and Jake had to push with a fair amount of force in order to gain access.

Once inside, Jake did not receive a warm welcome.

As soon as he entered the vicinity every bit of activity in the pub halted. There was an eerie silence as all eyes fell on Jake. The barman stopped pouring a pint in mid-flow, a scruffy looking man stopped throwing his darts at the dartboard, nobody put a glass to their lips and if a pin dropped you would definitely have heard it.

The hostile reception reminded Jake of the scene in the film *An American Werewolf in London* when two backpackers entered a Yorkshire pub.

It was a very strange atmosphere for such a well-populated public house. The dim lighting added to the unpleasantness of the situation. The silence continued and Jake felt the staring eyes burn through his wet clothes and beyond the surface of his skin. It was not a pleasant encounter as the only sound he could hear was the rain beating heavily on the old sash windows. Jake got the impression that the staring was not for recognition of who he was, but more to suggest that he was an unwelcome stranger in a world where he did not belong.

Eventually, the silence was broken.

"What can I get you?" shouted the barman across the room. His tone was a little menacing and his speech was deliberately slow.

"A scotch and Coke please," replied Jake.

The pub then returned to its business as if the barman's voice had acted like that of a conductor instructing his musicians to continue with their music. Jake felt a sense of relief rush through him as the burning eyes gradually let him be. He proceeded to the bar and held out a £5 note.

"First drink of the night is always on the house. Besides, you look like you need a drink. Have you seen a ghost or something?" asked the barman.

"Not exactly," replied Jake, still not fully relaxed but feeling slightly more reassured. "Thanks for the drink."

"Just passing through are you?" quizzed the barman.

"No, I've not long purchased the old house about three miles or so west of here, Abba Manor. Do you know it?"

The room fell silent once more. All eyes were once again firmly fixed on Jake. Jake uneasily lifted the glass to his lips, oblivious to the fine taste of the single malt whisky that he would usually fully appreciate. The barman, complete with extremely bushy white sideburns, leant forward as he spoke in a deep and serious tone, "That place is evil son, and it wasn't always known by that name. It has a certain history of tragic events. It's truly cursed. Please, son, heed my warning and leave while you still can."

Jake attempted to laugh off the barman's revelations, but inside his stomach was squirming. First the taxi driver and now the barman. Was anyone in this area free from superstitious opinions?

A scruffy-looking man stood up from roughly two tables behind where Jake was standing. "You'll not be staying for another drink then?" It was more of a direction than a question.

"Leave it alone, Alec," said the barman. "The gentleman means no harm."

Jake turned around to confront the hostile Alec. "Look, I'm not looking for any trouble but I'll say when I'm ready to leave. Unless I'm told to move on by the management that is." Jake tipped his head to the barman in acknowledgement to who he regarded was in charge. It played to the barman's desire to feel important which was Jake's intention.

"You're not welcome here," spat Alec. "You may not intend to bring trouble to us, but as long as you are living at *that house* trouble will follow you. Bad trouble."

Jake decided to go for broke. "I came here tonight to befriend my new neighbours, but all I seem to be receiving is hostility. Perhaps it will help matters if I inform you all that I am originally from these parts. For some reason, you don't like to welcome strangers, I don't agree with that attitude, but listen; I'm not exactly a stranger. Now is there anybody here who I can perhaps buy a drink?"

"It's nothing personal," said Alec. "It's that house, it's evil."

By this time Jake was getting close to not caring, but a voice suddenly came from the other side of the lounge with a perfect interjection. "You're welcome to buy me a drink if you like, duck. And then you can join me at my table."

"Okay, what are you having?" said Jake, relieved to hear a friendly voice.

"Half a pale ale," shouted the lady.

"Half a pale ale for the lady," said Jake to the barman.

Once served, Jake walked over to the lady's table, unable to resist a passing stare towards Alec. The lady was roughly in her mid-to-late forties and looked Romany like in appearance. She was wearing an impressive amount of jewellery including a set of large hooped earrings that swung from her podgy lobes.

"Nanette Forester is the name, duck. Take a seat".

"Thanks," said Jake. As he sat down on the uncomfortable mahogany chair he noticed an ashtray overflowing with cigarette ends smoked as far down as possible. The law that bans smoking in public establishments, including pubs, was another decade or so away yet. Jake knew that the cigarette ends belonged to Nanette as each one was coloured by her bright red lipstick. She was smoking at present.

"And you are Jake Zennor. My daughter is crazy about you. She once travelled all the way to Paris to see you play with Blossom of Eden, and here you are now living almost on her doorstep. She'll have kittens when I tell her."

Jake was relieved to finally be in the company of someone who wished him no hostility. He was beginning to believe that his escape to the Peak District had been a huge misjudgement on his part. It was bad enough that he seemed to have purchased a house that the locals regarded as evil, but could he not even leave that house to be in the sanctuary of a local pub? This area is where he had always regarded home to be for Pete's sake and he was feeling more and more unwelcome by the minute. Perhaps things had changed too much around here for him to ever feel like he belonged in these parts again? Was it London where he now truly belonged and all that the busy city dictated, never meaning to return to his humble homeland again? Had he truly crossed a line when he made the big time, past the point of no return? Was Abba Manor sending him a warning to get out of here because he was no longer wanted? Had he turned his back on his humble beginnings? Okay, he was a successful musician but it had all been on merit and he had never meant to neglect his roots or forget where he had come from. Or was he simply seen as an unwelcome stranger – it certainly wasn't clear that a lot of people around here recognised him.

Nanette suddenly seemed like a lighthouse in a misty storm, offering Jake a lifeline of sanity. Although he had moved to the Peak District to shed some of the limelight, he couldn't help but feel a sense of relief to discover that Nanette's daughter was proof that he hadn't completely entered another galaxy.

"I moved back up here from London partly because I had very little quality time to myself, always being hounded by photographers or fans wanting autographs. Don't get me wrong; I do appreciate my fans because without them I would not be what I am today. It's just difficult to lead a normal life sometimes. Be careful what you wish for aye? I must admit though it's reassured me tonight knowing that someone has finally recognised me, I was beginning to feel like a bit of an outcast. For the very first time in my life, it appears that my fame has actually made me feel some security."

"Don't let your ego get too bruised," joked Nanette. "Most folks in this village don't know their arse from their elbow; many are like that prat Alec. They're totally oblivious to what happens outside their safe little community. They walk around with their head up their arse. One day in London would kill them all off with cardiac arrests brought on by shock. They piss me off sometimes with their ignorance and narrow-mindedness, take no notice of them."

"You seem pretty clued up, Nanette. Is there any truth in all this shit I'm hearing about Abba Manor?"

Nanette took a long drag of her cigarette and thought long and hard before answering Jake's query. She blew smoke into the air and then lowered her eyes to meet Jake's.

"It's not fair to lie to you, Jake. People are scared of that house and things have undoubtedly occurred there. Unnatural things. The majority I'm sure is based on hearsay and the police have never revealed anything conclusive to the community. There is a lot of Devil Worshipping going on in the Peak District, and particularly the fields and land to the west of here seem to be a major choice for such activity. There are plenty of good folk around too, though, don't forget that.

"Rumour has it that the last few occupants of your place, going back as far as living memory will serve, have all been worshippers of Satan. It is said that sacrifices take place up there, and chanting and distant screams can be heard on many a night. I'm sorry Jake, but it is said that Abba Manor has always been the meeting place for those who choose to dabble in darkness. It has also been rumoured that it has been the focal point for black masses to take place. But like I said, nothing is conclusive. Just be careful and watch your back."

Jake appreciated Nanette's honesty, he realised that she sought no pleasure in telling him this unnerving information. Nanette's words did little to help Jake in his quest for reassurance, though.

"Thanks for the warning. My manager, Abe, was meant to be checking out the property where I was buying, he obviously didn't do his research as well as he should have done."

"Don't be too critical, Jake. Don't blame Abe. What Estate Agent would reveal such detrimental information? Besides, you live at Abba Manor now, Jake. If there has been a chain of devil worshippers owning the property, it has now been well and truly broken."

"Apparently, Abba Manor wasn't its original name. Do you know what the house used to be called?"

"I'm sorry Jake, I don't. Come on; let me buy you a drink."

"No let me," said Jake, forever the gentleman.

As it turned out, Jake went on to purchase another four drinks to Nanette's two.

Jake discovered that he enjoyed being in Nanette's company. The conversation naturally moved on from *Devil worshipping* and *haunted houses*, and Jake soon put all his fears to the back of his mind. Any doubts or regrets he was beginning to have about returning to the Peak District subsided as Nanette made him feel at ease and nostalgically reminded him of the warm character of the folk he knew growing up as a child in and around Bonsall, not too far from where he was now living and drinking.

Nanette revealed to Jake that she was widowed, her husband falling victim to a tragic quarrying accident whilst she was pregnant with his child. No other man could ever match her Tommy, and she was glad that she had Bethany as a daily reminder of him, yet upset at the cruel fact that

Tommy and Bethany would never know one another. Jake discovered that Nanette's experience was very therapeutic for him in his grief for Alannah; they had a connection, albeit a tragic one. Beyond this night, Jake would often meet with Nanette and Bethany, and they all became firm friends. Bethany, who had already been a fan of Jake's music, now found herself in the very surreal world of having her icon regularly popping around for a cup of tea and a chat!

They say that you should never meet your heroes, but for Bethany, Jake didn't disappoint.

The night had come to a natural end, and Jake was surprised at how quickly last orders came around following his ability to eventually settle into the pub. This type of traditional country pub would rarely have the need to take advantage of any 24-hour licensing laws.

"I'll call us a cab," said Jake, punching in the numbers on Abe's mobile phone.

"Hello, Peak and Dale Cabs," said a voice at the other end.

"Taxi please."

"Certainly sir, where are you?" The accent was local.

"The World's End Public House and I'm going to Abba Manor via School Lane, as there are two passengers in total and my friend is to be dropped off first."

"Abba Manor, is that Mr Zennor speaking?"

"Yes, this is Jake Zennor."

"I don't mean to be rude Mr Zennor but are you going to wait for the taxi on this occasion. Earlier tonight one of our drivers knocked on your door and waited a good five minutes, but you didn't appear to be in. Time is money in this game, sir."

Puzzled by the operator's comments Jake replied sharply.

"Well, the mistake must be yours not mine. Archie picked me up. He told me to phone again later and he would see me home okay."

"Mr Zennor, I'm afraid we don't have a driver by the name of Archie."

"Well, perhaps I was poached by another cab firm, it happens all the time in London."

"It is unlikely. We are the only cab firm for miles around. You aren't playing a joke on us are you Mr Zennor?"

"No, of course, I'm not."

"It's just that we did have an Archie work for us about four years or so ago."

"Well, there you go then. He is probably working as an independent now."

"I doubt it Mr Zennor. He was killed in a Road Traffic Accident on his way to a pick-up one rainy night."

CHAPTER 5

Jake eventually retreated to Abba Manor via Peak and Dale cabs driven by one of their alive and kicking taxi drivers. Nanette had kindly offered her sofa for the night in case he had been too badly shaken, but Jake declined, conscious that his macho pride should remain intact. However, he did express his gratitude of the offer and promised to drop by and meet Bethany soon.

Jake was usually a cynical man with a firmly closed mind on such things as ghosts and ghouls. However, following the recent unexplained happenings even his scepticism was beginning to thaw. He had quite often needed to stand his ground in bar brawls and various altercations over the years, but this was now something different he was experiencing. How does one trade punches with a ghost? Could paranormal happenings really be taking place? Jake was in unfamiliar territory. He was used to being in control but he was beginning to feel less and less certain of current life in the Peak District and he did not like it. An unfamiliar dynamic was starting to surface: fear was beginning to creep into the life of Jake Zennor. A fear of the unknown. Jake was unsure how to protect himself against any external forces that may be at work.

Had Archie really been a ghost or was he simply an unlicensed taxi driver with the same name as a guy who died a few years back?

But what about the business card that Jake had been given which seemingly belonged to the bonafide Archie of yesteryear? How could that be explained?

In spite of a productive night's drinking with Nanette, Jake still managed to find room for a nightcap. More to the point, pouring himself a whisky delayed Jake having to turn the light out for the night.

Eventually Jake surrendered to bed. After such an intake of alcohol, Jake would usually fall asleep almost at the same time that his head hit the pillow. But not tonight. The alcohol took little effect as fear and anxiety conspired to create a sobering barrier to sleep. Jake kept a candle alight near his bedside so that he wouldn't need to surrender to the dark completely. He attempted to put things into perspective as he lay there, but his mind kept racing. Inwardly he felt ashamed that he needed to seek protection from the flickering light of a candle and realised that this was only his first night staying in Abba Manor. How would he cope with the many nights ahead?

Get a grip Jake. He thought to himself. *Okay, it's dark and isolated but isn't that a perfect alternative from having to share life with the parasitical paparazzi in London? Yeah, I'm much better off here…and Alannah would have loved it here too…Oh, Alannah, I wish I could see you again. I hope you can hear my thoughts, babe, I miss you so much. If only…*

Just as Jake was beginning to convince himself that his destiny did really belong at Abba Manor, he became interrupted by the sound of a piano playing. He sat upright with the shock and his eyes widened. *Who the hell is playing my piano? In my house?*

He jumped out of bed using the candle as a guiding light and rushed downstairs. His eyes quickly fell upon the piano, but to his amazement, no one was sitting there playing it! Indeed, the music had stopped altogether just as his eyes had made contact.

There was an eerie silence. Jake's stomach began to squirm. He was confused but trying desperately to search his mind for a reassuring explanation. Was it a car passing the house? The hour was late but he understood that a small amount of traffic was always required to travel during the night. A truck driver perhaps? A truck driver would travel during the night and listen to the radio in his vehicle as a mechanism to stay awake on his gruelling journey. But Jake realised that the narrow country lane that passed before his house was not exactly a main route and he would be surprised if anyone, let alone a truck driver, would seriously be using it at this unearthly hour. Deep down he also conceded that Abba Manor was situated too far from the road for it to have been a car radio that he had heard. Puzzled and scared, Jake returned to bed.

Jake nestled his head on the pillow and once again kept the candle alight as a pathetic attempt at protection. Not much later the piano music started again and it was the same repeated phrase as before. The melody possessed a haunting refrain but also a very pleasant quality, however under the circumstances; Jake simply couldn't appreciate its beauty. Jake rushed downstairs for a second time, almost tripping on the bottom step. Again, the music ceased to play as Jake appeared at the scene. He was beginning to wonder if he had drunk too much alcohol after all, but he felt stone cold sober. Then Jake's fear reached a climax as he heard a new noise, this time from behind him.

Jake's usual reaction would be to turn around and deck whoever had dared to enter his home uninvited, but Jake sensed this would not be the average burglar standing behind him and was convinced that if he turned around, he was going to be confronted by something unnatural. He was frozen to the spot. He feared that behind him would most likely be a spirit. Or even worse. In desperation, Jake, not a religious man at all, began to recite The Lord's Prayer… "Our Father, who art in heaven, hallowed be thy name, thy Kingdom…"

"Meow!!!"

"What the…?"

Jake turned around and relief drained from him like water through a spout as the candlelight revealed a young black and white cat. It was no more than a year old and its shabby appearance suggested it did not have an owner. Jake placed down the candle in order to allow him to pick up the cat.

"Hello boy, you gave me a fright. How did you get in here? What's your name then? Have you got a name? You haven't got a collar, have you?" The cat responded to Jake by licking his nose and beginning to purr. The feline, remarkably like many animals, possessed the ability to be a good judge of character and had obviously sensed that Jake was a soul that could be trusted.

"Hey, that tickles," said Jake as the cat continued to rub against him. "Shall I adopt you? Would you like that? Would you like a home? I could certainly do with the company. In return, you can protect me from the ghosts and ghouls of Abba Manor. What d'ya say?"

Jake was able to carry the cat's skinny frame in one hand and retrieve the candle in the other. He made his way back up the stairs with his new companion, safe in the assumed knowledge that the cat must have simply walked across the piano keys. Jake concluded that it must have been a fluke that some kind of melody seemed evident as the paws hit the notes.

How wrong he was!

Jake had only climbed halfway up the stairs, still holding the cat, when he was interrupted by the same haunting melody that he had heard earlier. He turned sharply determined to catch the culprit in the act this time, but again the candlelight revealed nobody sitting at the piano.

Instead, he was astonished to witness the piano keys playing on their own.

CHAPTER 6

Jake finally fell asleep that night and was awoken next morning by a tickling paw at his nose. The cute feline was no guard dog but there was a mutual understanding between Jake and the cat that they were both in need of a friend. Jake had decided to name his new tenant Elgar after the famous Worcestershire composer. Although Jake's career was based on contemporary music, he was a classically trained pianist thanks largely to a dedicated school teacher who had realised Jake's potential at a very early age. Through his mentor, Jake was able to appreciate classical music with the respect it deserved. The widowed teacher, Mr Courtney, had often sympathetically waived the fee required for extra tutoring, preferring instead to be enriched by the natural talent of his pupil's ability than demand a payment from Jake's devoted mother. Silently realising that the Zennor household's humble finances would not be able to regularly stretch to listing piano tutoring as a main priority, the matter was never discussed, and Mr Courtney, being a true gentleman, was eager not to cause Jake's mother any embarrassment. Eternally grateful to Mr Courtney's constructive contribution to his musical career, Jake always made a point to include a thank you credit to a certain Victor Courtney on the sleeves of his albums.

Elgar pawed mischievously at Jake's face again. As Jake stirred he could still hear the melody in his mind's ear that had mysteriously been played on the piano the night before. Despite the bizarre circumstances in how he had come to hear this piece of music, on reflection, Jake couldn't help but admire the tune and he was intrigued as to how it sounded like it could be an excerpt from a classical piece of music, yet still possessed a quality that enabled it to easily sit within the modern world without seeming out of place. It was indeed a piece of music after Jake's own heart.

Eventually Jake submitted to the cat's request to greet the day and threw on a T-shirt which partly covered the top of his boxer shorts. He picked up Elgar and proceeded downstairs to the kitchen. After handing Elgar a saucer of milk, Jake sat at his kitchen table with his usual bowl of cereal. Abe had managed to provide a selection of necessary furniture from local suppliers for when Jake moved into Abba Manor, yet a range of original furniture had been inherited with the property. The piano that appeared to have a mind of its own being just one item! More furniture was to be delivered later that day, including Jake's belongings from his previous home in St John's Wood, London.

Jake began to scan the kitchen for a radio; he enjoyed listening to the national breakfast show whenever possible. He couldn't locate one from his seat, but it became irrelevant as he began to realise the beauty of his environment and appreciated the silence, which was only delicately broken by the sound of Elgar lapping at his milk and the intermittence of a sheep bleating or the refrain of a songbird. It made a welcoming change from the intrusive sounds of the city. But the silence also gave an opportunity for Jake's mind to wander. Typically, he thought of Alannah. Abba Manor would have been perfect for her to be free of her complex troubles in the world. She would have adored the peacefulness and tranquillity of the countryside. Why had he not discussed with her the idea of moving to the Peak District? Tears began to fill Jake's eyes and he could only hope that her spirit was somehow still with him.

Suddenly the moment was interrupted when a knock came at the front door. Jake walked cautiously to answer it, not knowing what to expect reflecting on recent experiences. His mind began to gather speed. Was it Archie at the door? Was there going to be anybody standing there at all, or was it some invisible entity like the 'piano player'?

Jake opened the door with caution.

"Hello, Mr Zennor. I've come to fit your phones. Eugene's the name."

Relief oozed from Jake. With all the commotion Jake, had clean forgotten that Abe had arranged for the landline phones to be installed in Abba Manor. The voice belonged to a gormless and harmless looking lad, appearing to be no older than in his early twenties. He was wearing a grey coloured uniform, which appeared too small in size for him, especially on the length of the arms, and a baseball cap facing the wrong way, which was obviously not meant to be part of the telephone provider's corporate standard of dress.

"Oh yes, I've been expecting you. Come in," invited Jake. "Fancy a cuppa?"

"No thanks, Mr Zennor," replied Eugene. "But do you mind pinching me?"

"I beg your pardon?" asked Jake.

"Sorry, I just can't believe I'm going to install phones into the home of *the* Jake Zennor. I've got every record you've ever made, including imports from abroad. Can I have your autograph when I've finished the job?"

Jake smiled. "No problem. You'd best come in and start work for now, though. You've got a lot to do."

"I know," said Eugene looking at his worksheet. "A phone in no less than 12 rooms, including a special waterproof phone in the shower. My, how the other half live. I'll get on with it right away."

"Cheers mate, I'm a bit paranoid about the radiation caused by cordless phones hence the amount of land lines required," said Jake.

"No worries, it keeps me in a job and I would imagine that mobile phone reception is a bit hit and miss in such a remote location as this anyway."

"I'm not a fan of mobile phones either really. Perhaps they'll catch on one day."

Eugene worked hard, wanting to make an impression on Jake no doubt, and after close to four hours of committed labour he was just putting the finishing touches to the final telephone installation when he felt a distinct air of coldness emerge behind him. He turned around but quickly determined that there was nobody there. With the shake of his head, he returned to his work, assuming that he must have imagined the presence that he had sensed.

It was not long after that he was feeling the cold air again, only this time it seemed more intense. He turned around again, but as before there was nobody there. This time, the experience was too much of a coincidence not to unnerve him. He resumed to his job again but the temperature was now becoming so icy cold that he began to hurry his task of working on the phone installation. As he breathed he could visibly see the arctic atmosphere producing a mist of dancing fog from his mouth, and his fingers were quickly becoming numb as he fiddled with the phone and his tools.

Soon after, the youngster was sure that he heard a faint laughter cutting through the icy temperature. Feeling startled he turned around once more. Again, there was not a soul to be seen. He called out in desperation. "Mr Zennor. Mr Zennor is that you?"

But there was no reply.

"Mr Zennor, are you there? Have you opened one of those big windows or something? It is like a fridge in here." As he said the words he was able to hear the hiss of the radiator, dispelling any theory that he might have had at all as to why it was so icy cold in the room and completely at odds with the freezing temperature. He also quickly realised that the door to the room and all its windows were shut. The icy temperature didn't make any sense. The youngster's terror began to increase.

"Mr Zennor are you there? This is not funny you know? This is really freaking me out. Please stop."

Silence.

"Mr Zennor, are you there…Is *anybody* there?"

Still, silence.

The air was now so cold that it was becoming unbearable Eugene continued to see his breath in the freezing air before him and as he anxiously returned to his work his fingers were not able to function properly due to the coldness. To his own amazement, he managed to finish the job and fretfully gathered his tools.

His fear increased when he became certain that he actually felt the icy grip of a hand at the back of his neck.

He turned around once more expecting to see Jake after opening the door to the room, but instead, there stood a figure of a man, far shorter than Jake in height, wearing what appeared to be a very expensive looking period costume. They were the sort of clothes that Eugene had only ever seen in history books, films or television period dramas. The figure was unnervingly ghostly pale in complexion.

He could see that the door was firmly closed and it was obvious that the figure had not entered the room via any conventional entrance.

Astonishingly, the figure then began to slowly vanish before the youngster could determine what was happening. The disappearance was gradual and began to occur from the feet upwards, climaxing when the head remained visible in mid-air for what seemed an eternity for the startled telephone installer. The expression on the ghost's face did not change throughout the apparition until immediately before the moment that it disappeared. An inane smile appeared which then broke into an unnerving cackling laughter that faded in unison with the gradual disappearance of the ghostly head.

Terror gripped the youngster.

When the whole of the figure had finally vanished Eugene fled from the room, out of the house, into his van and drove at high speed away from Abba Manor.

On hearing the commotion, Jake ran to the door only to see the van turn out of the driveway.

Strange lad thought Jake. *I thought he wanted my autograph!*

CHAPTER 7

"So who packed the bottles of beer?" called out Che to the three men ahead of him.

"Why didn't you pack the beer yourself if you felt it to be such a crucial inclusion to the packed lunch?" replied Jake.

"Because it would make my rucksack too heavy that's why?"

"Oh really, and fuck everybody else?" Roland, Che's brother joined in the debate.

"You know me Bruv, I'm a selfish bastard."

"At least you're an honest one," interjected Fergus.

"Anyway, don't worry about any lack of alcohol, Che. At the end of this walk, we reach a cracking pub where we can sit down and have a few beers. Believe me, they will taste a whole lot better after earning the right to drink them," said Jake.

One of the main reasons for Jake's decision to return to the Peak District was to be able to meet up with some of his old mates again. Jake had been amazed how fame had become the dividing wall in identifying who his real true friends were. People whom he would have considered to stay the distance in terms of loyalty suddenly became jealous and began to keep their distance once he found stardom, whereas other less significant acquaintances suddenly latched onto Jake as if they had been bosom buddies since the beginning of time.

Che and Roland Summers had remained loyal friends to Jake before and during his fame. Before they became good pals their parents had even been close friends, back to the days when people could leave their back door open to wander freely in and out of each other's homes. Jake often affectionately recalls the times his dad would pop down the local pub on a Sunday afternoon with Henry Summers or arriving home from school to find his mother and Jenny Summers engaged in incredibly lengthy and articulate discussions on ordinary everyday matters, for example, the state of the weather.

Jake had been delighted when on his return to the area Che and Roland had instigated the idea of going on an 'expedition' across the tors and dales of the Peak District. The two brothers had welcomed Jake's return to the area and had even arranged a surprise coming home party for him, miraculously being able to keep things secret and conjuring up a number of old school friends. The party had been a rip-roaring success with the climax being a drunken Jake singing karaoke accompanied by the equally intoxicated Summers brothers who had always been game for a bit of fun.

Accompanying them on the mountain walk was Fergus Sutcliffe, the bass player from Blossom of Eden. In spite of the band's split, Jake had always remained close friends with Fergus and also the band's former drummer Saul Jackson.

Fergus was a very shy, reserved and genuine individual and unlike Jake didn't really fit into the mould of the conventional rock star. With his gangly frame and large pointy nose, he never possessed the same good looks to match the other members of the band, although he still managed to indulge in his fair share of eager groupies that were constantly nearby in the early days of the band's rise to fame and into their most successful years. Fergus was more than content to stand in the background whenever the band performed on stage and allow his meticulous bass playing to become the centre of attention rather than his limited stage presence. However, the modest Fergus didn't realise that he possessed an intriguing stance when approaching his bass playing which connected with millions and added to the band's persona. With his head bowed down enabling his hair to completely cover his face, the hunched-over Fergus became lost in the music and his lengthy guitar strap meant he plucked expertly at his bass strings just below his crotch area. This signature method of playing bass became copied by many inspired bassists across the bands of the world.

Since the band's split, Fergus had completely retreated from the public eye on an artistic level, choosing to live off his plentiful earnings from his days with Blossom of Eden. He enjoyed this quiet life with his Japanese wife, Naoko Shinji. In spite of his shyness, Fergus had the ability to become an articulate and tireless campaigner for various causes that he believed in, such as animal rights, protecting the environment and even sympathising with the cause of surfers and their campaign for cleaner British waters around the British coastline, in particular, Cornwall. Fergus channelled all his creativity into these causes and very rarely picked up his bass guitar anymore, although he had never been a major songwriter in the band anyway.

The weather had been surprisingly kind to them so far on their trek, although it was a little muddy underfoot due to the heavy rainfall that had occurred during the night. The four men had fully expected that it would be inevitable at some point to have to walk through the challenging elements so often associated with the English weather and were pleasantly surprised to discover the sun shining so brightly and for so long.

They came to a small rock face that wasn't too dangerous but it required the need to change from walking into scrambling: the necessity to use both hands and feet to venture any further towards the summit, but not challenging enough to actually be considered as a climb.

Just as they reached the top of the scramble, Jake slipped on the wet surface and some rock broke away causing him to jar his knee.

"Shit that hurt," he squealed.

The Summers brothers managed to support either side of Jake and carry him to the footpath that had reappeared now that they had reached the top of the rocks. They helped Jake to sit down.

"Are you okay to carry on?" enquired a concerned Fergus, his long curly hair gently blowing in the breeze.

"Yeah, just give me a minute. I think I've got a cartilage problem again in this left knee, I often get some pain and locking."

"It must be as a result of all those times that you've run across the stage in your concerts like an Olympic sprinter to impress your female fans," joked Che.

Jake laughed. "It's more likely to be due to those charity football matches I play in."

"You might require an operation," said Roland.

"I think a lobotomy is required before any knee surgery," joked Che again.

"Very funny. You're not helping you know," said Jake. "Okay, I think I can carry on now," declared Jake, as he ceased rubbing his knee and returned to his feet.

The four men continued their walk. Jake's knee remained sore but he didn't want to spoil the party and silently walked through the pain barrier.

The stunning scenery helped to distract Jake from any pain that he may be feeling in his knee. The clear day enabled them to wonder at the miles of green rolling hills, tors and fields. They had long since left the car park that held Fergus's 4x4 vehicle and they had ventured so far and high that they could no longer locate the car park when scanning the magnificent scenery. The odd village or hamlet appeared like tiny scattered pieces of children's building blocks, and very few roads could be spotted either as they simply faded into pale insignificance like threads of cotton trailing over the unspoilt landscape. Any vehicles that could be noticed appeared like small ants marching along the threads of cotton.

When the surface became relatively even, Jake was able to cope better with the walk, but eventually, the footpath took the small group to the foot of a steep peak and Jake was concerned that his knee wouldn't be able to make the strenuous climb.

"I think this is one peak too many for me, guys."

"Lightweight," Che mocked his friend good-heartedly.

"It's my knee, I don't think I can make it."

"It's okay," offered Roland looking down at the map he was holding. "We can go up over the peak and meet you at the other side, Jake."

"How come, Bruv?" asked Che.

Roland revealed the contents of the map.

"Look, all you have to do Jake is follow the wall around the base of the peak and eventually it reconnects with the footpath at the other side of the summit where we will meet you. There are simply two routes on offer to the eventual footpath that we need: either up and over or around the side."

Jake could see the depiction of the wall on the map's print leading to the footpath at the other side of the peak, confirming exactly what Roland had told him. He removed his eyes from the map, looked across the land and could see the beginning of the limestone wall that had stood there for hundreds of years.

"Okay. I'll meet you at the other side. I don't wish to spoil any fun for you guys. You go ahead and climb the summit. It looks like the final peak of the walk anyway according to the map. I wish I could come with you but I doubt my knee will hold out."

"It could be dangerous for you, Jake," said Che in an unusually sensible tone for him.

"Perhaps. I won't bother chancing it. I'll be fine. I'll see you in about 45 minutes or so then," said Jake.

"Remember, just keep to the wall and you can't go wrong," said Roland. "It leads to the footpath."

Jake watched his friends begin to climb the summit before turning to limp towards the limestone wall.

As he walked along the wall he couldn't help but be fascinated at the literally thousands of stones that had been so articulately placed all those centuries ago. He found it hard to comprehend the amount of time that it must have taken to build the wall, and indeed the huge workforce that must have been deployed. He wondered how his three friends were getting on, enjoying one another's banter in order to motivate their efforts, while Jake only had the sheep to talk to. He laughed to himself as he concluded that a conversation with the most intellectually challenged sheep would be far more rewarding than discussing anything with the tabloid press, including that cheeky bitch Lucy Ives. However, he quickly became annoyed at himself as he realised that although she angered him he found her to be an extremely attractive woman. He grudgingly began to undress her in his mind when suddenly his trail of thought was interrupted.

The wall disappeared!

Jake wasn't sure if the map had been printed inaccurately, or since its print the wall had been disturbed in some way, but one thing was for sure: Jake had reached the end of the wall and he was nowhere near the other side of the summit or on the footpath where he was meant to meet the others. Worse still, Jake realised that the wall had acted as a barrier to avoid the sheerness of the hillside and if he were to carry on without its support he would surely fall to his death.

Jake considered returning back along the wall to the start of the summit, but this would mean he would have to cover some considerable distance to return to that point and then be faced with the difficulty of climbing the peak with his injured knee which was what he had wanted to avoid.

Jake was in a dilemma as to what he should do.

Jake looked up from where he stood and he could see that to climb up the side of the summit from this angle was impossible. There were no footholds or visible route upwards. To approach the summit could only be achieved from the starting point in which his three friends had done. To make matters worse his injured knee began to throb, and he realised that he was restricted from displaying any decent mobility.

Jake stood rooted to the spot for a good ten minutes or more, not quite knowing what to do next, frantically searching his mind for a solution. Eventually, he felt so helpless that he decided to shout for help.

"Fergus, Roland, Che. I need your help. Can you hear me, guys?"

The only sound was the bleating of nearby sheep.

"Fergus, Roland, Che. I need help. Can you hear me?"

There was still no reply from his three friends. Jake concluded that they must be too far away to hear him and could even possibly already be at the other side of the summit waiting for him to appear.

He looked at the sheep around him and noticed that they were able to walk quite remarkably against the sheer terrain of the hillside. He knew he wasn't a sheep but he was now becoming desperate. He convinced himself that if he took enough care and concentrated fully, then he could attempt to continue walking along the side of the steep ground without the support of the wall. Deep down he knew this could well be an act of lunacy but he felt that he had no other choice.

Suddenly as he was about to step out onto his extremely risky journey, a cloud appeared from nowhere, enveloped him and masked his visibility halting him in his tracks. It was difficult to understand how this cloud had suddenly appeared, considering it had been an exceptionally good day for weather and the sky had remained perfectly clear and blue.

Jake realised that he would have to wait for the cloud to pass before he could attempt to recommence his crossing, but curiously the cloud refused to clear.

Jake began to have visions of mountain rescue helicopters searching for him or a St Bernard dog finding his frozen body in days to come. Jake realised that his throat was dry as he pictured the barrel of brandy attached to the dog's collar and decided that it would be a welcoming ingestion at the moment.

Jake waited and waited, but the cloud simply would not clear.

Then suddenly Jake heard music from beyond the mist.

He couldn't believe what he was hearing. It was that same haunting melody that he had heard on the piano in Abba Manor, but on this occasion, it appeared to be accompanied by the playing of harps, making the piece sound not only haunting, but now also angelic.

Jake couldn't understand where the music could be coming from. The refrain continued as Jake remained in the safe haven of the cloud.

A feeling of tranquillity pleasantly swept over Jake as he sat calmly, amazed and mesmerised by the beautiful music.

Jake began to believe that the cloud could only have arrived at that precise moment in order to prevent him from foolishly attempting the crossing along the dangerously steep hillside. In short, it appeared in order to save his life. Although not usually the most spiritual of men, he concluded that he might be experiencing some kind of divine intervention.

Perhaps it was Alannah somehow protecting him?

But then his thoughts entered a darker mode. What if the cloud and angelic music were representing something else? Something he didn't want to be a part of. What if he had already died and this was now his calling?

Just then the cloud slowly disappeared and the beautiful music faded as he heard a voice confirming that he was still very much in the land of the living.

"Jake, don't move. Grab hold of the end of this rope. I may not have packed bottles of beer but I never go on a climb without a rope."

"Che! Fuck me am I glad to see you."

Che had tied the top end of the rope around a rock and supported it with a mountain hook buried deep into its face. He was standing nearest to Jake some seventy feet or so higher holding the rope, but both Roland and Fergus also had a firm hold.

"Jake, it's your only hope. Tie the rope around your waist and we will try and haul you up. You will have to use the land for support the best you can."

Jake did as Che suggested, but he didn't fancy the prospect of being hauled up the side of the mountain. One false move could easily result in disastrous consequences. Jake instinctively looked down and instantly wished he hadn't. It was a long way to the bottom with nothing obvious to break a fall.

The three men pulled, feeding the rope through their hands as Jake attempted to gain height scrambling on the limited greasy footholds on offer. It was hopeless, Jake couldn't get a solid grip on anything and worse still - he slipped. Feeling his life flash before him, Jake fell helplessly down the hillside.

But then somehow he stopped.

"It's okay, Jake. We still have hold of you but Che is in trouble now," yelled Fergus.

The momentum of Jake's weight heading south had caused Che to slip over the edge. Fortunately, he had managed to keep hold of the rope although it had caused a nasty friction burn to his right hand. Luckily his foot had wedged between two rocks preventing him descending any further. Roland managed to reach down to his brother and pull him back to safety, literally dragging him up by his coat. A sigh of relief was breathed in unison as the men reflected on the scary moment. However, there was no time for dwelling on 'what ifs' because the outstanding problem of retrieving Jake still remained.

"Listen, guys," shouted Jake. "Keep pulling on the rope and I'll try and climb up it at the same time. It is useless trying to use the land for support."

Jake could see Che's thumbs up signal to give the idea his approval.

As Jake climbed he could feel his arms burn with pain as he ascended up the rope. Suddenly he wished that he had a better appetite for gym work and less of an appetite for booze and fags. Che was also experiencing pain on his injured hand and all three of the *rescuers* could feel the pressure on their arms and thighs as they fed the rope through their hands, dug in their heels and pulled Jake's weight upwards. No matter how painful the ordeal became, there was a mutual recognition that progress was being made and adrenaline and determination ensured that the task was not going to beat them.

His arms feeling like lead, Jake had almost reached the top when the usually calm and collected Fergus let out an uncharacteristic wail. "THE ROPE IS ABOUT TO BREAK!"

With Jake edging towards safety, Fergus had glanced over to the rock which had secured the rope and noticed that the pressure of Jake's weight and movement had caused the rope to fray against the craggy surface.

Suddenly, Fergus's warning was realised as the rope finally gave way and snapped. Jake, who was literally one last final reach to safety, began to fall, but somehow Che had managed to grab him by the arm as he dangled over the cliff face. Using all his vigour, Che slowly pulled Jake to eventual safety, using every last bit of hidden strength that he possessed.

"Cheers buddy," said a grateful and relieved Jake as he hugged Che, his friend and saviour.

"No sweat mate just quit the hugging will ya?"

The four men laughed, quickly forgetting their ordeal in the realisation that Jake was going to be okay before they safely continued along the ridge to the summit and down its descending footpath. They spoke about their experience and even joked about it as they ventured onwards, but Jake chose not to share with his friends the strange intervention of the cloud and the accompanying music that he had heard. He assumed that none of the others had heard it, as they too hadn't mentioned anything, and they would have surely ripped the piss out of him even more for being so scared that he had 'imagined' music playing whilst being stuck up a mountain!

As he inwardly reflected, Jake began to speculate just what had happened to him. Was it possible that he had experienced some kind of divine intervention? If the answer was yes, what he didn't understand was why he had been saved? *What made him so special?* Philosophically he concluded that perhaps it just wasn't his time. For some reason, his number hadn't come up. *Surely it was as simple as that.*

"I can taste that beer," stated Che.

"We will have earned it as well," replied Roland to his brother.

The four hikers had survived the most gruelling aspects of their expedition, clearing miles of tors, summits and of course surviving Jake's ordeal at the final peak. There remained just one relatively unchallenging dale to cross before reaching their rewarding final destination of the country pub.

There was the need to cross an old wooden stile in order to access the dale and Jake waited until the others had crossed, not wanting to hold them up with his sore knee. In actual fact, he cleared it fairly easily.

As the friends walked along the field they marvelled at the beautiful scenery. The dale was set in a stunning valley with rolling hills either side of the path. It gave the impression that the footpath had appeared in order to part the magnificent waves of green just like in the familiar biblical story involving Moses. When the four men looked straight ahead it seemed as though they were looking down a beautiful roofless tunnel with the light blue sky beautifully complementing the distant green hills and its dotting of cotton wool sheep.

The ground was still sodden underfoot from the previous night's rainfall and the four men's walking boots were heavily caked in mud making the footwear barely recognisable.

"It seems to be getting even muddier underfoot now," commented Roland.

"This field is clearly void of a natural draining system," commented the ever-knowledgeable Fergus. "Unfortunately, the hottest sun and climate can take days to free a truly saturated field such as this from mud and water."

"This ground does seem unusually muddy I have to say," added Jake.

They carried on a little further, egged on by the calling of the public house and its impressive array of cask ales that lay in waiting. Jake had also decided that a meal was now also required. Everyone agreed that they had worked up an acute appetite as well as a thirst, and they had long emptied the contents of their rucksacks. After all, they had commenced the walk not much after 6.00 am, which now seemed such a long time ago.

Roland had led the way since entering the dale, which for him became an unfortunate decision. Suddenly, out of the blue, he began to sink into the ground quite dramatically. It happened so quickly that the ground had swallowed him up to his knees before anyone had even realised what was happening.

"He must have stepped onto a quick-sinking bog," shouted Fergus. "We've got to get him out."

"No, Che. Wait," said Jake restraining his friend. Naturally, Che's reaction had been to dutifully rescue his brother without a second thought but Jake had read the danger. "If you go storming in there we will have both of you to pull out."

Che reluctantly recognised the logic in Jake's words.

"Well, what can we do?" said Che frantically.

"Here we can use this," said Fergus holding a long branch that had fallen from a nearby hawthorn tree. They had lost Che's rope when rescuing Jake from his mountainside ordeal, now incredibly a second rescue of the day was upon them. And Roland was sinking fast.

Jake hastily grabbed the branch from Fergus and took a step forward but instantly his boots began to sink into the mud as well.

"I can't lift my feet! It's like fucking cement!"

Just then Fergus ran past a helpless Che and gave Jake an almighty push slamming him into the mud and causing him to leave one of his boots behind in the muddy ground.

"What the fuck are you doing, Fergus?" Said a startled Jake.

Che looked on in a bewildered state, sharing Jake's concerns.

"You need to spread your weight as if you are on ice. It will prevent you from sinking. I'll hold your ankles while you reach the branch out to Roland." It was good advice from Fergus which Jake now recognised.

By now, although it was only within a matter of seconds, the mud had engulfed Roland almost to his waist. Both he and Jake desperately reached towards one another but the branch was out of Roland's reach. Roland continued to sink into the mud as if it was some sort of malevolent form of quicksand.

Che had quickly pulled himself together and insisted on skimming across the bog like a lizard in an attempt to come to his brother's aid. He took the branch from Jake's outstretched hand and replaced it with his own hand securing a firm grip with Jake. He then stretched out his other arm holding the branch towards his frenzied brother who could now only be seen from his chest upwards. Roland's natural reaction after failing to grab the branch had been to try and push down on the ground in order to raise himself above the mud, but this meant that his arms also sank into the bog and became inadvertently trapped.

"Roland, you've got to try and free an arm," yelled Che desperately. "The branch is in reach now."

"I can't Che," replied Roland hysterically. "It's like fucking concrete."

"Try Bruv. You've got to try."

With all the strength that he possessed in his entire body, Roland tried to move his right arm. Realising that he was literally fighting for his life he somehow found a hidden strength that saw his hand break the surface of the muddy ground and dramatically grab onto the branch.

"Way to go Bruv, now hold tight while we pull you out."

Apart from the now free arm, at this point only Roland's head and shoulders could be seen as the mud had now enveloped him almost all the way up to his neck.

With Fergus as the anchor man, the three men pulled with all their strength to try and free Roland but he was well and truly rooted. A look of despair came onto Che's face as he saw his brother's chin begin to sink into the mud.

"Again! Fucking pull again," he ordered and Fergus and Jake willingly obeyed with as much strength as was humanly possible.

Astonishingly some progress was made. A smile came across Che's face as he witnessed his brother's neck pop up out of the ground.

"That's it boys, well done. We are doing it. Pull again quickly."

Jake had taken to climbing along Che's arm and actually embracing his friend's torso so that maximum momentum could be achieved when pulling and to avoid any injury to Che's arm. Unfortunately, this also enabled Jake to be able to see Roland's terrified face and his heart went out to him.

The three men pulled again for all they were worth.

Fergus was the only one being supported by relatively solid ground and he was able to dig his heels into the earth and lean back as he pulled Jake's legs with all his might as if he was taking part in the most significant tug of war that there had ever been. But then Fergus unexpectedly found himself falling backwards as he catapulted along the ground and unintentionally released hold of Jake's legs.

They had managed to free Roland by about another 10 centimetres when the branch had suddenly snapped, causing Fergus to fall and separating the link between the brothers.

Tragedy then followed.

"NO!" shouted a frantic Che, as he witnessed his brother helplessly sink the same distance again, but at a much more alarming speed than it had taken to momentarily free him.

It was useless. Jake and Fergus quickly realised that this was a truly desperate situation now. There seemed no way of grabbing hold of Roland and he was sinking incredibly fast.

"I love you, Che. Take care of yourself, Bruv," said a resigned Roland.

"It's okay Roland. We're going to get you out."

"It's too late, Che. We're out of time. Jake, you can have my share of pints when you get to the pub. Take care of Che for me; God only knows what he will get up to without me to keep him in line."

A tear rolled down Jake's face and also a smile in the face of adversity at Roland's ability to keep a sense of humour at his darkest moment. Could this really be happening? It dawned on him that if he wanted to say goodbye to his friend it would have to be now or never. "So long buddy."

Fergus could only put his head in his hands shattered at the prospect of the failed rescue mission.

Before long, Roland's head had disappeared into the soggy earth leaving just his hand sticking up out of the mud into the air.

The three men poured out their emotions with a mixture of sobs and laughter as Roland kept his dignity and sense of humour to the very end. His hand waved goodbye to them until it could wave no more, signalling that Roland had drawn his final breath. The lifeless hand then too ultimately sank down into the bog.

Jake tried his best to console a hysterical and distraught Che whilst he contained his own anguish. Fergus could not speak.

The funeral of Roland George Summers had been a bitterly sad occasion. It was barely incomprehensible how such a young and promising life could have been snuffed out in such heart-rending conditions. Jake was relieved that the Press had largely failed to connect him to the tragedy for Roland's sake; the last thing he wanted was for the media to make a mockery and a circus out of Roland's passing. One rogue photographer from the local press had appeared at the church, but Che had persuasively confiscated his camera and explained how it was in his best interests to refrain from attempting to report anything.

Fortunately, now it seemed, Roland had never married or had children preferring never to take life too seriously and living it to its full potential. The priest had commented on how Roland had seemed to have packed more than a lifetime of experiences into his few years on Earth. In spite having no immediate family of his own, Roland had been a very much loved and now missed individual. The church aisles and village graveyard had been packed to the rafters with weeping friends and family, and it was decided that it was only fitting that Roland's funeral should be a celebration of his life and a reflection of the joy he brought to others rather than focussing on the tragic circumstances of his loss of life. So, a wake had been organised in the same village hall that ironically Roland had organised for Jake's welcome home party.

At the wake, Jake and Che maintained the tradition of bad Karaoke, belting out favourite songs of Roland's. Che had even managed to joke to Jake about how crazy it had been to have had to dig Roland up only to put him back in the ground again! An irony that would have played to Roland's own sense of humour.

Eventually, a quiet moment presented itself and Jake felt that he needed to discuss with Che the events of that fateful day when they went walking across the Peak District.

"Che, I'm sorry to bring this up mate, but do you ever think about how that even happened to Roland?"

"Fuck me Jake; bring the party down why don't ya?"

"I know, I'm sorry, but it just doesn't make sense. It's been playing on my mind a hell of a lot. I know that it had pissed down the night before but I can't understand why such a treacherous bog would appear like that. To be that lethal and to that extent."

Che noticed the worried look on Jake's face.

"What are you thinking, buddy?"

"That what happened to Roland is possibly my fault."

"Don't be daft mate, how do you work that one out? We all tried to save him and you could see that the daft bugger bore none of us any grudges at the end."

"It's just that my house that I have bought. Abba Manor. I have been told that it has always been connected to evil and perhaps had the power to orchestrate evil things to occur. And I'm worried that I have unearthed something there, you know, perhaps disturbed a sleeping evil and that is what caused the bog to appear."

"Listen, Jake. I've heard the rumours about that place myself. But that is all they are rumours. Come on mate, in all these years I've never taken you for a believer of shit like this."

"I thought that myself but things have been happening. Things I can't explain. I've heard music playing in the house in the middle of the night. What's more, I even saw the music being played on the piano with my own eyes. I saw the keys being pushed down as the notes sang out, but I swear that there was nobody sitting there!"

Che stared at his friend for a moment trying to take in what he was being told. He knew Jake wasn't prone to telling lies, but he found his revelation a bit startling and difficult to digest. Finally, he spoke.

"Listen, Jake. Do you consider yourself to be an evil man?"

"No, I don't?"

"Okay, neither do I and neither did Roland. Now listen to me. I saw a horror film once about a guy who buys a haunted house and it was proven that an evil house can only attract evil people and as you are not evil Jake, then I think the bog was just the weird elements of science and not the supernatural. My big brother's death was fuck all to do with you mate; you loved him as much as I did."

"But what about the music?"

"Is it nice music?"

"Well yeah, it is beautiful."

"Then again it's not evil. If there are ghosts in existence they do not always have to be evil, Jake. Now stop worrying. What happened to Roland was just a freak of nature; it pissed down with rain causing an almighty bog to form that just happened to become as deadly as quicksand. It's a drag but that's all there is to it. Now please can we change the subject?"

Jake respected his friend's wishes. In spite of his own nagging need to understand, Jake didn't continue to discuss the bog in the dale, the music of the night or go on to mention the cloud appearing on the mountainside. Perhaps Che was right; the bog was just constructed by the elements of nature and was not connected to anything more sinister. Jake also realised that Che needed to come to terms with his brother's death the best way he could and Jake filling his head with new theories was not going to prove helpful or bring his brother back.

In the days, weeks and months yet to come, Jake would continue to torture himself over Roland's death with the pain feeling almost as acute as it did now. Why had he lived and why had Roland died in the space of just a few hours? Why had the cloud appeared at that vital time to prevent him falling to his death, yet why had there been no such intervention when Roland helplessly sank to his muddy grave? It was a mystery that would haunt Jake Zennor day and night.

Unfortunately, despite Che's persona at the wake, he never did really come to terms with Roland's death. As the days surpassed, time never became a great healer for Che and his grief quickly escalated into a spiral of drinking and unusual aloofness towards his friends and family. The once wisecracking and attractive man soon became replaced by a drunken and depressed soul. Friends, including Jake, tried desperately to help and support him but without Roland by his side Che became lost and a shadow of his former self. Che struggled without the guidance of his older brother. He would describe his life as having a huge chasm without Roland being in it, as if a part of him was missing and perhaps had died too, along with his brother on that terrible day. Like his brother, Che had never married nor had children. He did have a regular girlfriend in Heidi Thorne, but he had shut her out so much emotionally since Roland's death the relationship inevitably ended.

One day news came through that Che had been killed in a motorcycle accident. Eyewitnesses claimed that he had taken the bend too fast on a slippery road and lost control of his motorbike careering straight into the jagged rock face that ran along the side of the highway. His closest friends feared that he might have intended to drive into the rock on purpose, choosing to end his life.

Roland's final words to Jake had been to take care of his brother. With Che now also dead, Jake felt that he had failed Roland's dying wish.

Following Jake's attendance at the second funeral of a close friend on his return to the Peak District, the feelings of guilt and uncertainty tormented his brain. He was only 35 years of age but already he had suffered the loss of both his parents following a road traffic accident and now one of his closest friends had been killed in similar circumstances. He had also seen another friend tragically suffocate to death underground and had needed to try and come to terms with the suicide of his fiancée.

This was far too much tragedy for a man of 35 years to have to deal with.

And Jake couldn't help feeling that most, if not all of this tragedy, was down to him.

CHAPTER 8

The driving rain fell hard as the evening drew to a close. Jake was listening to a self-created compilation cassette tape, the volume level turned slightly higher than usual in an attempt to eclipse the sound of the fierce weather. Jake had quite an eclectic taste in music. Of course, he had his staple favourites such as Lennon, Elvis or Hendrix but he had to concede that his current rivals from the Grunge, Britpop, and in particular the Madchester scenes were banging away favourably on his eardrums.

Even above the music the three loud bangs at the door were easily heard. The sound even managed to wake the snoozing Elgar, who raised his head as he lay before the comforting warmth of the open fire. Jake wondered who could possibly be at his door on such a terrible night of weather conditions.

Nanette perhaps? Jake had made it clear that she was always welcome at his home, but would she really have bothered to make her way to Abba Manor when faced against such challenging elements?

Similarly, Jake very much doubted that Abe would be up from London again so soon, and he typically would not have wanted to travel in this type of weather. If Abe had been a professional footballer, he would have been the kind to wear gloves and tights whilst out on the field of play.

The knocks came again. Whoever was responsible certainly seemed eager to make a connection, but Jake concluded that the harsh weather conditions must surely be playing a part in their insistence.

When Jake opened the door he realised that the enthusiasm displayed through the persistent knocking wasn't necessarily inspired by the severe climate. To his utter surprise, it was the appealing if somewhat wet face of reporter Lucy Ives that stood at his door.

"What the hell do you want?" exclaimed Jake, inwardly feeling a certain weird sense of admiration for Lucy in her ability to find him, especially in such ferocious weather conditions. "How the hell did you track me down?"

"That's my job," replied Lucy with a friendly smile, as if their previous unpleasant encounter had never even happened.

"I should shut this door straight in your face so that you can return to the rock from which you've crawled from under," stated Jake.

"Come on Jake, you wouldn't really send a girl out into a terrible night like this all alone. Even when it's a heartless bitch like me. I take pride in the meticulous way I conduct my research and I know that underneath that brash exterior lurks a chivalrous gentleman. Besides, I'd like to clear the air between us. We got off on the wrong foot the last time we met. Let's simply draw a line under it and start again. What d'ya say? After all, I have come a long way to talk to the great Jake Zennor."

Jake was still angry and distrusting of Lucy, but this feeling slipped further and further into his subconscious as her flirting helplessly took effect on Jake. Lucy's tone of voice delivered through that cut-glass accent, and the gentle look in her eyes was caressing Jake's ego to maximum effect. Jake hated to admit it to himself, but even the way the rain had messed with Lucy's dripping hair, and with the cold water trickling down her face, this saturated look had made her appear especially attractive in a very natural kind of way. Boy, was she sexy?

It was entirely possible that Lucy did wish to genuinely make amends, contemplated Jake in his manipulated mind. It seemed best to go with the flow and hear what Lucy had to say, at least for the time being. With his anger diminishing by the second, though not entirely, Jake felt it only proper to invite Lucy in from the doorstep and out of the appalling weather conditions.

"Come on, you had better come in," surrendered Jake. "But only because of this terrible rain, don't think you are forgiven for that charade of an interview you conducted the last time we met."

"Thanks," said Lucy as she gratefully crossed the threshold. "Don't worry I'm not a vampire."

Jake frowned.

"You've invited me into your home, Jake. If I were a vampire your invitation would grant me licence to attack you. A vampire's powers are useless inside a potential victim's home – unless they are invited in."

Jake didn't answer and shut the door forcefully, which made Lucy jump. "Drink?" he offered begrudgingly.

"As long as it's not laced with arsenic," giggled Lucy, in an attempt to ease the obvious tension.

Jake didn't react. He prepared Lucy a white wine and soda water from his well-stocked drinks cabinet and then frostily handed it to her. His firm facial expression never faltered.

"I'm impressed," said Lucy. "You remembered my tipple."

"What do you want then?" quizzed Jake coldly, making it clear he was not interested in small talk.

"I told you, I want to apologise."

"Oh yeah, and what else?" Jake remained suspicious. "I'm sure if you wanted to clear the air you could have easily phoned me instead of travelling all this distance, especially in such adverse weather conditions. London is a long way to travel from just to say that you are sorry."

"I don't have your phone number Jake, and I'm sure that a superstar like you is not listed with directory enquiries."

"However, you did manage to locate my address."

"Oops, I did, didn't I? You are not convinced of my intentions are you, Jake. Look, as I have already said, we just got off on the wrong foot last time we met. Besides, it was worth coming all this way just to see such a beautiful and authentic property. I can see why you retreated to Derbyshire, Jake. Alannah would have loved it here too, I'm sure."

"Okay, get out now." The mention of Alannah's name convinced Jake that Lucy had only arrived to seek the information that she had failed to obtain from their initial meeting.

Lucy totally ignored Jake's request to leave, walked over to Elgar, who was still nestled by the fire and picked him up. "Oh isn't he adorable. You are such a big softy when it comes to something with a pretty face aren't you, Jake?"

"What's that supposed to mean?"

"Well come on, all those different women that you have been photographed with over the years. Tell me, when did you finally realise that your infidelity would have an effect on your relationship with Alannah. Let me guess, when she killed herself perhaps?"

Jake surprisingly remained controlled despite his inward anger beginning to increase again.

"You know what? You haven't got a clue what you are talking about. You do not know the first thing about Alannah's relationship with me. I thought you stated that you were good at conducting your research."

"I conduct it well enough to know what a two-timing piece of shit you were to Alannah. You need to face up to what you did to that poor girl, Jake." Lucy's friendly persona was beginning to disappear as she began to use her words like weapons.

"I loved Alannah. I was engaged to her for Christ's Sake. We were going to be married." Jake's anger bubbled away inside.

"Oh, that's alright then," replied Lucy more than sarcastically. "Tell me Jake, what possessed you to do it to her, to cheat on her time and time again? She was beautiful, she was everything that you or any other man ever needed."

"You think I don't know that? You know nothing. She was all I needed and more," the rage festered in the pit of Jake's stomach.

"So why screw all of these other women?" pressed Lucy, gleefully twisting the knife.

"I didn't screw them all," Jake was reaching breaking point, hardly able to contain his fury.

Undeterred, Lucy pressed on with her verbal onslaught and interrogation.

"You screwed enough of them to drive your fiancée to suicide. Are you such a greedy egotistical bastard that you like to reap as much as you can? Simply take the plates on offer?"

"You're way out of line, Ives," yelled Jake.

"Wasn't sex good enough with Alannah?"

"I wouldn't know!" Jake finally screamed.

Silence fell.

Lucy looked puzzled.

"What do you mean?" Enquired Lucy seeking clarification.

"I mean we never had sex. Alannah and I never had sex."

"I don't understand. She was beautiful. Were you both waiting until you were legally married or something? It's a bit of an old-fashioned approach in this day and age isn't it? And how unbelievably noble of *you*, in particular, Jake."

A single tear ran down Jake's cheek, which Lucy caught sight of before he turned away.

Up until this point, Lucy had felt totally justified in her line of questioning. She had travelled all this way to let the bastard have it with both barrels, had looked forward to the confrontation even, but now she was wondering if she had overstepped the mark because perhaps not all was as it seemed.

And she found herself wondering that despite all her pushing of Jake Zennor's buttons, was she actually prepared to finally hear the truth. Judging by Jake's emotional reaction, she was concerned that her digging had unearthed something that would have been better left sleeping.

"Okay Lucy, I'll give you something that you can write about," sobbed an unusually resigned Jake as he sat down.

On seeing his master in distress, Elgar jumped out of Lucy's grasp and settled immediately on Jake's lap as if to verify where his true allegiance belonged out of the two humans before him.

"You can write about Jake Zennor, no better than a murderer in most people's eyes. Jake Zennor, the fallen angel. Jake Zennor, the failing pop star…finally reduced to a blubbering mess."

Lucy didn't mock. "You really did love her, didn't you?" Lucy now spoke with a genuine concern.

Jake replied by a simple nod of his head. This world-renowned pop star, an idol to many who time and time again had performed his songs with such confidence to packed-out arenas suddenly appeared a broken man before Lucy. She resisted from viewing the incredible situation as any sort of victory. She even felt some sense of privilege that Jake had chosen to let his guard down to her of all people. She knew enough about him to know that not many people, if any, would have seen this hard-edged rock star with his inner emotions so vividly exposed.

"Okay, Jake. Tell me the truth just once, and I'll be out of your life forever. I promise. Help me to understand what has really happened here."

Jake wiped his nose with the back of his hand and once again gave a resigned nod of his head. In his sub-conscious mind, Jake realised that talking about what had really happened with Alannah, no matter who the recipient to the information was, could only help in his healing process and grief. Jake had never gone along with the 'showbiz' accessory of having a personal shrink to chat with, although ironically in Jake's case, some form of counselling may possibly have proved beneficial in his grief for Alannah.

Lucy waited patiently allowing Jake time to feel comfortable about opening up to her. She knew this was about to be a big deal.

Before long Jake began. "Alannah knew about the other girls. We loved each other deeply but we never had much of a physical relationship. She had certain *complications* about intimacy if that's the correct term for the complex feelings that she felt. Believe it or not, she actually encouraged me to seek other sexual relationships, as long as I always came back to her and I didn't necessarily shout to her about it. As long as my other liaisons were purely physical with no emotional ties she was content.

"It's ironic really if I'd had my way I wouldn't have had the tabloid posse paint me half as colourful as they did, even though some of my male fans thought it was great that I seemed to be hooking up with girls left, right and centre.

"I certainly could have been more discreet at times, and I do consider myself weak, but I didn't actually get physical with every girl I met. An innocent dance on the dancefloor, or a gentlemanly escort home with no strings attached, suddenly gets magnified to mammoth proportions and twisted to suit the publication. There should be a lot less of such twisted journalism now I'm out of London perhaps? Believe me, the womanising lifestyle certainly didn't happen as much as you'd like to believe. But yes, there were times when I still had needs, I'm only human and Alannah understood that. At times, I was weak and boy did I feel guilty, but like I said she really was cool with it all.

"She was happy being in a relationship with me but she had the black dog hanging around far too often. Depression is an awful thing, Lucy. Alannah knew that I loved her for who she was inside and that I didn't view her as a sex object. It was difficult not to be all over her like a rash because she was so beautiful, but I knew never to push the physical side of our relationship. Alannah was secure in the knowledge that I would never seriously seek the *love* of another woman. She knew I loved her."

Lucy appeared curious but genuinely non-judgemental. "What made her think this way, Jake? You were going to be married, yet you hardly shared her bed and you were both okay with this? Please, help me to understand."

Jake brushed a tear from his cheek. "That's how deep our love ran. We had an unconditional love I guess. A love in a million, a billion, a trillion – I don't know! You see in Alannah's eyes I could give her a love that wasn't tainted or dirty. It was a love that was pure because sex just didn't matter or form part of the equation. And in spite of my handful of sexual relationships with other women, I was a man she could fully trust. I'm not proud of sleeping with other women, and I could have done more to keep the wolves from the door, but the press, of course, like to put their own twist on things. Most of the time the photos in the newspapers were actually innocent liaisons with girls that I just knew socially. They were often totally platonic friendships. And get this. Sometimes the 'kiss and tell' stories that were printed were actually given by girls I've never even met! The stories were total fabrications and were even supported by pictures of a girl superimposed in them standing next to me! But sleaze sells, doesn't it?"

Lucy listened on attentively.

"I swear to you, Lucy. Alannah understood and actively encouraged this arrangement because she thought it would help keep me. She had a very delicate and confused state of mind and this was her way of keeping a sense of security. She figured that if I had sexual liaisons elsewhere when we were not sharing a physical relationship ourselves, then I would have no reason to get restless and walk out on our love. The truth is I would never have left her anyway but only she knew how to square things for her own piece of mind.

"The ironic thing is I found her so fantastically beautiful that she was the only girl I wanted to make love with, but I always understood her fragility. That was our strength - we understood each other.

"Alannah knew that when all was said and done, she was the only woman I ever wanted. I guess it's hard for someone on the outside looking in to understand."

"What made her not want sex, Jake? Like you say, she was beautiful. Surely she was proud of her body? It is difficult for me to understand why she thought this way about sex and why she ultimately felt the need to kill herself. She seemed to have everything going for her. Why was she in such a confused and delicate state of mind?"

"Alannah had a cross to bear since her childhood. It was something that I'd taken the time to listen to her about, another reason why she loved me so much I guess. She told me how I was the only man who had ever listened to her. The few guys she had before me were only interested in that beautiful body of hers, you know, to be a bit of eye candy on their arm – but Alannah was so much more than that. Once they knew that the bedroom aerobics were few and far between they soon pissed off. But not me."

"This cross she had to bear. What was it?"

"I had to hear how that perverted bastard had tortured her and how he had hurt her, both physically and mentally.

That bastard hadn't been around for years but he was still hurting her every day. Hurting her in her mind." Jake was becoming frustrated at his own words.

"Go on, Jake. You're doing really well."

"She told me how she had lay awake crying as a little girl, terrified and confused because it was *a little secret that must never be shared with anyone.*"

"Oh my God," said Lucy. "Alannah was sexually abused by her father?"

"Yeah that's right, and the day that she killed herself she had left me a note. A suicide note left only for me and that's why the parasites of the media have never truly known why she chose to kill herself. I made believe that there had been no suicide note left at the scene. If your profession felt it necessary to persecute me for thinking I'd pushed her too far by screwing around then I was more than happy to be the diversion from the awful truth of the matter. I can let Alannah rest in peace with her dignity intact."

"But why suddenly did this awful stuff from her childhood push her to commit suicide after so many years living with the knowledge of the abuse, especially as you were helping her through it?"

"Because I found another sheet of paper with the suicide note. That dirty evil bastard had sent her a letter saying he was getting out of prison soon. For good behaviour believe it or not, and he indicated how they could 'pick up where they had left off.' He always knew how to torture her mentally as well as physically.

"Alannah actually had a history of suicide attempts and eating disorders, but I always managed to keep things out of the papers. I had the money to deal with extortion and blackmail if need be, but fortunately, that wasn't too often. Alannah didn't even have to know I was paying the scumbags off. I simply always wanted to protect her. But I failed. I didn't protect her in the end, did I?"

"You can't blame yourself, Jake."

Jake wiped his eyes with his hand. "At least Alannah's suicide note informed me how much she loved me and how she was grateful for my years of support. It wasn't enough, though; she would never ultimately be able to get over her history of abuse. I have willingly paid for top counsellors and psychiatrists over the years in a bid to free her of her demons. I'd have done anything to help her.

"I guess the letter exercised personal contact from the old man and this was just too much for her. It must have really messed with her head. If only she could have waited a few more hours until I was home. I knew I shouldn't have left her alone." Jake looked to the high ceiling, his eyes filled with tears. "Oh Alannah, don't you know that I would have protected you from anything and anyone." He broke down sobbing.

Lucy hurried to Jake and embraced him in an attempt to comfort him.

"Jake look at me," she said compassionately. Jake looked up, Lucy gently guiding him by the chin before cradling his head in her hands. Their eyes connected with a mutual honesty.

"Jake, I was wrong about you. I am so sorry that I have been such a callous and assuming bitch. You, on the other hand, Mr Zennor are a truly beautiful man."

"But a failure. You know, on that fateful day when I lost Alannah I placed more emphasis on my music than I did Alannah. I left her alone while I went overseas to try and save my stupid career. Well, I've failed with my career and worse still I couldn't even save her, could I? The only person I've ever really loved. I hate myself for not being there when she needed me most."

"Jake, you can't blame yourself for another man's evil. Alannah died knowing you loved her. You have to believe that she has carried that special love to wherever she is now, and that love is keeping her safe where her father and nobody else can ever hurt her again."

Lucy reached into the inside pocket of her coat and removed a small tape machine. Jake was astonished to see her remove the recording cassette from the device and fling it into the open fire.

"I won't be printing a word of what we have discussed today. I'm truly sorry Jake for all the crap that I've put you through. I've been such a narrow-minded idiot. I'm truly ashamed of my behaviour towards you. Alannah's secret will remain safe and I promise you that you won't be hurt by me anymore either. I will not write a single word and I will drop the story immediately. Please forgive me."

Lucy gently wiped away the tears from Jake's face and then a tear from her own cheek. She cautiously leant forward and found herself kissing Jake on the lips. Not sure if she'd done the right thing, she whispered softly, "I'm sorry, Jake. The emotion just got to me there for a moment. It's just, well, I would give anything for an ounce of a special love like you and Alannah shared."

They gazed into one another's eyes. The hostility and anger that was once so evident between the two of them had ironically been replaced by a strong desire for one another. Before long they were kissing passionately. Elgar sensed that three was a crowd and made himself scarce as they slipped from the chair onto the softness of the rug beside the open fire.

Jake began caressing Lucy's neck with his mouth as he lay on top of her. She sighed with appreciation. He moved down to her blouse and kissed the soft flesh beneath each buttonhole as he opened them until the blouse finally fell open. Lucy confidently rolled over so that their position changed with ease as she now sat upright across his crotch. She removed her unbuttoned blouse and black silky bra to reveal her breasts. Jake looked at them admirably in the firelight, and Lucy guided his hands over them. She then wrenched Jake's T-Shirt over his head and leading with her tongue kissed him pushing her well-proportioned chest into his. She gradually moved her mouth down his torso until eventually she had unbuttoned his jeans and lowered his boxer shorts. She proceeded to beautifully and thoughtfully caress him with her mouth and tongue.

Before long proceedings resulted with Jake being inside her. Their lovemaking became free of any inhibitions considering their relationship before today and their sexual chemistry entwined perfectly, each indulging in their own pleasure but eager to attentively please the other with thoughtful improvisation.

Within the pleasure of Jake's mind entered some confusion. Here for the first time, in a long time, he was actually *making love* again. This didn't feel like a meaningless episode of casual sex, amazing considering his resentment towards Lucy up until this point. But had he really resented her? He had certainly never found her to be unattractive in the physical sense. And after all, isn't there a thin line between love and hate?

And there felt no need for him to display any kind of sexual sacrifice with Lucy like he had done with Alannah. This felt like he was truly making love. Better still it felt like *they* were both truly making love.

But should he feel guilty considering the essence of his relationship with Alannah?

Yet it felt so right.

It felt so good.

Alannah had been uncomfortable at the thought of engaging in the act of making love.

However, it was obvious that Lucy didn't share this uncomfortableness. And why should she?

And Jake had to concede that he didn't believe that there was anything wrong what was happening either. He was enjoying the touch of a woman it and he shouldn't feel guilty about something that felt so right. He had simply been in an unusually tragic relationship with Alannah and he had respected her wishes to enjoy their life on a platonic level. And he had more than enjoyed that platonic relationship with her. That worked for them and it was no big deal.

But now Alannah was gone. Yes, he missed her, he will always miss her, but he was still here. He was still alive and he didn't need to hold back on his desires anymore if it felt right.

Jake's thoughts returned to total concentration on the matter at hand. Feelings of pleasure swept through his body. Feelings that had laid buried and dormant for so long. Jake could sense Lucy's obvious pleasure as he stroked her smooth skin while she let out breathy noises of bliss from her lips. It felt good to be bringing pleasure to someone in this way.

Afterwards, they rested a while holding and stroking one another, not speaking. Content, but finding their *new* situation a rather surreal and unexpected experience. It was not much later that Jake led Lucy to the bedroom where the lovemaking continued throughout the night.

CHAPTER 9

The violent shaking of Jake's oak bed shocked Jake and Lucy from their peaceful sleep.

As they woke into reality, they became harrowingly puzzled as to what could be causing the aggressive movement of the bed.

No entity could be seen to explain what was happening.

Lucy wanted to scream but terror silenced her. She looked at Jake in despair.

"It's okay," said Jake observing her fear. "Weird things happen in this house but I don't think we are in any danger. I don't think we are meant any harm."

Lucy managed to grab Jake in spite of the shaking bed and cowered her face into his chest. He was almost as scared as she was but he realised he had to remain strong for Lucy's sake.

However, their terror intensified when howls of laughter could be heard all around.

Suddenly the bed began to rise towards the ceiling, as the laughter grew louder. The bed levitated in mid-air for what seemed an eternity, carrying the combined weight of

Jake and Lucy with ease, before suddenly plummeting back to the floor with a loud thud.

The laughter halted abruptly as the bed crashed on the floorboards.

Suddenly there was silence.

Jake held Lucy tightly in a desperate attempt to reassure her.

Fortunately, they were not hurt, but Jake was both mystified and concerned as to what was causing the unpleasant experiences in his new home.

Lucy buried her head even further into Jake like a scared woodland creature retreating into its burrow when sensing danger.

The silence was broken by the now familiar phrase of music being generated from the piano positioned downstairs. It was the same haunting melody that Jake had heard on the night that he had become acquainted with Elgar.

"Jake, what is going on? I'm scared shitless," said Lucy, then she allowed a moment to pass recognising that Jake was unable to offer any explanation. "And what's that tune? It's beautiful."

CHAPTER 10

"You can play pool?"

"I have many hidden talents," replied Lucy.

"Oh really, and there's me thinking that you had shown me everything already," Jake's mind gleefully returned to the image of his and Lucy's time in the bedroom – before the bed had shook like an earthquake!

"There's plenty more to come yet, Jake. You ain't seen nothing yet."

"I can't wait."

"Let's just concentrate on playing pool for now, Stud."

"Ooh, you little tease."

"So who is going to break?"

"Ladies first."

"You may regret that decision; I'm going to kick your ass."

"You wish."

Shortly after moving into Abba Manor, Jake had the pool table installed into one of the ground floor rooms. It was a particularly excellent room to utilise; it was one of the few in the house that allowed natural light to spill between its walls, due to its positioning against the rising of the sun, coupled with the large bay windows that stood impressively tall. The room also provided a majestic view over the rolling hills of the peakland countryside. In stark contrast, most of the rooms in Abba Manor were dark and cold adding to the ambience of it being a haunted house – which Jake was begrudgingly beginning to accept.

Nevertheless, ghouls and all, Jake had set about transforming his home into a typical rock star's paradise, even applying for planning permission for work to begin on installing the obligatory swimming pool. Each time he splashed out on such extravagance Jake would square things in his own mind by donating anonymously to a charity or two. He didn't particularly see himself as someone who craved for material things, but he couldn't deny that the clichés of a rock and roll lifestyle played to the way he liked to live his life. After all, he had arrived from such humble beginnings in Bonsall, that surely once achieving financial success it simply made sense to spend the cash and to try and enjoy it. He had never bought into the proverbial 'rainy day' theory.

As Lucy bent across the table to take aim and break the triangular stack of pool balls, Jake couldn't help but admire her from the rear. Jake hadn't wanted the traditional green coloured cloth on the table, instead opting for a blue covering and he liked the way Lucy's denim-clad legs blended with its shade. Her figure was clearly stunning from all angles, and as she leant forward, he felt like grabbing her from behind there and then but managed to somehow resist the urge. He also watched the pool cue move within her hands like a submissive rigid cobra and found himself wanting to trade the cue for himself so that he could feel her expert fingers caress and squeeze him once more.

"Your turn," she said innocently, turning around and unwittingly shaking Jake from his fixation on her.

He recovered well. "I thought that you were going to kick my ass? You haven't potted a single ball from that break."

"And neither will you. I've left nothing for you to gain an advantage."

Jake weighed up the position of the balls and conceded that Lucy was correct, there was nothing on offer to pot. He therefore attempted a 'safety shot' by gently kissing one of the spotted balls with the white ball. Jake was reasonably pleased with his attempt; there didn't appear much that Lucy could do in reply.

How wrong he was!

Lucy quickly potted a ball into the middle pocket by using the cushion to rebound it upon. The pot seemed near impossible and Jake had not noticed its likelihood beforehand.

"Looks like I'm stripes then," declared a self-satisfied Lucy.

"Must have been a fluke."

Lucy leant over the table again for her follow-up shot. This time, she needed to approach it from a different angle and as she leant forward Jake could see the exposure of her cleavage. It took all his willpower not to rush over and intervene with her pool-playing, she looked so beautiful.

Jake felt both guilty and confused having these thoughts. Not because of Lucy. Lucy seemed to possess a sex drive almost as strong as his, but what would Alannah have made of their relationship - which at the moment was highly physical?

The arrangement that Alannah and Jake had agreed upon had never been a major issue, but Lucy had awakened something inside of him.

And Jake had to concede that he liked it.

Jake had willingly suppressed his sexual appetite with Alannah, respecting her issues and understanding the need to do so due to the abuse that she had once suffered. But although their relationship was fuller than most in many ways, in terms of beauty Alannah hadn't always been easy to resist as she too was drop-dead gorgeous. However, the physical side of their relationship had never been the primary connection between them.

During his time with Alannah, Jake had indulged in casual sex with only a handful of women, not nearly the amount that he had been accused of in the press. The liaisons had meant nothing. They had purely served a purpose as a means of sexual relief and no subsequent relationships had developed. And until now there had been no one since Alannah's death on any level.

But with Lucy it was different. The feelings he had for her confused him. Yes, he lusted after Lucy with a strong need to be satisfied, but when he touched and stroked her the feelings were markedly different than with any of his casual conquests. When he was intimate with Lucy he was only concerned about her and her pleasure alone. His own became secondary.

And after their lovemaking, Jake loved to lie awake simply to watch Lucy sleep.

Jake knew he was falling for this girl in a big way. The same girl who not too long ago was responsible for some very different feelings, including anger and resentment.

"I'm off to get a cold beer from the fridge. Do you want one?" Jake felt as though he needed to cool down if he was going to get through this pool game without ripping Lucy's clothes off.

"Yeah, okay. I need to take a pee actually. Is it okay if I use the downstairs toilet?"

Jake smiled. "For Pete's sake, Lucy. You don't have to ask my permission to use the flaming toilet."

"I was raised to always use my manners."

Jake smiled again, before leaving the room first, while Lucy placed down her cue and quickly decided to soak in the stunning view of the rolling countryside beyond one of the large windows. She was still admiring the view and had not yet left the room to use the toilet when Jake reached the kitchen.

Elgar had circled and rubbed against Jake's legs as an indication that he wanted to be fed, nearly causing Jake to fall, and in doing so significantly slowed down Jake's quest to grab the beers from the fridge. Elgar purred loudly as he savaged his pouch of trout and sardine enriched cat food. Eventually Jake made it to the bottom shelf of his fridge door in order to obtain two bottles of lager. As he shut the door he heard the toilet flush indicating that Lucy had finally left the scenery behind in order to answer her call of nature. They met in the hallway and walked back together towards the games room.

"After you," offered Jake.

"No after you," smiled Lucy.

"You're trying your hardest to prevent me from being a gentleman, aren't you?"

"You'd better believe it, Stud."

So Jake entered the doorway first. "Oh, I see that you are so good at pool that you managed to pot all the balls before you even left the room to use the toilet, including all of mine."

Lucy looked confused. "What do you mean? I left the table as it was. I haven't taken a single shot while you were away."

"Yeah right, I bet you cleared the table illegally didn't you? It was the only way you were going to kick my ass," Jake began to chuckle.

Lucy looked at the pool table and there was not a ball in sight – nothing but empty blue cloth. All the balls had mysteriously disappeared into the pockets of the table.

"Jake, I swear to you, I looked out at the scenery from the window and then went for a pee without even looking at the table, let alone taking another shot."

Jake reshuffled the bottles of beer so that both were being held in his one hand, before reaching out to stroke his girlfriend's hair. He realised by the expression on her face that Lucy was telling the truth.

"It's obvious then isn't it?" spoke Jake in a resigned tone.

"What is?" said Lucy.

"We are not the only ones playing in the games room today. It must be the ghosts of Abba Manor making their presence known once again!"

Lucy shuddered. "Pass me that beer quickly, Jake. I'm gonna need it!"

CHAPTER 11

"Are you sure this is a good idea?" asked Jake.

"Trust me, babe," answered Lucy. "If you want to know exactly what is going on around here this is the best way."

"What makes you such an expert?" said Jake unconvinced.

"I've read about these things."

"The only stuff I've ever read or heard about Ouija boards has always seemed dodgy. I heard that you can release bad spirits if you don't know what you're doing."

"Are you scared?" teased Lucy.

"Of course not."

"Okay then. Draw the curtains, light the candles and we'll begin."

Jake reluctantly complied with Lucy's instructions while she carefully placed the Ouija board onto the authentic oak table. The table was another piece of furniture that Jake had inherited with the property, along with the piano that played by itself! Unfortunately, it seemed that as well as some of its impressive furniture, original fittings and even a small collection of paintings, Jake had also inherited the hauntings of Abba Manor. The paintings, although well-crafted, were unnervingly dark in their use of colour and appeared spooky to Jake and Lucy. There was one portrait in particular which really freaked them out. It hung at the foot of the creaking staircase and depicted an unknown and evil-looking character dressed entirely in black. The dark eyes of the portrait eerily followed the viewer around no matter what angle he or she happened to be positioned.

The use of the Ouija board had been Lucy's idea to try and unearth some sort of explanation as to the paranormal activities that had occurred since Jake's return to the Peak District.

Although the shaking of the bed had distressed Lucy, on reflection she became intrigued and excited that Abba Manor could possibly be a haunted house and the investigative elements of her nature demanded that she find out more. She was also keen to genuinely find some answers for Jake, whom she now found herself caring for more and more.

"Ready," said Lucy, now feeling some nerves herself in the pit of her stomach.

"Ready."

The couple looked at one another with anticipation and slowly placed their index fingers on the overturned glass.

Lucy began the dialogue with whoever could be listening.

"Is there anybody there?"

"That's original," mocked Jake.

"Shush," half-snapped Lucy. She repeated her question. "Is there anybody there?"

There was no reply.

"Is there anybody there?" Lucy asked a third time.

Silence.

"This is bollocks," said Jake, but his cockiness was partly a smokescreen to hide his apprehension.

Jake shouldn't have mocked what he didn't understand.

All of a sudden the candles went out for a good four or five seconds before relighting themselves.

"Is there a breeze in here?" asked Lucy.

"All the windows are shut," replied Jake.

The candles went out and relit again.

"Holy shit," said Lucy.

Jake widened his eyes and then composed himself. "What's your name?" he asked.

No reply.

"Who are you?"

Still nothing.

"Can we help you with anything?"

The glass began to move and slowly began to spell out a word, gliding to each letter in turn.

M-U-S-I-C. The glass had spelt out the word 'music'.

"Did you move the glass, Lucy?"

"No way. I thought it was you."

Suddenly a deep red fluid began to ooze from the walls. Jake and Lucy unnervingly looked at one another as they each realised that it looked a lot like blood. The blood flowed more strongly until a mass of red fountains gushed down the walls, turning the floor into a pool of disturbing scarlet liquid.

"Oh my God! Do you think that somebody was murdered here, Jake?"

Jake was helpless to provide an answer.

Despite the alarming development seemingly deriving from the use of the Ouija board, Jake and Lucy's curiosity drove them to continue placing their index fingers on the glass.

Their curiosity was soon massaged as the glass moved again and repeated the spelling.

M-U-S-I-C.

Jake and Lucy looked at one another with widened eyes.

"That's how I earn my living," stated Jake, not quite knowing who to.

The glass then moved slowly but deliberately towards the words of "YES" and "NO" on the Ouija board, before deciding on its choice to divert its course and land on the affirmative word.

Then suddenly the old piano began to play the same haunting melody that had been heard before.

And the crimson waterfalls continued to flow.

"What the fuck is this all about?" probed Lucy.

Jake signalled with his free hand to silence her, not wanting to interrupt the flow or the connection with who or whatever had transpired.

Suddenly the glass picked up speed and abandoned moving towards any letters in particular. Instead, it went into a continual pattern of random spirals on the board. The spirals became faster and faster until they became quite frenzied.

"Why are you here?" asked Lucy in desperation, she had become quite uncomfortable with the manic spiral movements of the glass, especially as it was now moving independently of hers and Jake's fingers.

To her relief, the glass ceased from spiralling but then began to move once more returning to its method of steady movement towards the letters of the alphabet. It continued to move independently of Jake and Lucy's touch.

D-E-A

Lucy squeezed her eyes shut as she feared what word was destined to be spelt.

Her fear was realised as she opened her eyes again.

T-H.

The word DEATH had been spelt out.

Lucy and Jake glared at one another not quite knowing how to react. This was now becoming very scary. They could each feel an intense sense of energy around them in the room, presumably due to the connection that they had made with the spirit world.

Elgar, being a cat, was acutely sensitive to any supernatural existence just like any respective member of the animal kingdom and he arched his back as he also sensed a presence. He hissed at something as his eyes became transfixed on something that only he could see. His fur was standing on end like an extreme spiked hairstyle belonging to the most dedicated of punk rockers.

"What exactly do you mean by all of this?" inquired Lucy to the apparent spirit, not wholly sure if she really wanted to know the answer.

The answer that did emerge, transpired to surprise and confuse both her and Jake.

L-O-V-E became the sequence of letters slowly provided by the glass.

Jake breathed a sigh of relief. "Well, that's better."

All the time the piano music continued to play.

"You seem very emotional. Can we help you?" offered Lucy.

The glass moved to the word "YES".

"Please, tell us how?" asked Jake.

Once again the word M-U-S-I-C was spelt out.

The energy then decreased as if the final spelling of the word 'MUSIC' had exhausted the connection that had been made from another world.

The candles then went out for the final time and a door slammed abruptly in another room.

The piano music fell silent at the exact same moment, as did the gushing blood from the walls, which actually seemed to retreat back into the brickwork without a trace.

Somehow all evidence of the blood had totally disappeared! The room appeared exactly as it had done before Jake and Lucy had taken to the Ouija board.

"See I told you it would work," stated Lucy, although there was not a hint of smugness in her voice.

Jake nodded thoughtfully. "I certainly can't deny that doors to another world can be opened using this thing, Lucy. The problem is I think we are now left with even more questions than answers."

Jake and Lucy swore to one another there and then that they would never dabble with an Ouija board again.

CHAPTER 12

Jake was becoming increasingly disturbed at the unexplained happenings at Abba Manor, and he felt a compelling necessity to tackle the situation.

Excluding the odd invite to christenings, weddings or funerals, Jake hadn't been to church since he was a young boy, and this had only been due to the stern insistence of his mother. However, on this particular Sunday morning, Jake was encouraged by his desperate situation to attend church. He felt a sense of hypocrisy attending church in his hour of need, considering his lack of religious undertakings over the years, but he convinced himself that he had led an ethical enough lifestyle in the main and therefore any force of good, whether that be via God or anything else, would open rather than close a door on him.

A few heads turned as Jake entered the church, inadvertently interrupting the service which had long since begun. The sprinkling of teenage girls couldn't believe their luck, many only being at the service due to their parent's protests and therefore finding themselves in similar circumstances to Jake all those years ago.

Now, of course, seeing a bonafide pop star enter the church, they were certainly glad that they had made the effort to attend, albeit not for perhaps for the right reasons in the eyes of their parents. But Jake's presence suddenly had an unintentional helpful effect for the church – *'Maybe it's cool to attend church after all'* they thought.

Jake had certainly made an entrance befitting of a rock star, continuing to wear his designer shades even once inside the dimly-lit church. However, there had been no intention on his part to display any disrespect or attempt to upstage God in his own place of worship. Wearing shades indoors was just something he often did out of 'rock star' habit.

Father Irwin continued his sermon, although he too could not escape Jake's unexpected entrance. The kindly priest could not help but smile within as he contemplated that when the word inevitably spread through the parish of Jake's presence today, then surely next week's service would attract a record attendance.

He had recognised Jake at once. Not because of his fame, but because this was the same little boy, Jake Zennor, that he had seen reluctantly 'dragged' to his sermons over twenty years earlier by Polly Zennor, Jake's mother, a woman highly respected in the close-knit community of the time.

In spite of Jake's lack of enthusiasm for religion, Father Irwin realised that Jake had always basically been a good lad at heart. Indeed, during Jake's youth, stories would regularly reach the priest from the elderly members of the community whom Jake had helped in various ways. The energetic Jake would fetch the odd bit of shopping or do a spot of gardening for the most vulnerable members of local society. As far as Father Irwin was concerned, no matter what dizzy heights Jake's career may take him, to him he would always be just another member of his flock.

Father Irwin was intrigued however as to why Jake had chosen to walk into his church today so many years later. Despite his best efforts, the pace of the service inevitably quickened with the priest's anticipation. He was eager to speak with Jake again after all this time and satisfy his curiosity.

Jake had stood in front of thousands of people at a time performing his music with admirable confidence and self-belief, but here he was in the company of no more than 50 people feeling extremely out-of-place and uncomfortable. Putting the teenage girls that were present to one side, the older generations of people staring at him reminded him of his entrance on that rainy night at The World's End Pub. Fortunately, Nanette and Bethany were sitting at the rear of the church and there was room for him to sit next to them on the wooden bench. Bethany instantly became the envy of the other young females as the rock star smiled as he sat next to her. Closely too.

Once the service had ended, Jake said goodbye to Nanette and Bethany with the firm promise to see them again soon, before hanging around to speak with Father Irwin once the excitable crowd had finally cleared.

"Hello, Father."

"Hello Jake," welcomed Father Irwin in his softly spoken Irish accent. He placed his right hand on Jake's shoulder to enhance the warm greeting. "It's been a long time. It's good to see you back in the parish. How are you?"

Jake instinctively removed his shades before answering. "I think I might be in a spot of bother, Father. And I'm hoping that you may be able to help me."

Father Irwin listened attentively as Jake went on to explain about all the strange happenings that had occurred since his return. This included the ghostly taxi driver, the violent shaking of the bed, the mysterious potting of the balls on the pool table and by no means least, the haunting piano that was able to play by itself.

Jake did, however, choose not to inform Father Irwin of his and Lucy's experiment with the Ouija Board, fearing that the priest would not have approved at their irresponsible plunge into the occult.

Father Irwin listened carefully to Jake's predicament and was wise enough to know that however incredible the story seemed to be, the truth was clearly being spoken. A man who represents the epitome of goodness realises that the equivalent forces of evil must also exist.

"I can see that you are clearly troubled, Jake."

"I'm a loss as to what to do, Father."

Father Irwin gave a reassuring smile as Jake realised it was his turn to listen. Father Irwin described a wide spectrum of the paranormal to Jake, from spirit possessions of living humans to mischievous poltergeist activity. Jake was amazed at just how knowledgeable the priest was about the subject. Jake never pressed but he could sense that a lot of what Father Irwin was articulating could only be based on personal experience. He was astonished to discover that exorcisms and the like did not only appear in Horror novels and Hollywood movies, they were actually real life occurrences!

Father Irwin went on to inform Jake of an Exorcism that he had been party to in the Irish County of Roscommon. A young girl from a small community had become possessed by a devilish spirit. Many of the villagers were convinced that she was simply suffering from a form of mental illness, and many more ignorant locals claimed that she was a witch - a willing servant to the Devil himself.

However, Father Irwin explained that sometimes the Catholic Church had to accept when the need for an Exorcism arose. It was not something that the Catholic establishment, even as high as Rome, would draw attention to themselves, and most exorcisms would be conducted behind closed doors in the knowledge of only a chosen few.

The poor girl, who was barely in her teens, had savagely killed a horse and several sheep with a pitchfork, whilst shouting out expletives in a voice that did not seem to belong to her. The voice was much too deep and appeared of another gender entirely, let alone belonging to that of someone of much greater years to the girl.

Father Irwin remembered the disturbing laughter that had mocked him and his two companions as they stood before the spirit, making reference to their white 'dog' collars and pathetic uniform indicating they were slaves of the church.

Tears momentarily filled his eyes as he chillingly recalled the green stench liquid that projectile vomited from the girl's mouth and the fierce stare of hatred in her burning eyes.

He also told, while she was still possessed, of the girl's ability to rip the heads off chickens using only either her bare hands or her jaws, all the time still mocking with cackling laughter knowing that her performance was a disturbing spectacle.

Nevertheless, following a fierce battle using all the powers that Christ offered, the evil spirit was eventually removed from her body and she once again returned to the angelic girl that she had once been, never having any recollection of her possession.

The astonishing tales that Jake had heard from Father Irwin had totally convinced him that he had done the right thing in approaching the priest for help. By simply confiding in him, Jake already felt an enormous amount of pressure being released from his tense being and felt a warmer sense of security about the situation knowing that the Holy man was now part of the equation.

Father Irwin suggested a blessing of the house in the first instance and hoped that the need for any other intervention wouldn't be required. However, he warned Jake that he needed to be prepared for whatever action was ultimately necessary if good was to conquer evil.

The two contrasting men headed immediately to Abba Manor, but not before Father Irwin had collected his Bible, a crucifix and a bottle of Holy water.

Father Irwin and Jake could hear their own footsteps on the crunching gravel as they walked up the daunting driveway to the door of Abba Manor. Father Irwin had specifically requested that Jake park the car at the foot of the driveway as part of the priest's preparation to absorb the elements of the house as he approached it by foot.

Jake found himself deliberately slowing his pace in order for Father Irwin, who was now approaching seventy years old, to walk beside him comfortably. The years had slightly taken its toll on the kind man whom Jake had always respected since a youngster, regardless of his own opinion on organised religion. Father Irwin's hair was now thinning and grey. His waistline had spread too, but to Jake, this seemed to enhance the warmth and character of the man in the same way that Father Christmas was perceived and endeared by a young child.

These days, Father Irwin walked with a limp caused by arthritis setting into his left knee joint and hip. This did not go unnoticed by Jake, and he felt it a testament to the man that he was prepared to walk up the driveway in order to convene the situation in the most comprehensive manner.

They had not been walking long when Father Irwin turned to Jake to speak. "You know, it's amazing to think that I have served this parish for over 30 years but I have never had any cause to have any dealings with this house, until now. All the previous owners during my lifetime have never come close to the church. I'm no fool, Jake, and I realise that organised religion and the church are not everyone's cup of tea, but this house has always been surrounded by mystery and suspicion. I find it strange even by the law of averages that Abba Manor has never had just one spiritual proprietor."

"You're not doing much to relieve my fears, Father."

"I'm sorry, Jake. I should know better than to succumb to hearsay."

It was clear that Father Irwin didn't warm to the house as he got nearer the eerie building. The windows, although large, were very dark providing very little insight to the rooms, which only fed the imagination to what could be lurking behind the old walls. Abba Manor was by no means an inviting place to approach.

When they finally reached the door, Father Irwin paused to catch his breath and reached into an inside pocket. Holy water was thrown upon the old wooden door before Jake had time to turn the key.

The old door slowly creaked open and the two men entered the property.

"I can definitely feel a presence Jake; it has hit me instantly."

Father Irwin began to scatter more Holy water from his bottle as he proceeded further into the hallway.

"In the name of the Father, and of the Son, and of the Holy Spirit." Father Irwin then crossed himself. "Amen."

Jake instinctively did the same.

The priest continued.

"Peace be with this house and with all who live here. May the God whom we glorify with one heart and voice enable us, through the Spirit, to live in harmony as followers of Christ Jesus, now and forever. Amen."

"Amen."

"When Christ took flesh through the Blessed Virgin Mary, he made his home with us. Let us now pray that he will enter this home and bless it with his presence. May he always be here with you, share in your joys, comfort you in your sorrows. Inspired by his teachings and example, seek to make your new home before all else a dwelling place of love, diffusing far and wide the goodness of Christ."

Father Irwin's words were spoken with true passion, and Jake couldn't help but feel admiration for the manner in which Father Irwin was conducting his business.

Father Irwin paused for a moment and closed his eyes. He took in a deep breath before opening them again and he turned to speak to Jake. The tone of his voice was soft and reassuring.

"Don't worry Jake, it will be okay."

Jake nodded and left Father Irwin to roam the house at his will, in order to bless the other rooms of Abba Manor. At first, the old man climbed the creaky stairs to continue with the blessing.

The process of blessing the upstairs of the house passed unremarkably, but as Father Irwin was sprinkling Holy water in the final bedroom before the need to venture to the lower rooms, he was interrupted by the sound of beautiful music being played on a piano which he realised to be located downstairs. He smiled and found pleasure in reflecting that God's work had been done well in providing Jake with such undeniable talent.

Elgar meanwhile had been following Father Irwin into every room that he had blessed, and now that his work seemed to be done he felt pleasantly obliged to acknowledge the cat's presence.

"Well hello, little kitty. Can you help me to try and persuade your master to have a go on the church organ for me one of these days?"

"I'd be glad too," came Jake's unexpected reply from right behind him.

Father Irwin nearly jumped out of his skin.

"How did you get up here so quickly? Wait…I don't understand…I can still hear the music. The piano playing, it's not you, Jake? Is someone else at home with your talent? I was under the impression we were alone."

"Mmmm. Alone? Not exactly, Father. The piano music is not being played by me, or anyone I know actually. Isn't it beautiful, though? And haunting?" Jake spoke so matter-of-factly as an indication that he was getting used to the idea of the piano playing solo, after all, no harm had come to him because of it. He also felt more secure having Father Irwin present. Jake somehow felt more protected by the presence of the priest.

Father Irwin, however, still appeared somewhat startled.

"It... It's certainly beautiful," came the priest's reply.

Father Irwin ventured downstairs as quickly as he could considering his physical ailments, and sure enough discovered the piano playing by itself. He stood transfixed, mesmerised as he watched the keys push up and down by themselves in perfect harmony. "Well I'll be damned," he said.

He sprinkled some Holy water on the piano, perhaps as more of a test than a blessing.

The beautiful music simply continued.

"I have blessed this house almost from top to bottom, Jake, and hopefully, that will eradicate any evil spirits that may have been here. But of one thing I am sure. There is nothing evil about that music, Jake."

"Thank you, Father."

"May God be with you."

"And also with you."

CHAPTER 13

Jake didn't have anything, in particular, to occupy his time and was debating whether to venture outdoors and explore some of the delightful places that the Peak District had to offer. He felt that his mind needed occupying so that it wouldn't dwell too much on the whirlwind occurrences since his eventful return north.

He toyed with the idea of visiting the nearby town of Crich. The word Crich simply means "hill" giving a clue as to its location resting on a south-eastern foothill of the Pennine range. It was a town his father Cyril would often take him to as a child. His father being a bus driver enjoyed taking his only son to the tramway museum that is situated there, and he prided himself in being able to educate the attentive Jake on the finer detail of the history of the transport system. Jake remembered fondly of being taken with the bright colours of the trams, such as the Dutch imported orange tram that had once transported the citizens of Amsterdam and the many bright red trams that were also on show. Exploring a transport museum was not exactly 'rock and roll', yet for Jake undeniable memories of fondness had been secured, and to go and have another look in these later years should prove a pleasant enough experience he concluded.

These days, Jake had noticed that a popular television series called Peak Practice, which depicted a fictional country doctors' practice, had been filmed largely in Crich, and Jake was intrigued to discover what effect the series had had in the village.

Jake himself once penned a song entitled "Pennies from Heaven" inspired by Crich's historical connections to currency, although he never referred to the town and its history directly in the lyrics so Peak Practice could perhaps be considered Crich's first real brush with fame. In 1788 a pot of copper Roman coins had been found at Shuckstone Cross and in 1761 more Roman copper coins had been found on Crich Cliff, astonishingly dating from the reign of Hadrian, he who is famous for the significant defensive barrier known as Hadrian's Wall built in the Roman province of Brittania. Hadrian's Wall now serves as a component of the border between England and Scotland.

Jake had finally decided to grab his coat and venture out to Crich when a knock at the door echoed throughout Abba Manor. By now, Jake never quite knew what to expect when somebody, or something, called at his door.

He desperately hoped that it was Lucy.

Jake missed her terribly since her return to London, more than he ever thought he could. She was one of the few good things in his life at the moment. He longed to hold her, stroke her, touch her, laugh with her.

Wait. Laugh!

Jake began to realise that the deep-cutting void that had been left by Alannah was finally beginning to heal. Of course, he could never forget Alannah, but Jake now understood the need to move on. Before Lucy had entered his life, each day seemed to drift into the next with no apparent purpose. His grief seemed to leave him frozen in time, but now he was actually *living* again and not just *existing*.

Jake approached the door with caution.

As he turned the large brass handle he wondered if he was to be greeted by pleasure or pain on this occasion.

It was definitely pain.

Some would even argue that today's visitor to Abba Manor could be considered evil.

Before Jake stood a tall, slender man. His piercing eyes cut through Jake knowingly. His hair was jet black in colour and immaculately swept back and tied into a ponytail. His fingernails were longer than the average male and complemented the immaculate appearance of his hair. He was almost as tall as Jake but their build was not similar. Jake's shapely physique was in contrast to the natural skinniness of his visitor. The caller's appearance also held a Latin flavour.

"Hello, Jake. Aren't you pleased to see me?"

Jake had hoped that he would never have the displeasure of meeting the person that stood before him again, let alone at his own front door. Jake had recognised him instantly. It was Nick Santini, Jake's former songwriting partner of Blossom of Eden and one-time best friend. Nick was of mixed blood; his father an authentic Italian Restaurant owner, settling in England after meeting Nick's mother, who like Jake was a native of Derbyshire by several generations.

Once upon a time, the two boys had shared and enjoyed their adolescent years together, bunking off school to listen and analyse Beatle songs and fool about on their guitars, until they fused an uncanny ability to pen their own music.

Despite the obvious talent that resonated between them, the friends were not content to simply remain a musical duo and liked the idea of being part of a bigger band just like most of their musical heroes. They were only 17 years old when they formed Blossom of Eden, and largely due to the songwriting ability of Zennor and Santini the band were snapped up at the tender age of 19 by a major record label at the end of the 70s.

Blossom of Eden became a global success on a colossal scale before they even reached their early twenties and the band became one of the most major musical forces of the 1980s, before splitting towards the tail end of the decade. However, as the good times rolled through the years, Jake painfully watched his best friend gradually become a victim of his own success. He treated people like dirt and enjoyed doing so. Nick only cared for one person once he made the big time and that was Nick Santini.

Nick was unresponsive to his friend's attempts to advise and reason with him, eventually becoming so nasty and pathetic that Jake gave up caring for his songwriting partner, and instead began to focus his sympathy for the victims of Nick's appalling behaviour.

Jake had seen glimpses of Nick's dark side before they had become famous, such as using an air rifle to shoot at sheep, birds and cats. Jake could never understand how his friend could find pleasure in hurting an animal. In those days, though, Nick's better nature did seem to outweigh his cruel streak and Jake found him on the whole great fun to be with as they got involved in simple mischief together.

It was typically Nick who would get them into fights with the local boys or with the city gangs if they made the trip on a Saturday night into the centre of Derby, but it was always Jake who was left to finish the fight, standing up for his wayward pal to prevent him getting a pasting, which most of the time it was what he actually deserved.

With the fame, of course, came money and status, and while Jake always remained grounded, Nick's dark side escalated and became more severe. He wouldn't think twice about paying a hit man to break someone's legs for very trivial reasons, an exercise he orchestrated undetected on several occasions, and another example of his wickedness would be callously lashing out and striking a groupie when she had served her sexual purpose and he had grown tired of her affection. Jake detested how fame had made him such a cold-hearted and nasty bastard.

Needless to say, Jake and Nick had not parted on good terms when the band split. Nick had taken the band to court, demanding that a larger proportion of the royalties were owed to him, falsely claiming that he had been the band's sole founder member and amazingly stating that he had been the only band member to write any of the band's songs, previously giving Jake an equal songwriting credit simply as a generous favour to his old-school pal. Fortunately, Nick failed with his ludicrous lawsuit, but he did somehow manage to strike a typically underhand deal in obtaining sole publishing rights and copyright to the entire Blossom of Eden catalogue. This resulted in the astonishing situation that if Jake ever wanted to perform one of his own compositions from the Blossom of Eden days, he would need to seek Nick's permission to do so while Nick reaped the financial rewards as Jake sung his heart out!

Towards the end of the band's demise, Jake and the other members hated the way that Nick would overstep the mark with the groupies, treating them like his personal property and tossing them to one side once he had had his fun. By their own admission, none of the members of Blossom of Eden had been saints but they were basically decent human beings, especially compared to the likes of Nick Santini. They had all willingly indulged in the wild times of sex, drugs and rock and roll – after all that had been one of the fundamental aspirations of starting a band, but Nick began to regularly have sex with suspected underage girls. This disgusted the rest of the band and in hindsight, Jake regularly found himself these days wishing he had done more to intervene, but then again Nick had always denied they were underage anyway when confronted.

Even Abe had convinced Jake to let sleeping dogs lie back in the day, outlining how any adverse publicity could have harmed the band's reputation.

It was ironic that now, Jake was the one who was receiving adverse publicity since Alannah's suicide.

And even since the split, despite all of the bitterness that Nick has caused, no member of Blossom of Eden has ever exposed Nick for what he was really like behind the public façade, even though Nick would never have shown them the same amount of loyalty in a million years.

"What the fuck do you want?" spat Jake.

Nick gave a conceited smirk before replying.

"Now that's no way to greet your best friend, Jake."

"Best friends don't screw each other over."

"All in the past, Jake. Water under the bridge my friend, as far as I'm concerned. Come on mate, let's bury the hatchet."

"I'd like to bury it into your nasty fucking skull."

"Come on Jake, it's time to kiss and make up."

"Why? What's in it for you?" Jake was already convinced that Nick could only have shown up for his own gain and had no genuine desire to call a truce.

"Come on, don't be like that. So I've made mistakes, it was just business that's all. It was never personal. Let's be mates again, I never did want our friendship to be compromised."

"You've got a fucking nerve. You tried to claim that you wrote my best songs and when that little scam failed you still somehow ended up fucking owning them. And if you truly want to make amends are you planning to pay Fergus and Saul a visit too?"

"No. They were never my mates, Jake. Not like you. They were just puppets to play my music."

"They are good lads, Nick. All you have ever done is use people. What the hell happened to you, man? You turned into such a wanker. I'm only going to ask you one more time, Nick. What do you want?"

Nick paused and then gave another annoying smirk before replying.

"Ten grand please mate."

Now Jake's suspicions were cemented.

"Ten grand! You must be fucking joking and if you are not joking, you are either very brave or very stupid. When I think of all the times I stopped you getting your face smashed in, I was such a mug. Well, nothing will give me greater pleasure right now than to make up for all those saved beatings by kicking the crap out of you myself. I pay you enough money when I want to sing one of my own fucking songs, why should I give you ten grand?"

"Calm down, buddy. Talk to me. We had some great times mate, you know that. What about all those hours we spent talking through the night, drinking those bottles of Bourbon dry."

Jake was having none of it. "You were a different guy back then. Just tell me what this is all about and then you can fuck off out of here."

"Tell me, Jake, do you miss Alannah?"

"None of your fucking business?"

"I'm sure that you do, and I'm sure you'd like to keep her memory alive with all the dignity that it deserves."

"Get to the fucking point, Santini," snarled Jake, his volcanic temper beginning to erupt.

"It must have been *hard* for you mate - or perhaps not I guess, ha. Never having sex with the woman you love. You should have put it about a bit more like I did. No ties, no *memories.*"

"You are walking a fucking tightrope, Santini."

"Mind you, Jake, I'm not sure that even I would want to go up someone after her own dad has."

Enough was enough and Jake saw red as his patience finally ran out. He punched Santini straight in the mouth, cutting his lip and knocking him to the ground.

The scumbag cowered as he pathetically attempted to scramble backwards on the floor as if he could somehow escape the towering Jake.

"Don't hit me again Jake, please," whimpered Santini, attempting to stem the flow of blood with the rear of his hand. Jake paused, his fists still clenched. Knowing that Santini was no physical match he reluctantly allowed Nick to stand.

"If you hit me again, Jake, I'll make it twenty grand."

It took every ounce of willpower, but Jake managed to restrain himself, quickly realising that some type of extortion was on the cards here. He decided to listen to what the scumbag had to say for now and if necessary he could always floor him again afterwards.

"What are you talking about, Santini, and how do you know so much?" Then Jake had an awful thought. "Oh my God, have you been talking to Lucy? The bitch. I'll fucking kill her after I've killed you that is."

"Lucy? A new woman in your life, Jake? Well, well, well. Alannah's barely cold and you're already keeping her side of the bed warm with another. Don't worry, it's not your new bird who sang like a canary. I'm sure I can get some dirt from her, and perhaps even on her, another time. For now, let's talk about Alannah and her interesting past with Daddy."

"You disgust me. I didn't think that even you could sink to blackmail, Santini. I won't let you crap all over Alannah's memory, do you hear me? Anyway, who would believe you?"

"Ah, but I've got it from the horse's mouth you see, so are you willing to take the chance pretty boy? I've got a letter giving a blow-by-blow account from a certain Mr Ashe, you know the father of Alannah Ashe, on how he used to spend time with his daughter.

"He wants to write a book and confess all to the world, you know the sort of thing. *I've served my time but this is the real relationship between me and my daughter, the dead fiancée of rock star Jake Zennor.* He wants me to put up the money for the book and its marketing, pull in a few favours in the publishing industry. It's amazing how many people are as warped as I am you know." (The accessibility of 21st century independent publishing wasn't anywhere near as advanced in the 1990s.) "Obviously, with my weight behind the story, it will be better received. I'm sure you've noticed that I've had a number 1 hit recently. That's one more than you, old friend. The old man recognises my talent for words, he has hinted at me possibly even ghost writing the book from his sordid little memoirs which he created in the clink. You know, I might just do that; it could be a nice little earner, it could help catapult me back onto the front pages too. But ten grand from you, Jake, that's all I'm asking for. I'd say it's a very small price to pay in order to keep everything hush, hush. I'll tell old man Ashe the deal's off. I'm sure that I would make a lot more than ten grand if I was to finance the book, but as you're a mate, Jake, I'll do you a favour. What do you say?"

Jake promptly knocked him to the ground again.

"Show me the letter."

"Ok, ok. Can I stand up first?"

"For now."

Nick wearily got to his feet and produced a letter from his inside pocket.

Jake snatched it from Nick and proceeded to read it. It dawned on him that Santini was speaking the truth. He didn't bother to rip it up as he could tell that it was a photocopy and realised that a scumbag like Santini would have the original stored away safely.

Jake thought for a minute, trying to weigh up his options.

He could beat Nick Santini black and blue but would that prevent Alannah's memory from being laid bare for all to see? Although Jake would momentarily be satisfied, Santini would surely ensure that the story unfolded into the public domain.

Jake composed himself and reluctantly realised that ten thousand pounds was a small price to pay to protect the woman he had loved in life and death. His only regret being that the money was going to a low-life called Nick Santini and a scumbag like that should not be allowed to profit from Alannah's tragedies.

"Okay, Nick you win. I don't have that kind of money to hand so will a cheque do?"

"How do I know it won't bounce? I mean your career isn't doing so good these days is it, Jake? Funny that really. Since the split I've had a number one single myself, did I mention that? I always knew that I was carrying you lot, best thing I ever did was to break away from Blossom of Eden." Santini was enjoying twisting the knife, but Jake chose not to take the bait, for now, he just wanted this matter over and done with as quickly as possible.

"Look, I can give you about three grand cash and a cheque for seven grand. If you want any money now, it will have to do. To be honest the price is cheap if it means that I don't have to see your ugly face again."

Santini smiled. "As we are old mates Jake, it's a deal. I know I can trust you. It's your biggest fault, Jake, you're just too nice. A bit of that ruthlessness that I've got might make your solo career almost as successful as mine."

"At least I can sleep at night. Anyway, your bubble will burst, Nick. A career in music is a marathon, not a sprint; I'll be around longer than you will. Keep looking over your shoulder because one day your karma will be right behind you waiting to pull you under. Your pretty face won't last forever, especially if you cross me again."

Jake closed the door refusing to invite the scumbag into his home. He went into the kitchen and withdrew three thousand pounds from his safe, which was hidden behind the unlikely refuge of an oil canvas of a Robert Bakewell New Leicester Sheep. He reluctantly returned to Nick with the cash and wrote him a cheque for the remaining balance.

"As I trust you, Jake, I won't count the money. I'll put the original letter in the post to you, recorded delivery, and you have my word that Alannah's old man won't receive any help from me with his mission to spill the beans. It's been a pleasure seeing you again, Jake."

"Well don't keep in touch. You've got what you came here for this time; don't think you can push it. Now get away from my house while I'm feeling generous enough to still let you breathe."

"I'll see myself up the drive then," and on those words, Nick left.

Santini hadn't pulled far onto the drive, inadvertently concealing the view of his Porsche behind an oak tree. As he proceeded towards the top of the drive he noticed that his car was missing. It appeared that it had been stolen.

Justice, perhaps?

Could Jake's warning of karma creeping up on him be happening so soon? Realising that he couldn't return to Jake's house with his tail between his legs he decided to walk up the country lane beyond Abba Manor. As he walked he looked up to the sky and was unnerved by the swiftness in a change of the cloud formations above him. Fairly soon darkness began to fall too and in a heartbeat, the pleasant weather conditions quickly turned to dreary rainfall.

Santini eventually reached the top of the lane where he came to a T-junction and decided to rest and gather his thoughts. He noticed an old Georgian red pillar-box and he removed the original letter from Alannah's father from his back trouser pocket, placed it in an envelope, which was already addressed to Jake and posted it. The bastard had had it all the time. Jake had kept the photocopy too, so now all evidence of the letter was effectively laid to rest. It was nothing short of a miracle that Santini had actually managed to keep his side of the deal – albeit he was willing to chance the omission of the recorded delivery system.

Santini felt bittersweet. He had just made himself ten thousand pounds richer but he was still missing his car. *Never mind*, he thought, *it's insured, I'll just use the Jaguar tomorrow instead.* It was amazing how frugal he could be with money, considering the riches he already had. The taking of £10k from Jake had been more about the victory over his old buddy rather than the amount he had pocketed.

Santini was troubled though on how he was going to get back to London when suddenly a taxi pulled up out of the blue. Perhaps his luck would hold out a little longer. The rain was now falling heavier and lightning was illuminating the sky at frequent intervals. The driver slowly lowered his window in order for him to talk to Nick Santini.

"You look as if you need a ride, mate?"

"I'll give you £500 to take me to London, and make it quick." As ever Santini showed no hint of manners or common courtesy.

"Sure thing. Hop in," said the taxi driver.

Santini climbed into the rear of the taxi.

"London you say, mate? You are a long way from home. For such a long journey, I think we had best be on first name terms. The name's Archie. Pleased to meet ya."

It was the same ghostly taxi driver, Archie, who had taken Jake to The World's End pub on that rainy night.

Nick Santini being his usual arrogant, ignorant self did not engage in much conversation until after about 25 minutes of the journey when he felt that the route was a little strange and he said in a sharp tone, "Arnie, where the hell are you going?"

"The name is Archie, sir."

"Yeah, whatever. Haven't you heard of motorways up this way? We've been climbing cliffs for miles now."

"I thought that Sir would perhaps appreciate the scenic route."

"Well, I don't, you inbred moron. If you want your money, you had better put your foot down."

"Gladly," said Archie, and with that, the cab seemed to accelerate at an unnatural pace. They were moving at about 120 miles per hour within a matter of seconds, taking bends at a dangerous rate as the car climbed the windy roads of the peaks.

"Is this fast enough, Sir," said Archie grinning.

Archie's erratic and dangerous driving was unsettling Santini.

"Do you realise who you've got in your cab? Do you know who I am?"

"Oh yes Sir," said Archie, his tone contrastingly more menacing now than it had been. "I know exactly who you are and I know exactly the kind of little shit that you are." Archie then immediately slammed on his brakes without warning, causing Nick to fly forward and smash his nose on the headrest of the passenger seat before him.

"Tut, tut. Really Sir, you should be wearing your seatbelt you know. Or perhaps you are far too important to wear a seat belt? But as you can see, even little shits like you bleed. Your blood is just as red as the next mans, only yours probably runs a little colder."

Barely conscious Santini moved an arm in the direction of the door handle.

"Let me out. I need to get out here."

"But Sir, you haven't paid your fare," said Archie now in an ever-increasing sarcastic tone.

Nick managed to reach into his pocket and pull out the contents. Still dazed he threw the money towards the front of the car, not realising it was the complete £3000 along with Jake's cheque.

He went for the door handle again. All the locks on the doors shut simultaneously, surprising considering Archie's car was built way before central locking systems were commonplace in British motors.

"Please driver, what's going on here? Please let me out. I'm sure I've more than matched the fare you quoted. I have no beef with you, mate. Look, I know I'm in the middle of nowhere, but please let me out."

Nick's arrogant behaviour had been vanquished and his manner now oozed with a whimpering, desperate and pathetic tone. "Will you let me out...please?"

Archie scratched his chin, biding his time as he toyed with Nick's fear. He was receiving great satisfaction watching him squirm. Finally, he answered Nick's plea. There was only ever going to be one answer.

"No."

Archie slammed his foot on the accelerator and sped clean off the side of the cliff. The car glided through the air filled with the noise of Archie's cackling laughter and Nick Santini's helpless screams. Archie's laughter continued but his presence vanished along with the car and cheque leaving only Santini and the money flying aimlessly through the air until the miserable rock star finally hit the ground below.

He didn't stand a chance. Nick Santini died instantly.

CHAPTER 14

With a mixture of terror and amazement, Jake watched the white hands dancing across the keys of the piano, playing that same haunting melody that he had become so accustomed to hearing. This was the first time that hands had actually been visible to Jake and he became mesmerised as they expertly pushed on the ebony and ivory colours. Until now only the keys of the piano themselves could be seen, moving up and down in perfect unison to the music. Yet still Jake could not see any arms attached to the hands or any arms attached to a body. So why now could he see hands caressing the notes of the piano? Why had this moment been chosen to reveal the hands? And why was there still no revealing of a whole person?

Jake then became confused. His mind switched to trying to understand how he was able to see the hands playing the piano from the bed where he lay when there was a flight of stairs and walls and floors separating them. He was in a totally different room and he was in his bed. Yet he could see them so distinctly. *How could this be?*

Then he realised why the hands appeared so ghostly white in colour. A pair of immaculate white gloves covered them. So immaculate that there appeared no evidence of a seam or stitching. The gloves fitted the contour of the hands and fingers so perfectly it was as if they were a second skin. Ghostly white skin.

Then the hands slowly left the piano maintaining a life of their own, but the piano continued to play by itself, just like the night that Jake became acquainted with Elgar. The hands maintained the ball-shaped position of a trained concert pianist and moved across the floor like two graceful dancing spiders. The fingers and thumbs were like ten miniature ballerinas' legs, the movement so light and dainty.

The eerie hands reached the bottom of the stairs and even had the audacity to stop and turn to one another as the music continued. They appeared to look at one another as if they had eyes, before beginning to slowly climb the stairs, as if some telepathic communication had taken place between them. Jake could sense they were coming, could even see them in his mind's eye, but he was helpless in being able to do anything about their journey.

The hands moved slowly and deliberately, yet still with an air of grace. They reached the top of the stairs and waited a while. Jake was inwardly praying that they might head off in the opposite direction of his bedroom, but his prayers were not to be answered as once again they began to move in unison. Towards his door.

The door was already ajar there being no need for the hands to push it open. They made their way across the dark wooden floorboards and onto the woven mat that lay before Jake's bed. He prayed inwardly again that they wouldn't bother him, but he knew it was a hopeless task. He knew that it was only a matter of time before they climbed up the bedpost and landed on his duvet. He knew that they were teasing every inch of fear out of him before they eventually climbed along the bed and reached his throat.

Jake somehow realised that the hands' mission was to strangle the life out of him. Yet although he knew this, why was his body preventing him from stopping them? He lay in his bed paralysed and no matter how hard he tried he simply could not move. The restriction of his movements was stronger than a mere paralysis of fear. His whole being was subject to a physical paralysis caused by something, not of this world. All Jake could do was helplessly wait to meet his fate, like a fly does when trapped in a spider's web.

Then they inevitably began to move up the bed.

Jake sensed that if the hands had the power of laughter, then they would be cruelly laughing at his predicament as they moved in for the kill.

They moved slowly to prolong their victim's anguish. Jake desperately tried to move again but it was impossible.

Jake could now feel them at his midriff, ironically their light movement causing a tickling sensation through the thin bedclothes. Then they slowly moved further along the surface and eventually closer to Jake's face.

Jake knew that this was it. This was the moment that they were going to wrap themselves around his neck and strangle him to death.

Jake was terrified.

One by one he felt each finger embrace his neck, moving slowly and deliberately to prolong the terror. In spite of the close-fitting gloves, the fingers felt icy cold. As Jake felt the tenth digit rest in place he felt the hands begin to apply pressure to his neck. The icy squeeze of the hands demonstrated how they were clearly determined to halt his breathing.

The hands squeezed harder and harder.

Jake felt the life draining from him; he tried to move once more to stop the pain, to desperately try to save himself, but still he could not move. Jake helplessly began to feel himself slip away.

Jake then began to see a bright light which was terrifically blinding, but in the distance, he could make out the faces of his deceased mother and father. They were smiling and seemed very happy.

He could still feel the hands squeezing at his throat.

Then he could see Alannah, standing to the right of his parents. She too was smiling and was drawing him closer to her with the gentle calling of a hand gesture.

Jake could still feel the presence of the hands upon his neck but the pain was now curiously diminishing.

What should he do? What could he do?

Although he longed to interact with all three people again he felt this was not his time to go. He tried to move again without success.

Jake attempted a further time to move but it was hopeless. The unexplained paralysis was simply too overwhelming.

Then he tried again with all the strength that was locked deep within him…

The phone rang out five times before it eventually woke Jake to a full state of consciousness…and boy, was he happy to trade his sleep for the sound of the voice at the other end of the line.

It was Lucy.

It made a welcome change to be awoken by the serene voice of the woman now enhancing his life, albeit her career restricted their ability to meet up more often. Lucy's phone call had broken the now too familiar pattern of Jake waking up in cold sweats. Unlike today, Jake was not always having his sleep broken by a welcome distraction. He had experienced similar dreams of near death experiences before today, causing him to wake in a cold, anxious sweat. They seemed so frighteningly real. Jake was getting used to waking in complete darkness following various terrorising threats to his life, including almost suffocating in an airtight darkened room and being buried or burnt alive. *What could these recurring dreams of near death possibly mean?*

"Hi honey," Lucy said affectionately. "Have you seen today's papers?"

"I don't read them remember," Jake replied. His answer was surprisingly lucid considering the bad dream that he had just experienced. He chose not to tell Lucy about it.

"And you haven't listened to the radio news either?"

"No babe, to be honest, you woke me up. What time is it?"

"About 8:30. I'm sorry to wake you Jake, but I've got some news I must tell you about. Before long you may have the press wanting to talk to you."

"Why? What's happened?"

"It's about your old sparring partner, Nick Santini."

Jake sat bolt upright, any lingering lethargy was fully blown away by Lucy's revelation. Jake paused silently for a moment and an emotion of horror rushed through him. He instinctively concluded that Santini had double-crossed him. *The bastard's kept the money and still gone to the press.* Jake realised that Nick was more than capable of performing such a devious act.

"What about him?"

"He's dead, Jake."

"Dead? How?"

"He's been found at the bottom of a cliff, by a couple of ramblers. Early indications are that he's been there for a few days." Lucy elaborated on the details in the newspaper she had before her.

As she read, Jake managed to get out of bed and downstairs to his post for the day. Carefully perching the cordless phone receiver between his ear and shoulder he opened the original letter from Alannah's father that Nick had posted to him.

It was over.

"The police believe it was suicide," revealed Lucy. "He must have jumped."

Even more relief drained from Jake, fearing that he could somehow have been implicated in Nick's death. The location where Nick had been found wasn't too far away from Abba Manor and after all, Jake certainly had a motive. But then again so did a good many other people who had fell victim to the evil ways of Nick Santini.

"Really?" said Jake. "I must say Lucy; you sound curiously chirpy considering you are breaking the news to me that my one-time best friend is dead."

"Do I? Sorry, I don't mean too. I know you've hated each other for many years now so I'm not sure how you'd feel about it. Seriously, are you upset? I guess he was a big part of your life once."

"Don't worry Lucy, my tongue is firmly in my cheek. I won't shed any tears for Nick Santini, if only you knew the half of it."

Lucy failed to pick up on Jake's remark.

"Yeah, I won't grieve for him either. I probably shouldn't say this but I think the world is a better place with him dead. Do you know what they found on him?"

"What?" asked Jake intrigued. He knew it couldn't be the letter now.

"Photographs of child pornography and an address book containing contact details of known paedophiles. There was quite a bit of money scattered around too by all accounts, not that he'll be spending it anytime soon. He certainly won't be remembered as a martyr or an icon. The bastard deserves to be dead."

"Child porn? That's sickening. I had no idea even Santini could sink that low."

"Yeah, terrible isn't it. I hope he rots in hell. He certainly won't be a cherished memory like those who have gone before him will he? He will never be mentioned in the same breath as either Elvis, Lennon or Hendrix. Anyway, let's not waste another word on Nick Santini. If I am sounding chirpy, it's because of some other very good news I have for you."

"Oh yeah, what's that? By the way, you forgot to include Jim Morrison in your list of dead iconic rock stars." Jake couldn't help but wonder if he himself could soon be added to that illustrious list considering the unpleasant dreams that he was experiencing. Were they somehow prophetic?

"I'm coming to stay with you. If you want me to of course? And Nick Santini was never as talented or as good looking as Jim Morrison."

"Or as any of the others. Anyway, who said that I want you here?" mocked Jake.

"Ha-Ha, very funny. You know you can't bear to be apart from me really, Zennor."

"Okay, I confess. I have missed you not being around," answered Jake more sincerely.

"I need to do some detailed research in Nottingham for a few weeks. I'm feeding into a major tourist drive for the UK, so I'll be investigating all the history of Robin Hood for starters. I can be with you tonight if you are willing to meet me at East Midlands Airport? I'll be landing about nine. The company are willing to fly me up as I said that I can save them hundreds of pounds in hotel expenses if I stayed with you instead."

"You cheeky and presumptuous cow," laughed Jake.

"You say the nicest things, Jake. You're such a catch for me."

"You know I'm only joking. It'll be great to have you; I mean more for Elgar's sake of course. He's missing you more than I am me thinks."

"And me him more than you. It's Elgar who I really want to see."

Jake smiled with the banter. "I'll see you later. I'll be eagerly waiting at the airport."

"Glad to hear it. Bye"

"Bye." Jake punched the air as he hung up.

CHAPTER 15

Lucy woke to the sweet sound of birds singing in the tranquil countryside of the Peaks. The previous night of hot passion had resulted in the window being left slightly open, although there was now a slight chill in the room. She moved closer to Jake and kissed him on the cheek causing him to stir. "What time is it?" he said stretching.

"Who cares," said Lucy. "I could just laze here forever."

"Well at least the bed's not shaking today," said Jake.

"You certainly know how to kill a beautiful moment, Jake," said Lucy, playfully slapping his bare chest.

"Ouch," mocked Jake. "You shouldn't strike the man you love."

"The man I love? You're very sure of yourself Jake Zennor. I tell you what if you go and make me a nice cup of tea I might just begin to fall in love with you."

Jake smiled, stretched again and then dutifully climbed out of bed. Lucy slapped his bare backside before he slipped a pair of black boxers on. Finally, he ventured downstairs but it was not long before he returned.

"I'm out of milk! I'll pop down the village stores and get some. Will you be okay on your own?"

"Err, I should think so. I'm a big girl now, Jake."

Jake got serious for a moment. "I know, but will you really be okay considering what can go on here. The bed might shake or the piano might start playing. You know how it is. You could get spooked."

"No, honestly I'll be okay. You know what, Jake? I've been wondering about these ghostly goings on. Do you think that it could be Alannah?"

Jake paused a while and seriously considered Lucy's suggestion before answering. "Alannah? No, I don't think so. She wouldn't deliberately set out to scare me. And as beautiful and as clever as she was she never had a talent for music, so at least I don't believe that the piano playing could be caused by her."

"But perhaps she disapproves of our relationship? It would certainly explain the bed shaking that night. And when one departs this life to reach the other side, perhaps you begin to possess all sorts of new talents. Perhaps she can now play the piano or can at least use it as a vehicle to communicate with you Jake, knowing that you are involved in music."

Jake fell silent again contemplating Lucy's theory. Finally, he shook his head and dismissed what Lucy was saying.

"I'm sure that she wouldn't disapprove of us, Lucy. I told you that she actually sanctioned me to fool about with other women when she was alive."

"But Jake, we are not fooling about, are we? We are in a serious relationship. She might object to you actually being in love again."

Jake walked over to the bed and took Lucy's head in his hands. He attempted to reassure her. "Look, Lucy, I'm sure that Alannah would want me to be happy. She wouldn't object to me finding happiness with you. I'm convinced that if she is looking down on us now it can only be with her total blessing."

"Do you really think so?"

"Yes, I really think so. Now stop being daft. I'll go and get that milk."

"Okay," said Lucy beginning to find her loving smile again. "You do that; I'm spitting feathers here. Some people need drugs and some people need alcohol. What I need first thing in the morning is a nice cup of English tea. Without it, I can't face the day. Tea is my vice and it will never change."

"Oooh, you're so Rock and Roll." Jake looked around the bedroom for clothing that would not compromise his speed. He opted for a plain burnt orange T-shirt, that probably wasn't capable of combating the current temperature outdoors for his quick errand to the shop, and he also discovered a pair of jeans that lay crumpled in the corner of the room. It was not clear if the jeans had recently been washed and were waiting to be ironed, or if they had simply been discarded and forgotten one evening when the need to sleep had been the pressing priority.

Jake did not bother to locate any socks, fiddling with them and actually finding a matching pair would be far too time-consuming. He was far too keen to rescue his damsel in distress and produce the requested cup of tea that meant so much to her. And to be honest he fancied a brew too.

Jake then put on his trainers that were conveniently handy. He did not bother to tie the laces, instead opting to tuck them into the sides of the footwear, hoping that they would last the swift trip to the shop and back. Once his attire was complete, he gave Lucy an affectionate wink of the eye before he left the room. Jake didn't bother to brush his hair hoping that a quick run through with his fingers would suffice.

Lucy sank her head back into the pillow and began to relax. Her mind wandered, filled with thoughts of Jake and how lucky and content she felt now that she was sharing her life with him. She smiled to herself when she thought of his little cute mannerisms that enhanced his attractiveness, like the way he twisted his ear when he was thinking. She also liked the way his eyes widened in unison with raised eyebrows when he was interested in a topic of conversation or enthralled in a TV programme. What made it more endearing was that when this was pointed out to him, Jake was in complete self-denial that he could portray such gestures. Lucy loved to playfully tease him about it.

Lucy then began to wonder if Alannah had liked these things about Jake too, or had she even known of any other traits of Jake's that Lucy had yet to discover. In spite of what Jake had said to her, Lucy still wasn't convinced that it wasn't Alannah who was contacting Jake from beyond the grave, and she began to question if she had the right to be in Jake's life. Lucy wondered if she and Jake had got together too soon after Alannah's death and was somehow being disrespectful to her memory.

Lucy's trail of thought was abruptly interrupted by an unexpected loud bang. Feeling shocked, she sat upright clinging onto the sheets as if somehow they could suffice as a protective shield. Lucy called out Jake's name, hoping it was him who had returned but in reality, she knew it was too soon. She listened for his reply but there was silence. Even the singing birds had seemingly become mute. *But Why?* Had a ghostly presence appeared? Was it Alannah?

Lucy felt scared, but she desperately tried to convince herself that the bang must have been her imagination whilst she had been deep in thought. She listened hard but could hear nothing, which momentarily relaxed her.

Wide awake now, and without any immediate follow-up to the loud bang, Lucy decided to take a walk into the en-suite bathroom to take a pee. Once she had flushed the chain, she went to the sink to wash her hands and face. As she turned the taps she screamed when the water poured out bright red in colour. It was just like the time when the walls bled during the Ouija board activity, only, this time, it was the taps that were bleeding. She turned them off and watched the remainder of the blood trickle away down the plug hole.

Lucy shook where she stood and didn't quite know what to do. Finally, she slowly plucked up the courage to turn the taps on again; and fortunately, this time, the water came out crystal clear. Lucy let out a sigh of relief and forced herself to conclude that there must have been some rust in the pipes that needed to clear or some other logical explanation. The washing of her hands and face remained uneventful.

She sniffed at her armpit and realised that she could do with a shower. Cautiously she moved over to the shower and turned the switch, hoping that a repeat of a bloody flow of crimson fluid wouldn't occur. She needn't have worried. The water appeared fine and became very inviting for Lucy to step in and enjoy a refreshing shower.

The water felt good and relaxing, Lucy soaked up the pleasant heat and freshness of her shower. The temperature was perfect. As it ran over her attractive body it seemed to wash away her fears. She smiled to herself as she reminisced about the night of sex that she had enjoyed with Jake the night before. She began to rub shower cream over her breasts and between her thighs, remembering how good it felt when Jake had been touching her in her most sacred places. Then she thought that she heard somebody enter the room, but she didn't panic as she simply assumed that Jake had returned.

"Hey baby, let the cup of tea wait. Come and join me, the water's beautiful."

Lucy had her back to the shower door. It slid open and she felt a hand on each shoulder. A slow massage ensued then the hands slid down her back, under her armpits and finally onto her breasts. She kept her eyes closed as hot lips started kissing her neck. She turned around and opened her eyes, wanting to gaze into the beautiful face of her lover as he caressed her wanting body.

But the eyes she met did not belong to Jake.

The eyes were clearly a window to a soul as evil as the Devil's himself. Lucy screamed and she managed to push past the intruder and grab a towelling robe from the wicker chair nearby.

"Hello my dear," said the man grinning. "Please, there's no need to put a robe on. Why cover up such a beautiful body? Come on, let's carry on the fun. I can tell that you were enjoying yourself."

"I thought you were my boyfriend. He'll be back any second, I suggest that you leave if you know what's good for you."

The man's voice became more threatening in tone as he ignored Lucy's advice. "Don't worry yourself. You won't be the first pussy that I've shared with Jake Zennor. Now get on the bed and spread 'em like a good little beauty before I begin to lose my temper with you."

"No fucking way. I strongly advise that you piss off out of here."

The man shook his head slowly. Although he was of many later years than Lucy, he still sent a shiver down her spine as he glared at her menacingly.

"Now don't be a spoilsport. You are really beginning to try my patience. I suggest that you get on the bed and do exactly as I say, otherwise, I'm going to slice those lovely tits of yours right off."

As the intruder spoke his chilling words, he pulled out a knife from his jacket pocket. It consisted of a dangerous looking blade roughly six inches in length. The steel of the blade glistened; indicating that this psycho obviously took great care of his prized possession.

By now Lucy was terrified, but she attempted to hide her fear. Reluctantly she climbed onto the bed, not yet quite sure of what alternative options she had other than to comply with this crazy man. However, she didn't remove the robe, determined to hold onto her dignity for as long as possible.

The intruder began to remove his belt. Grinning like an evil Cheshire cat, he spoke again, in a calm, collected and menacing manner.

"Don't be shy. I think you're going to enjoy this as much as I am."

Lucy shut her eyes tight, hoping against hope that somehow she wouldn't play any part in what was about to happen.

With a belt in one hand and a knife in the other, suddenly the man had his stride broken - and his nose!

Jake had entered the room and had struck the intruder with full force into the face. The knife and belt fell to the floor with the impact. Although the man was a good few years older than Jake, he was a large frame and life in prison had hardened him. The intruder was Alannah's father.

Somewhat dazed but spurred on by anger and a deep-rooted wickedness, Reggie Ashe managed to compose himself enough to square up to Jake. "Come on then, Zennor" he growled, and he managed to throw a punch that connected well on Jake's chin, who wasn't expecting such a swift recovery from the older man. Ashe's nose was pouring with blood, but Jake had foolishly not followed up his initial assault.

Ashe's next move was an attempt to retrieve the knife. Jake, although floored, managed to kick out his leg which connected with Ashe hard on his knee. The wicked man screamed with pain and it allowed Jake enough time to get to his feet and prevent Ashe from obtaining the knife.

Ashe hadn't particularly hurt Jake; Jake had lost his footing due to the element of surprise rather than any killer punch, not expecting Ashe to come at him so soon after breaking his nose.

With Jake now fully prepared to fight, Ashe never got a punch in again as Jake laid into the unwelcome visitor without mercy. Despite the onslaught, Ashe was a resilient opponent and he managed to get close enough to Jake to grab him in a kind of wrestling-style hold, not least to stifle Jake's punches. Jake lost his balance and banged his head on the wardrobe but remained standing. There was just enough time for Ashe to grab the knife and he lunged at Jake. The blade caught Jake on the arm causing a nasty gash, but Jake had managed to largely avoid Ashe's attack by quickly stepping aside. The momentum of Ashe's lunge carried him past Jake and he crashed through the large bedroom window. A hawthorn tree slightly broke his fall but he was still badly hurt, bleeding profusely from the wounds produced from both the fall and the heavy blows that he had received from Jake. Finally realising that it would be sensible to concede this battle, Reggie Ashe somehow managed to get up from the lawn and venture slowly up the driveway away from Abba Manor.

Jake and Lucy looked down from the broken window.

"I'm going to go and finish the bastard off," said Jake.

"No, don't," pleaded Lucy. "I don't want you doing time for killing a low-life piece of scum like that, whether he deserves it or not. He won't be back after the beating you just gave him unless he is a complete nutcase altogether."

"He is," said Jake. "That was Reggie Ashe, Alannah's bastard of a father. It's amazing how a shit like him can be allowed out of prison so quickly."

"Well, he has gone now, never to return again."

"I wouldn't put it past him to return."

"Just hold me, Jake, please."

Jake slightly calmed himself and obliged with Lucy's request.

A beaten Reggie Ashe had managed to reach the top of the drive but he soon collapsed with a mixture of exhaustion and pain.

As if by good fortune, something that a man like Reggie Ashe certainly could never deserve, a car pulled up and the passenger door slowly opened.

Ashe looked up from the floor. He could just about manage to see through his increasingly swelling eyes and the streams of blood dripping into his line of vision. His nose was by now a very peculiar shape altogether. Jake had certainly done a good job on him.

"Please mate," he whimpered to whoever was in the car. "Get me to a hospital, please. I think I may be dying."

A beaming face leant across the passenger seat and came into view.

"Don't worry, squire," grinned Archie. "I'll see to it personally that you are put out of your misery."

CHAPTER 16

"Well, I'm glad that's over," said Lucy speaking from behind one of Jake's cushions. "That was a bit too scary."

She was referring to a Horror movie that Jake and she had just finished watching.

"Well, it is Halloween, Babe. One has to get into the *spirit* of things," said Jake as he ejected the DVD from the machine.

"Ha, ha very funny," replied Lucy. "Come on over here. I need protection from a good, strong man."

"I'll go out and find you one then," joked Jake again.

"It's a good job that you're a half-decent musician because you would never have made it as a comedian. Now come over here before the witching hour arrives."

Jake strutted over to the sofa and then sat astride Lucy. It was not long before they were kissing passionately; their magnetism often took them on a deep journey of mutual pleasure. They were fortunate enough to share a chemistry and rare quality in their relationship that enabled them to be both in love and in lust with one another. As Jake's hands caressed Lucy's willing body she soon forgot about the scary moments of the movie.

Suddenly their passion became halted by noises from outside.

"What 's that," said a startled Lucy.

"It sounds like some sort of singing," replied Jake frowning.

"No, listen carefully. It's not singing, it's more like… chanting…. Oh, shit that also sounds like screaming."

"It sounds close too. Some bastard is on my land. I'm going out."

"No Jake, it could be dangerous. Phone the police."

"Not my style, Babe. I fight my own battles."

"Jake, listen to me. You can't be sure how many are out there. You're not Superman you know. Come on, let's see if we can see anything from the window and then we can weigh up the situation."

"Ok."

Lucy cautiously pulled back the curtain. They couldn't quite believe what they saw. A raging fire had been lit and Jake and Lucy could make out figures of people seemingly dancing around the flames. A separate group of people seemed to be standing nearby.

"Are they on your land, Jake?" asked Lucy in hope that they weren't.

"No, that hill is beyond my boundary. Archie was right."

"Who's Archie?"

"Never mind," said Jake. "They may not be on my land, but look over there. They are!"

Lucy and Jake could now see a further group of people lit up by torches of fire who were a lot closer to Abba Manor. They were dressed in black cloaks and masks depicting various faces of animals. They were walking across Jake's land towards the hill where the strange event was taking place. It was an eerie sight, as the assembly appeared to be in convoy marching strictly in four lines, led by a seemingly nominated figure which paced roughly two metres in front of them. The leader was wearing the largest of all the animal masks, which included two long horns.

"Fuck this," said Jake as he ran out of the room grabbing one of the baseball bats that he kept inside the house for protection, just in case he would ever experience any would-be intruders. He realised that the anonymity he enjoyed from being in such a remote location could equally place him in a vulnerable position should a crazed or simply greedy person ever want to track him down due to his fame and stature. He knew only too well that the world was full of crackpots and weirdos who wanted a pop at celebrities for some twisted self-justified reason. It had happened to John Lennon with the most tragic of outcomes in 1980 and it would not be too many years later when George Harrison would be attacked in his own home. Lucy called after Jake not to go outside, but her pleas were in vain.

"Get off my land you bunch of freaks," shouted Jake. This was a typical hot-headed handling of a situation by Jake, who had spent all his life hitting first and asking questions later.

The cluster continued to walk, seemingly oblivious to Jake's request. Feeling annoyed, Jake ran directly in front of their path forcing them to refrain from ignoring him.

The group's leader raised his right hand and the group stopped dead at his command. He and Jake faced one another, albeit the horned mask restricted Jake from seeing too much of the leader's face.

"I said get off my land," demanded Jake, trying hard not to show he was now slightly unnerved as the masks and amount of personnel before him placed his potential opponents at an advantage. Jake realised that any confrontation that was about to unfold was not going to be akin to the simple bar room brawl he was more accustomed to.

The leader didn't answer immediately and the deadly silence ironically spoke volumes as Jake's mind raced of just what he was confronting here.

Finally, the leader spoke. His words were delivered slowly and deliberately. "We will be off your land soon enough. We only wish to reach our planned destination which is the hill beyond your house. I sincerely apologise if our presence has offended you in any way, but your land does tend to invite a rather attractive shortcut and I believed that this house was currently unoccupied."

Behind the long-horned animal mask spoke a cut-glass English accent. The tone of voice never altered, and Jake guessed that the voice belonged to that of a male aged roughly in his fifties. Jake didn't quite know how to react when the leader's response had not been confrontational, yet he still detected a sinister deep-rooted presence in the delivery that made Jake feel uneasy. Jake didn't know whether to strike the jerk with his baseball bat for taking the liberty of trespassing across his land or to simply stand aside and let the weirdo group pass unchallenged. As he pondered Lucy ran from the house.

The leader spoke again. "Good evening Madam," before re-directing his speech back to Jake once more. "Now if you care to step out of my way we can be off your land in no time at all and we can join the rest of our party."

"Party? Is that what you guys are doing? I don't think so. That singing I can hear from the hill doesn't sound much like party music to me, and how come I heard someone screaming?"

"Well, Mr Zennor. I'm sure that our singing is far from elegant when compared to your musical expertise, and sadly it seems that even our attempt to celebrate has caused you some offence."

Jake now felt a further sense of unease knowing that the leader had recognised who he was. He knew that he couldn't show a chink of vulnerability to the group, as the worst-case scenario would surely be to place him and Lucy in danger.

"So what are you celebrating?" inquired Jake.

"Halloween of course," replied the leader.

"And just what kind of trick and treating is exactly going on up there on the hill?"

"Mr Zennor, you really shouldn't mock what you don't understand."

Jake took one last hard look at the animal mask before him and stepped aside, allowing the congregation to carry on. The quicker theses weirdos were away from his home the better. The leader simply gave a slow nod of appreciation before taking the group onward.

Despite all his senses sending out warning signals, Jake's sense of curiosity was growing strong. Against all his better judgement, Jake turned to Lucy. "Let's follow them.".

"No way, Jake," pleaded Lucy.

"Aren't you intrigued?"

"Maybe but I don't like it."

"It's ok, Lucy. I just want to see for myself exactly what is going on up there."

Curiosity began to get the better of Lucy too and she reluctantly agreed.

"It might be fun," said Jake.

"Just make sure we hang well back. I don't want them to know we are following them. Who knows what they are capable of."

Jake smiled and they set off keeping well out of sight, their concealment helped by the natural darkness. A terrified Lucy stayed close to her lover.

As they got closer to the congregation at the hill, the singing naturally increased in volume. It was a harsh unmelodic repetition of words from a language unknown to Jake or Lucy. The chant eerily pierced the darkness to a tight rhythm of deep-sounding drums.

Once they had reached the destination they were able to watch proceedings from behind a tree, inconspicuously sheltered by surrounding foliage. The light of more than one raging fire revealed masses of entwined bodies having group sex. Animal masks remained fixed on their faces in stark contrast to the liberal shedding of clothing. It seemed that knowing who exactly they were making out with was a totally unimportant part of the ritual. Now that Jake and Lucy could clearly see what was occurring, they stood open-mouthed, not quite knowing how to react or what to say to one another.

Also evident was a large slab of granite within a circle of smaller stones. Despite the obvious commitment and indulgence by the individuals participating in the explicit scenes before them, Jake and Lucy each noticed that not a single foot, or otherwise, entered this circle of stones.

Instinctively, Lucy found herself buttoning up her top button, however, the curiosity and magnetism of the situation were just too strong for Jake and Lucy to walk away, ignoring the good advice being screamed at them by their inner natural instincts. Lucy was particularly fearful. She considered herself to be a woman of fairly liberal mind, not easily shocked and willing to experiment with a mutually monogamous partner, and she had always been of the opinion that most things were ok as long as it was between consenting adults. But this seemed a bit too freaky. She drew the line at a group of strangers engaging in random intercourse covering their faces with the features of animals! What she didn't realise was that far more sinister and dramatic events were about to unfold.

The leader stepped forward and approached a naked female, except for her mask of course which depicted the head of a woodland creature. As he acknowledged her she, in turn, handed him a crying baby, which had been secluded beneath a blanket. The leader took the infant and laid its naked form on the large slab at the centre of the stone circle. Another female then walked over to the leader carrying what appeared to be some sort of ceremonial knife, with a large curved blade and various jewels inset into its spine and handle. Even the way she carried it portrayed an act of rehearsed sacrament, the blade straddled across both her open palms and she walked with a deliberate slow gait. She placed the knife down just outside the circle on a silk cushion and the leader reached out to take it.

Jake realised what was planned to happen next and there was no way that he was going to be able to sit back and watch the sacrifice of an infant, no matter what the consequences were destined to be for him personally. In typical Jake Zennor style, he ran from his hiding place and directly at the leader knocking him to the ground, which was also sufficient enough for the knife to be spilt from his grasp. Jake was still holding the baseball bat he had brought outside with him and a single blow to the head was enough to knock the leader unconscious.

Lucy quickly followed and collected the baby from the large slab into her arms.

Jake turned with the baseball bat held aloft expecting an onslaught from the rest of the weird congregation but amazingly no one approached him. A lone voice that could have come from beneath any of the animal masks explained why.

"You have no idea what you have done. Only the master is allowed inside the sacred circle of stones. You are now doomed forever; he will take both your souls in place of the infant's."

"Bollocks," replied Jake in character. Jake wasn't sure if the *master* that was being referred to was the Devil himself or the piece of scum he had just knocked unconscious with his baseball bat.

A different voice shouted out, "Step outside the circle so that we can kill you. You may prefer a death conducted by us rather than the unmerciful taking of your souls if you remain where you are."

Jake realised that he and Lucy were outnumbered should they leave the shelter of the stone circle, and although he actually believed playing a part in saving the infant's life was more likely to ultimately protect his soul, he pondered on how this situation would end. He and Lucy couldn't stay in the circle forever, and who's to say that there isn't some sort of deputy leader in this madding crowd who may soon feel compelled to enter the circle. He also realised that he had the child's best interests to consider, but how he was going to get Lucy and the child out of this situation wasn't apparently obvious at this moment in time. Just then Lucy let out a scream, "Jake look out!"

The leader had resumed consciousness and he came at Jake clutching the ceremonial knife, but his lunge was cut short as a single bullet completely exploded the right side of his head. The knife grazed Jake's arm with minimal impact as the leader fell to the floor in a heap.

"You are surrounded by armed police. Do not move until instructed or we will not hesitate to shoot again. Place your hands behind your head and very slowly lie face down on the floor. Wait patiently and a police officer will come and handcuff you and escort you to our vehicles."

The police announcement was ignored and mayhem unfolded. Jake and Lucy could hardly believe the drama that they witnessed before them.

Many of the Devil Worshippers preferred to take their own lives than surrender their beliefs to the establishment. A mass suicide pact simultaneously unfolded as other less impressive ceremonial knives were driven into the own hearts of the Devil Worshippers or they leapt into the raging fires without hesitance burning their naked bodies alive. The sound of chanting was deafening amongst screams and allegiances to the Devil.

A handful laid on the floor obeying police orders, however even more attempted to tackle the police, but without clothing and guns, they were destined to end up fatally wounded. Fortunately, there were no serious police casualties.

Amazingly the Devil Worshippers had remained true to their word and had not entered the circle, so Jake, who had complied with the police's instructions, and Lucy still holding the baby had miraculously remained safe from any harm.

The mayhem gradually diminished, as the police were able to ultimately control the situation, easily outnumbering the few Satanists that were still alive.

The maddening experience finally came to an end.

Jake spoke to Lucy from his position on the floor.

"You phoned the police when I first ran outside didn't you?"

"Yes, I did, Jake. That's *my* style."

"Well thank fuck for that, babe. I owe you one." Although not instructed to, Jake had assessed that it was ok to return to his feet again. "It looks like there won't be anyone left to do any sacrificing next Halloween that's for sure. I wonder where this little mite came from?"

Jake gently stroked the baby's small amount of hair. Amazingly the baby had stopped crying despite the commotion and appeared to have sensed the safe haven of Lucy's arms.

A police officer approached Lucy and Jake and produced his I.D. "Detective Inspector Miles. Is the child yours?"

Lucy shook her head.

"Then, I'll bet a pound to a penny that this little lad's mother is one of these mad bitches lying dead. These nutcases actually breed for their sick beliefs. We've been trying to break this ring for a long time, intelligence hadn't led us to this place tonight but luckily your phone call did. The problem is Devil worshipping in Derbyshire is only the tip of the iceberg, it's an international problem, and the people involved are slippery bastards who cover their tracks very well."

"How can they practice this madness without detection?" inquired Jake.

"Because there are people involved who you could never imagine, and that even includes people from your profession Mr Zennor, but proving that sacrifices are actually taking place is hard to do and it's hard for people to believe. They ensure that the pregnancies are secret and hidden within the cult. The births of the children bred for sacrifice never become registered so unless they are actually caught in the act, or a body is found, murder can never be proven. Unfortunately, we are chasing our tails a lot of the time, but tonight seems to be a success story thanks to your intervention. We had no idea that this was the venue to be used tonight; we thought that they were planning a ceremony a lot nearer to Manchester, up in the Northern Peaks. I can see that we are going to have to review our intelligence. At least we can give the few sick bastards that we have captured here tonight a bit of a grilling, but as you have seen, they would rather die for their cause than co-operate. Well done to both of you, I'm just sorry that you had to get mixed up in this."

"It was worth it to save this little lad's life," said Jake.

"What will happen to him now?" asked a concerned Lucy.

"Social Services will become involved and find him a good home. In the circumstances, he is a very lucky lad. By the way, we will need some statements from you both, nothing to worry about. I would appreciate it if you kept tonight's experiences to yourselves in order for our intelligence to be more productive. We can't afford for things like this to get into the press and compromise our situation and investigations, especially as a high-profile pop star such as yourself has tragically become dragged into things Mr Zennor. I'm sure that you understand."

"Yeah of course," said Jake.

Lucy nodded.

"And Mr Zennor, there is just one more thing."

"Sure."

"In addition to the statement, I would be grateful if I could have your autograph please."

CHAPTER 17

Jake fell about laughing uncontrollably. "You can't go up a mountain dressed like that!"

"Like what?" replied Lucy.

"Wearing high-heel shoes and skin tight jeans, that's what. You'll break your ankle at the very least, and your jeans will prevent you from scrambling."

"Jake, a nice walk in the countryside I said, I didn't know we were scheduled to climb Mount flipping Everest."

"Not quite Mount Everest, dear. I told you we were going to see part of the Pennine Way. What do you think the Pennine Way is, a flaming catwalk? Jake sniggered at his mocking of Lucy, who had taken it in the good spirit intended but was now becoming a little irritated.

"Look you arsehole, I'll have you know that I have climbed Mount Snowdon."

"Let me guess, you went up the Pyg Track."

"So, I still bloody climbed it. Right up to the summit too."

"Our Blanche's youngest, Jamie cleared the Pyg Track 2 years ago when he was barely 6 years old. When you have climbed the biggest mountain in Wales, via its most dangerous route of Crib Goch, as I have, I'll allow you to lecture me."

"Whatever, you arrogant prick."

"I have to say there really was no need to spend the last hour putting your slap on either. After half an hour in the drizzle, your mascara will have run right down your cheeks."

Lucy threw Jake a look as if to warn him not to push his luck, so he quickly bailed himself out. "What I mean is Babe, you don't need to wear make-up, you are naturally beautiful without it.

"Creep," said Lucy, only half-smiling.

"Come on we can stop off in Castleton and I'll buy you some proper gear. My treat for teasing you and dragging you into this unconventional day out."

"Okay, but only if the boots come in pink," said Lucy straight-faced.

For a moment Jake thought that Lucy was being serious, but then he realised that she had turned the joke on him and they both simultaneously burst into laughter.

"Give us a kiss," requested Jake.

Lucy obliged with a sweet peck on the lips and a cuddle thrown in as an added bonus.

By now Jake had purchased two vehicles to transport himself around the Peak District. The first was a red-coloured Ferrari, which he actually found himself embarrassed to drive as he felt at odds with his working-class principles when sitting in the driver's seat. But being a part of 80s pop star culture didn't fade easily. It had all been about image and status during that musical era. Lucy had teased him a few times that the Ferrari was simply an extension of his penis. The other vehicle he had purchased was what he had used to get him and Lucy to the village of Castleton today, a 4x4 deep-green coloured Land Rover.

As they parked up in the picturesque village they noticed that other seasoned climbers and ramblers were around to tackle Jake's chosen destination of Kinder Scout. Standing at 636 metres above sea level it is the highest point in both Derbyshire and The Peak District. He was inwardly impressed that Lucy had not shied away from tackling the moorland plateau and challenges of Kinder Scout, despite his earlier mocking he would have gladly accompanied her on a much less challenging hike, such as Dovedale.

"If we are going to do this," she had said, "We'll do it properly."

Although Jake was ever mindful of the tragedy that had befallen his close friend Roland he had refused to let the incident prevent him from exploring the Peak District and all that it offered. However, he would forever avoid the route that had been taken on that fateful day.

They entered the shop in Castleton where outdoors and mountaineering attire could be purchased and courtesy of Jake's credit card Lucy finally became suitably kitted out in a much more sensible outfit for such a venture.

"I'll just change into this lot in the ladies' loos," said Lucy.

"Ok, I'll wait here," and with that Jake sat down on a circular metal-framed bench that ringed the trunk of an ancient tree.

When she returned, Jake couldn't help but notice how beautiful she looked even in climbing boots and a waterproof suit. She had tied her hair back giving a new dimension to the pretty structure of her face, and he felt the urge to take her back into the toilets and remove all the clothes that had taken her so long to put on.

"Okay, let's go, cowboy," said Lucy.

"I suppose I'll have to carry the rucksack," said Jake.

"Of course. I couldn't infringe on your macho capabilities now, could I? After all, you did climb Crib Goch."

"Okay, I guess I deserved that one."

Arm in arm Jake and Lucy set off on their mission up Kinder Scout.

Lucy declared that it was a good time to stop for refreshments. Jake couldn't refuse, despite his earlier teasing Lucy had earned the right to a break having taking to the climb like a duck takes to water. In truth, Jake had wanted to rest a good 20 minutes earlier but had continued without declaring anything, urged on by his macho pride.

They sat down on a section of turf and looked out across the Derbyshire landscape. They were near the Kinder Downfall, which was the highest waterfall in the peaks flowing at 30 metres and complementing the River Kinder. It was an ideal resting place.

"It's beautiful here. What a view," said Lucy. "The sound of the running water is so relaxing and tranquil too."

"It is gorgeous, isn't it? Nothing is better than getting away from it all by climbing high into the clouds. Just breathe in the clean air as well, it's wonderful." Jake exaggerated his intake of breath in order to pronounce his statement.

"What did you bring to eat then Chris Bonnington?" mocked Lucy.

Jake unzipped the rucksack revealing their contents.

"Ooh chocolate, lovely. Won't I be putting on the calories that I've just walked off though?"

"Maybe, I don't claim to be a dietician but I brought it to provide energy. Anyway, before we eat the chocolate I've been very healthy and made up some salmon sandwiches on wholemeal baps."

"Salmon, excellent. Omega 3 fish oils, the food that feeds the brain. I take it you don't usually have salmon that much then Jake."

"You cheeky cow," laughed Jake and he began to play fight with Lucy.

He pinned her down so that she couldn't move.

"Say you are sorry Lucy Ives. Go on say it."

"It."

"Very funny."

"Get off me you lump."

"Only when you've apologised."

"Never."

"Okay, you've asked for it." Jake knew of a tried and tested way to combat Lucy's audacity. He began to tickle her.

She laughed hysterically and wriggled in vain to try and get free, but it was no use.

"Okay, okay I'm sorry. I give in."

"You're forgiven," and with those words Jake looked into Lucy's eyes from above and couldn't resist turning the play fighting into a kiss. Lucy responded positively.

They finally broke for air.

"I feel horny," whispered Lucy.

"Me too. We can't here, though... Can we?"

"We haven't passed anyone for ages. Come on live dangerously. I've noticed some rocks over there, which I think we can get to just off the beaten track. They are nestling in the shelter of the waterfall; it seems such a romantic setting. Let's go behind them."

"Well, I guess it brings a whole new meaning to the Mile-High Club!"

Lucy stood up on the spot where Jake had her pinned and unzipped her mountaineering jacket. She then lifted her fleece and T-shirt to reveal a white sports bra. She licked her lips before raising the left cup for a brief moment and then playfully replaced the bra again.

"Oh lord," drooled Jake.

It was not long before they eagerly managed to scramble the short distance across some stepping-stones to the shelter of the rocks.

They both removed their jackets and used them to lie on.

Jake raised all of Lucy's upper clothing so that he could caress her breasts with his mouth and it was not long before she had one leg out of her waterproof trousers.

Lucy grabbed his hair. Jake knew what she wanted. He fumbled at his belt and jeans in order to release himself. He felt the cold air instantly hit his manhood and for a second was astonished that Lucy had not once mentioned the cold weather in her present situation.

"I want you, Jake."

Jake didn't need telling again and he was soon inside Lucy, kissing her neck which inspired her noises of pleasure.

The bizarre situation of making love in a near public place heightened the passion between them, until suddenly, they heard a noise to the west of them.

"Jake, what's that? Is someone watching us?"

"They will have wished they hadn't if anyone is there."

"I really enjoyed that refreshing experience but voyeurism isn't my thing."

"Don't worry Lucy, he won't be watching anyone again once I've gauged his eyes out." Astonishingly Jake was oblivious that it was they who had run the risk of being seen.

"Shit, the rucksack, Jake. We left the rucksack behind."

Just then they heard a sound again as if a presence was definitely nearby.

Jake quickly pulled up his lower garments and headed over towards where the rucksack had been left, leaving Lucy to somehow reassemble her attire feeling a little foolish now despite the wonderful experience.

"There's no-one here," called Jake.

"That's impossible," replied Lucy as she re-entered her leg into her trousers. "No-one could get away that quickly, you'd see them easily across this area."

"I don't understand it, I really can't see anyone, and the rucksack hasn't been touched."

Lucy quickly made her way across the water surface with the aid of the stepping-stones in order to join Jake again. "Perhaps it was a bird or a fox," she offered.

"The noise seemed too loud as if a good deal of weight was pressing on the undergrowth."

"Well if there was a Peeping Tom he has mysteriously got clean away."

Just then Jake noticed something in the mud. "This footprint looks fresh, perhaps this belongs to the pervert who was here." Jake raised his voice to call out. "Come out you pervert. Did you get a good look you twisted fuck? What's wrong, are you too scared to show yourself? Is that the only way you can get it up, spying on other people?"

There was no reply to Jake's provocative calling.

"Jake, this footprint doesn't look like a climbing boot. It seems to be the shape of some kind of sandal footwear. Who on Earth would wear sandals up here?"

"The same sick twat who spies on people shagging."

"Jake, don't you notice anything else unusual about this footprint."

Jake shrugged.

"How come it's on its own. There are no other footprints near it as if one solitary foot has just miraculously landed here on this very spot and then disappeared again."

Jake couldn't offer an explanation.

"Jake. I don't like this. This is weird."

Just then they heard something behind them. Simultaneously they turned around.

A man walked towards them dressed as a roman soldier complete with a tunic and sandals. He walked straight past them nonchalantly and seemingly oblivious to their very existence.

"Hey buddy, what's your game?"

The stranger ignored Jake's question and walked straight past them.

Jake became typically angry.

"Don't turn your back on me, pal." Jake reached out to grab his shoulder but incredibly Jake's hand passed straight through him as if he was a hieroglyphic and Jake lost his balance falling to the mud.

Jake and Lucy both noticed that the figure's sandaled feet were not leaving a trail of footprints either.

Jake and Lucy then watched open-mouthed as the Roman figure simply walked off the cliff face and then appeared to walk on thin air, miraculously not falling to the rocks hundreds of feet below.

The Roman then walked literally into a cloud where his entity merged to become one and he was no longer visible to the startled and confused couple.

CHAPTER 18

It was not long after the ghostly sighting of the Roman soldier on Kinder Scout, that Jake and Lucy experienced a second Roman apparition.

Their next sighting occurred along the A515 road that links the towns of Ashbourne and Buxton. They had spent a pleasant day gently rambling about the village of Tissington and on the homeward journey to Abba Manor, just as dusk was falling, they had decided to park in a lay-by to debate the possibility of travelling to Buxton for an evening meal, or to instead frequent one of the pubs in the more nearby villages.

Out of nowhere an entire Roman Battalion suddenly appeared marching along the road! And what was even more disturbing was the fact that the hundreds of soldiers could only be seen from above knee height!

Jake understood from the information on his road map that the A515 was originally one of the roads that had been built by the Romans during their time of settlement in England. He concluded that what he and Lucy had witnessed must have surely been a ghostly apparition of a bonafide Roman Battalion from all those years ago, but of course, the road had since been built up with the introduction of road improvements since the time of the Industrial Revolution and beyond. What they had actually witnessed was the soldiers marching on the original height of the road!

The apparition lasted for a period of roughly twenty seconds and no other cars had passed so as far as they knew, Jake and Lucy had been the only witnesses to this astonishing spectacle.

Ironically, the stretch of road where Jake and Lucy had witnessed the ghostly sighting of the Roman Battalion was close to the unlikely place of a discount bookstore, and it was at this bookstore that Jake attempted the next day to discover some answers as to what he was experiencing on his return to the Peak District. Not only the trend of Roman sightings, but he was also keen to seek answers to the state of play at Abba Manor.

Jake eventually purchased just two books in total after spending almost 2 hours scanning information from other literary sources, much to the obvious disapproval of the twin elderly lady booksellers who peered over their half-moon reading glasses from their counter, but who were more than happy to take the £30 cash from Jake for *The Romans in the Peaks* and *The Peak District and The Paranormal.*

Jake discovered that the Romans entered Britain in 43AD and then gradually headed north building their forts, roads and settlements along the way. They reached the Peak District in the 70s AD and Roman forts were built at Brough and Glossop. Jake was interested to find that a rich legacy of Romano-British Farmland and the evidence of lead mining was still in existence today. Like many spas dotted about the United Kingdom, the Romans had founded the Spa at Buxton and they had also built many roads across the Peak District region. So, this firm presence of Roman activity could have resulted in the sightings experienced by Jake and Lucy, but what didn't make sense were the sightings appearing almost 2000 years later!

One explanation offered by the hardback edition of *The Peak District and the Paranormal* was that Jake and Lucy had witnessed a type of *photograph*, an image preserved despite the passage of time. The theory being that a person or persons, as represented in the instances of the soldier and soldiers that Jake and Lucy had witnessed, attend a location so often in their lifetime that a terrific force of energy is built up and the energy produces a visual image that remains tied to that particular spot regardless of the passage of time. The example used in the book told the story of an elderly lady who would kneel at the same spot day in and day out at a church in the Peak District in order to say her prayers. Long after her own passing she can still often be seen praying at the altar, and even when the image is not evident there can be found fresh indentations in the cushion she used to kneel on, even when the church has been locked for hours. The book even boasted a conventional photograph of the apparition of the praying lady, one of the few possible spirits ever captured on film. This scientific theory gave credence to the Roman army marching partially beneath a road that had been built up over the passage of time. No longer the cynic he used to be based on the magnitude of recent experiences he'd encountered; Jake Zennor was not fully buying into the notion of scientific theories. Instead, he was beginning to believe that living at Abba Manor had opened a part of his mind, and Lucy's too, that had become sensitive to paranormal activity. This would explain why they were now having supernatural experiences even beyond the house.

Jake believed in his own judgement and he believed his own two eyes, and the sightings that he had seen had definitely been real as far as he was concerned. The book had offered a balanced view detailing that there was a possibility that ghosts and spirits could simply exist. The book put forward the concept that the form of those that had passed from this life can sometimes simply have the ability to roam this Earth again, particularly if the spirit felt that they had unfinished business. Jake was leaning more and more towards this theory.

Jake had hoped for the inclusion of Abba Manor to be in the book, but unfortunately, the book offered no stories of one of the oldest, and potentially scariest houses of the Peak District. Likewise, Jake frustratingly could not find any significant answers to the haunting music that was still repeating from the old piano time after time. He was left to try and draw his own conclusions about the happenings experienced at Abba Manor and the beautiful music he heard there. It was all proving very difficult to comprehend.

One chapter in the book did offer evidence on poltergeist activity: when a spirit has the ability to actually physically throw things and disrupt the norm usually in a noisy and catastrophic way. One inclusion in the book told of frying pans and television sets being thrown around a house in Belper. This could explain the time when Jake and Lucy were woken by a shaking and levitating bed. Could they have experienced the haunting of a poltergeist? And if a poltergeist is able to physically move things then surely it could play the piano? But Jake wasn't convinced. The piano music that presented itself at the piano in Abba Manor was so movingly beautiful it didn't seem to sit comfortably with the evidence of poltergeists. The essence of a poltergeist would surely bang at the notes of the piano abruptly and with no attempt whatsoever to make harmonious music. The music coming from the piano in Abba Manor was like part of a concerto or sonata of the highest level of composition.

Jake was convinced that he wasn't alone at Abba Manor and the book provided details of how animals have a phenomenal sense to identify supernatural presence and spirits. Jake contemplated that this could well explain the endless barking that he hears whenever a villager walks his dog across the entrance to Abba Manor and when Elgar stops dead in his tracks and seems to focus his eyes intensely on something in the room that Jake himself simply cannot see. Jake would become unnerved at how sometimes the cat's fur would even stand on end and how he hisses at whatever is invisibly lurking in the darkness.

So, from a period of intense research Jake had been able to educate himself and in turn join some of the dots, but frustratingly there still remained many unanswered questions about the activity that he was experiencing.

No matter what trials and tribulations occurred in Jake's life, he could always escape into the salvation of his music. Putting the book down he now opted to sit at the unique piano that he had inherited with the purchase of Abba Manor. He didn't set out to play anything in particular, but as he picked his way around various scales and chords, he inadvertently began to progress into a more familiar melody. It was the same haunting tune that he had heard the night that he became acquainted with Elgar and when he and Lucy were awoken by the bed being shaken. Jake couldn't quite fathom why the tune appealed to him so much, but the more he played it, the further inspired he became, getting totally lost in the mood of the piece. Jake developed the music further by adding chord progressions and structuring the piece into the format of a song, with the ghostly melody becoming a chorus hook, and then slightly altering it to create verses. He then began to sing lyrics to the music. The words seemed to flow like a fountain of spring water he was so inspired. He always felt that his best songs were the ones that had come to him instantly. The familiar melody entwined in the chorus complemented Jake's inspired lyrics as he sang: –

"Love lives forever, if it's kept true, Love lives forever for me and for you.

The wind can carry eternal love,

I can keep the faith because I know I've been loved."

"That's a nice song Jake," said Lucy as she entered the room. Jake had become so engrossed in the music, Lucy had completely startled him.

"Oh thanks, babe. It's just a little something I'm working on," replied Jake modestly.

"It reminds me a little like *Imagine*."

"I'm not sure about that, but there is a B flat in there."

"Mmmm, it does have a rare quality all of its own. And what's inspiring you to write something like that?"

"Nothing in particular."

"Do you think the words are a bit corny, babe? Love Lives Forever: not the most die hard rock and roll lyric, is it?"

"Jake, love has been the most obvious common denominator between people for centuries and love certainly hasn't been a taboo subject in songs for many of the greatest artists that have ever lived. People still need to hear love songs and songwriters like you produce the best ones when they write them from the heart. The song is truly beautiful Jake including the lyrics. Sing it again for me."

Jake obliged.

"Love lives forever, if it's kept true, Love lives forever for me and for you.

The wind can carry eternal love,

I can keep the faith because I know I've been loved."

"Are you sure you're not singing about Alannah? Those words could easily be about your relationship with her."

"No, not really, it's just this piano, it seems to be bringing a love song out of me."

"A love song about Alannah?"

"What is this Lucy?"

"I just wondered, that's all."

"You can't expect me to forget that she ever existed you know."

"I know Jake; I wouldn't want you to forget her. But she has gone. You've got to move on with your life. You tell me that you love me now, but if that were true would you really be composing a song about your former girlfriend?"

"Don't be daft, it's just a song."

"Listen to those lyrics you're singing, Jake. Love lives forever. I've *been* loved. You're looking back in the words of that song."

"They're just words. They just kind of fit right."

"And the melody you are using; it is that same one that we heard playing by itself, isn't it? You know what I think. It could have been Alannah trying to contact you."

Jake shook his head in disbelief. "Why are you coming over all possessive and jealous like? It's not like you Lucy."

"I am not being possessive; I'm just looking at what the facts seem to be here. Just think about it Jake, what will the media make of it, singing about her while you are now with me? They will trample all over her memory again. I know she wouldn't want you to live in the past. Don't take this the wrong way Jake, but I'm sure that part of her suicide was intended to set you free as much as herself from the pain she was feeling."

Jake became increasingly defensive and was not empathetic to Lucy's point of view. "You never even knew her; how would you know what she would have wanted?"

"I know by the way that you've described her to me that she was a decent human being and if she truly loved you she would want you to be happy now. If she is contacting you through that tune it could be her way of telling you to move on. Your lyrics should reflect optimism and looking forward. The tune is too beautiful to be coming from an unhappy soul."

"Alannah died unhappily and could not play the piano so spare me the psycho-analysis. And I am looking forward. I am happy, we are happy, aren't we?" said Jake in a raised impatient voice.

"Yes," replied Lucy diplomatically, attempting to get her point across but realising the delicateness of the situation. "But If you are not over her I don't want to get in the way. Perhaps you're still grieving. You know sometimes I feel I'm living in her shadow and that I can't quite live up to your opinion of her. You talk about her as if she was a saint, that she never did a thing wrong but that just can't be possible. It's not human nature to be perfect all the time. How can I compete with that? And now you're even writing songs about her. I have feelings too you know and my feelings are alive and here right now."

Jake raised his voice even louder with frustration. "For the last time the song is not about her, it's just a fucking song."

"So why are you getting so angry? Have I touched a nerve?"

"Oh, just fuck off," shouted Jake, instantly regretting the words.

Lucy paused before replying, "You shouldn't talk to me that way Jake, I don't deserve it. I'll leave you to write your songs and dwell on Alannah's memory if that is what makes you happy. Give me a call if you ever sort your head out, but if you leave it too long I might have moved on myself. You see I believe that life is for living Jake. I can't help you anymore, I feel I'm only in the way."

"Don't be daft," said Jake more calmly, attempting to play down the situation. "Look, I'm sorry for swearing at you."

Lucy began to cry. "I love you Jake, but I can't be second best or a substitute for someone you can't let go of. I'm sorry, it's over."

Lucy ran out of the room and out of Jake's life.

CHAPTER 19

Jake found himself standing before a large crowd ready to entertain them. This would usually prove to be nothing unusual, Jake had vast experience of playing before a large crowd. He had played at Glastonbury, Knebworth, Hyde Park, Molineux, Wembley, countless American football and baseball stadiums and of course in the grounds of Derbyshire's very own 'jewel in the crown' Chatsworth House to name but a few.

But this venue was different.

The crowd were different.

Instead of familiar chants for live performances of their favourite songs, the crowd would shout words of destruction such as "kill".

The arena completely encircled Jake and he was standing in the centre. He realised that he was not in the familiar presence of a football stadium, but instead he was standing in some type of coliseum.

He noticed that the crowd were not sporting designer labels or "We love Blossom of Eden" T-shirts. Instead, they wore tunics, akin to the generations of Roman times.

He then looked down at himself and noticed he too was wearing a tunic, but unlike that worn by members of the crowd, his was stronger, made of a metal substance. In short, he was wearing a tunic of armour. He then noticed that instead of seeing a guitar in his hands he could see the glistening of a sword, and at the end of the sword on the dusty floor lay a lion looking up at him with the innocent eyes of a domestic cat pleading for Jake to spare its life.

Surely he was dreaming. However, he couldn't be sure. His subconscious mind debated the likelihood of reality versus fantasy. The recurring dreams of the ghostly white hands had continued, but this was a new scenario. What could it mean?

The theme of Roman history in the Peak District had become apparent again, as in his sightings of the soldier on Kinder Scout who mysteriously disappeared into a cloud and the marching Roman Battalion that was visible from knee height on the A515 Roman road. Could these apparitions be playing on his mind and messing with his dreams?

But it all seemed so real.

Jake withdrew his sword from the tip of the lion's throat and spared its life. A strange exchange of appreciation between man and beast took place, and the lion ran off towards the opening used for the entrance and exit of the gladiators and animals that graced the arena.

The crowd were not happy. They booed and hissed. In his dreamy state Jake, could not decide if they were dissatisfied with the allowance of survival for the lion or because they were the very same public that had been blaming him for the death of Alannah. It was the same disconcerting feeling that he felt about the negative reception of his solo career.

Jake held his sword up to the crowd in defiance and slowly turned to face each area of the hostile crowd.

He then noticed that a part of the arena was different. The seats were more spacious and he could make out that cushions made of velvet supported the bodies of whoever sat upon them. This part of the arena was sectioned off and the sight of a Roman guard at each end of the privileged seats indicated to Jake that they were reserved for important people. He noticed that central to the seating was a throne and on this throne, Jake instantly knew that it was the Emperor of the day seated upon it. Jake was then shocked to see that on either side of the Emperor sat Lucy and Alannah. They were stroking and caressing the fat man and looking at Jake and laughing. About all of them was an obscene amount of fruit and chalices of wine, which Alannah and Lucy willfully fed to the overweight Emperor.

It was clear that the Emperor was not pleased with Jake's decision to spare the lion his life.

"Bring out the dark one!" he shouted to the guards at the gladiator entrance, his face red with anger and saliva and food spraying from his mouth.

Jake could not believe what he saw next.

A creature came from the darkness of the tunnel into the daylight of the coliseum. At least Jake believed it to be a creature for it possessed two identical heads that were in human form, which bobbed about either side of a kind of dragon's head. From the ferocious mouth of the dragon head came infernos of fire spectacularly distributed between unnervingly enormous teeth.

The bloodthirsty crowd were delighted at its presence and clapped and cheered at its arrival into the arena.

In spite of its huge size, it was able to move with grace on its two muscular legs. The creature also had two powerful looking arms. Its skin was both scaly in parts with a green colouring but also possessed patches of unsightly thick black body hair.

Curiously it held an orchestra conductor's baton instead of a sword, made of a bright gold substance, but Jake realised that it looked capable of puncturing a gladiator's armour.

The creature moved slowly towards the centre of the arena where Jake stood.

Lions, tigers, leopards and huge men were pitted into the ring in a futile attempt to halt the creature's progress, but it simply tossed them aside like rag dolls and pierced their hearts with the conductor's baton. Those that were spared life paid for their attack by their eyes being gouged out by the baton. The baton seemed to be made of a substance that was indestructible.

The creature finally made a move for Jake and Jake managed to dodge the baton-wielding arm and in doing so Jake was able to nick the calf of the creature's left leg with his sword. This began to appease the crowd as they revelled in the David versus Goliath type battle.

The creature was angry at the wound and went for Jake again. It grabbed hold of Jake and flung him across the arena with ease.

It was clear that the beast's tactic was to toy with Jake. He would let Jake suffer a slow, painful and humiliating death as a notion to please itself, the crowd and the fat Emperor.

The beast picked Jake up a second time and flung him to the other side of the arena, he landed right before the Emperor, Alannah and Lucy who were both still cackling at him.

He looked up at the three of them wishing, hoping that they would somehow intervene.

"Please Caesar," begged Jake. "Please show me mercy."

Jake's request was ignored as the Emperor casually shooed Jake away with a hand gesture.

Jake turned to see that the beast was coming towards him once more.

Jake had little strength left from the assault and was feeling dazed.

The beast moved closer.

Jake tried to move but he was paralysed. He simply could not move.

He tried to wake from this awful nightmare, but he could not wake, finding himself in a kind of sleep paralysis.

Perhaps he was not dreaming. It all seemed too real.

The beast moved closer still as the crowd cheered it on knowing that a kill was in sight. It was astonishing how they could switch their allegiances so easily as long as they would see a gory end to the ultimate victim. Earlier they had wanted Jake to kill the lion in their misplaced notion of entertainment.

The two human heads began to speak to Jake. They both had manic curly hair like a mad professor.

Their voices were distorted but they spoke in perfect unison.

"So you think that love lives forever do you? Only hate lives forever, you fool. Everybody hates you. You are going to die; I am going to kill you and there is nothing you can do about it."

Above the terrifying voice, he could hear Alannah and Lucy still mocking him.

The beast drew up the baton that was dripping with blood from its previous killings. Any moment now it was destined to be thrust into Jake's chest.

Then suddenly the beast let out a squeal. It was hurt, but how?

It spun around as the lion clung onto the scaly back of the beast using its claws like deep-rooted anchors and savagely mauling at the monster. One of the three necks became severed as the lion's bites were so ferocious and one of the mad professor's heads rolled along the dusty floor of the arena. Not long after the other human head was also decapitated.

Although weakened the beast was still strong enough to finally free itself from the lion, tossing it down and slaying it with the indestructible baton.

Suddenly Jake was able to move a single arm and taking his chance he pushed his sword firmly into the inviting chest of the beast. The crowd cheered, switching allegiance once more as the beast fell to the floor writhing in pain and eventually dying.

Jake turned his attention to the brave but dying lion that had intervened to save Jake's life. As Jake looked into its gentle eyes he could see that it was the same lion that Jake had earlier allowed to live.

"Thank you," said Jake.

Somehow the lion was able to speak in a human voice uttering three words before it slipped from the living world.

"Love Lives Forever."

Then the lion changed into a young man. A young man who was now dead but had obviously lived a life of kindness when on this Earth. Jake did not recognise him.

Then the body changed again into Alannah. Tears rolled down Jake's face with a cocktail of confused emotions. Sad that she was once more dead, but pleased that she was no longer party to the Emperor's sideshow and was no longer the unrecognisable cackling form that had watched the atrocious proceedings from the prestigious seats of the arena.

She looked so peaceful now lying before him; just like she did on that sad and unforgettable day when Jake had found her dead on their bed.

Tears rolled uncontrollably down Jake's face. "Sleep well darling."

He stroked her hair. Then the hair that he was stroking began to change from deep chestnut to honey blonde. It was changing into another familiar head of hair.

Then the face of Alannah began to change.

"No" screamed Jake. "Not Lucy. Lucy is alive, she is not dead. Please

God, not Lucy too."

Then Jake woke up in a confused state with sweat dripping from his whole being. His dreams were becoming more and more disturbing.

CHAPTER 20

The days passed and neither Jake nor Lucy made contact. Jake missed her more than he ever thought he could, but he would not allow himself to pick up the phone. He regretted falling out with her, and the dream of her dead body staring up at him with lifeless eyes had seriously freaked him out, but in his mind, he felt that she had given him an impossible ultimatum. How could he choose between her and the memory of his deceased fiancée? In the circumstances, it surely wasn't selfish of him to want both. *Was it?*

Jake felt that it was an unnecessary and unfair choice to have to make. He believed that Lucy should have been more understanding of the situation and that she had largely created the chasm that now lay between them. He couldn't forget Alannah and he should not be expected too. And at the same time, he knew that Lucy was here and now and he loved her. In some ways, it was quite simple in his mind. Looking back, he had some of the fondest memories anyone could ever have. His time with Alannah had been so very special. But while he was with Lucy, he felt excitement at the thought of when they were next going to meet. He could not only enjoy the moment with her he could always look forward with genuine anticipation. Just thinking of her would give him butterflies in his tingly stomach and she had the ability to make him long for her like a schoolboy did with his first crush. Foolishly perhaps, there was also an element of not wanting to compromise his macho pride in chasing her, no matter how deflated he felt. She had walked out on him so it was up to her to make amends.

The swirling whirlwind of guilt Jake felt didn't help him either. It was not only the guilt over Lucy that tormented him. He should never have sworn at her the way he did no matter how provoked. He felt guilty about failing to recognise Nick's cravings for underage sex. He, Fergus and Saul had often suspected that Nick's choice of groupies often seemed to be of tender years but he always managed to convince them that the girls were of a legal age. Groupies aside, Nick had been a childhood friend but Jake had never picked up on any signs of his paedophilia, something that absolutely repulsed Jake and his heart went out to any of Nick's victims that there may have been. How could he have been so blind all those years?

It hit him twice as hard to know that his one-time friend had indulged in the same disgusting practice of child abuse that had ultimately tortured his fiancée Alannah so much that she had needed to take her own life. Jake's conscience was eased slightly as recent investigations seemed to reveal that Nick's cravings for child pornography escalated following the split of Blossom of Eden. With the other band members about he must have suppressed many of his sick desires, or during the time that he subsequently spent on his own, he found avenues to nurture something disgusting that lay within him and he built on his obsession. Jake was pleased that at least Nick had met a fitting death to end his abuse of any more children or young people. Nick's death was one that Jake didn't feel any guilt about. Yet the guilt surfaced when he couldn't understand why it was *he* who was still living and breathing whilst he had lost his fiancée Alannah and two of his closest friends in Che and Roland Summers. Why was he spared when those he loved and cared about had met an untimely end? Perhaps it was fortuitous that Lucy had left the scene because he would hate to have her death on his conscious too. It was as if he was jinxed.

Jake tortured himself over and over again about not being there the day that Alannah had taken her own life. If only he had come home just a few hours earlier. If only he had hidden his tablets and bottle of whisky. If only he had gotten to the post before Alannah had. He hadn't seen it coming and was always questioning himself whether he could have done anything to prevent her suicide.

He felt this way about Che as well. It was often suspected that he drove his motorcycle straight into that rock face on purpose. Even if it was a tragic accident could he have done more to alter Che's state of mind and self-destruction following Roland's death? Roland's final request to Jake had been to look after his brother. Jake felt that he had failed them both. Jake wondered could he have reached further and pulled Roland out of the treacherous bog that fateful day when they had hiked across the Peaks? Why had the cloud miraculously appeared to save Jake from a fatal fall down the mountain side, yet not much later no such intervention had come along to save Roland?

Although it is expected in life to bury one's parents before one's self even they were taken away from Jake far too soon, again in terribly tragic consequences. Jake had enjoyed the dizzy heights of fame and success while at the same time having to still cope with the knowledge that his parents had not lived to share any of it. He knew that they would have been proud of his achievements and he could have supported them financially as well, buying them a nice property by the sea and allowing them to enjoy their final years together in style, but alas this chance was cruelly snatched away the night that they were killed in a car accident when Jake was just 17 years of age – the very same age when Jake had formed Blossom of Eden. His only coping mechanism at losing his parents had been to throw himself into his music, and no doubt the poignancy of his lyrics and the tenderness in some of his musical arrangements had assisted in the rise and success of the band.

In spite of his first-hand knowledge of Che's self-destructive route in the face of tragedy, Jake himself was drinking far more heavily since the split with Lucy and was pretty much cocooned in the haven of Abba Manor, not having a lot to do with the outside world. The conspiracy theories that were beginning to surface about the death of Kurt Cobain should have gripped him a lot stronger than they did, and the fact that Blur's "Country House" had beaten Oasis' "Roll With It" to the number 1 spot in their heavily publicised race for the top of the charts had completely passed him by. He was, however, becoming increasingly lost in his own music. It was just as therapeutic for him to sit at the piano for hours on end, as it was to drink the endless bottles of scotch that passed his lips. It seemed that music, along with cigarettes and alcohol (nothing to do with the anthem-like song by Oasis of that title), were his only friends in his insular world.

The old piano was like a magnet pulling Jake through a journey of endless inspiration. As he worked, his hours upon hours of sitting at the piano could be measured by the markings made in the wood: the scorched markings from his smoking cigarettes as they perched at the end of the keyboard and the rings of whisky stains caused by the endless glasses of scotch placed on the piano lid. The one song that kept penetrating the repertoire was "Love Lives Forever" and Jake had perfected the song to its highest possible peak of composition. He had composed string arrangements to complement the song, along with some powerful guitar and percussion. Jake began to believe that this was the greatest song that he had ever written, and Jake had undisputed high standards in relation to his past musical legacy. He had heard that recently the remaining Beatles had reformed, using some surviving Lennon demos to create two new songs and to support their wide-ranging *Anthology* project. Although excited as a fan, even this news didn't phase Jake as he focused on his own masterpiece.

Despite his indulgence in his music, Jake couldn't get Lucy out of his head. Furthermore, the words she had said not long before they parted were beginning to make sense. "Alannah would want you to be happy." Perhaps happiness at the moment would mean throwing himself into his work and putting his love life to one side. This thought shone like a distant light through the confused state of Jake's mind. *Should he be loyal to Alannah's memory? Should he make it up with Lucy? Was his relationship with Lucy too soon? What would Alannah think of Lucy?*

Jake looked in the mirror through bloodshot eyes caused by the endless drinks of whisky and lack of sleep. He ran his index finger over the dark circle under his right eye soaking in the realisation that he didn't look good. His hair was uncharacteristically unkempt, he needed a shave and a good deal of sleep. He managed a wry smile as he contemplated that everything that contributed to his current state was perhaps a conspiracy of fate for him to embrace the grunge look that was having far more musical success than he was currently. But that wasn't Jake. Being a star of the eighties his image and style went hand in hand with his musical prowess, he wasn't about to start wearing shabby cardigans in a bid to resurrect his career. Jake realised that he had to save himself, and quickly. A new zest of emotion ran through Jake like an electric current, it was time to wake up and smell the coffee. He also realised that in addition to the drink, fags and music there was someone he could always rely on. He felt compelled to pick up the phone. A familiar and reassuring voice quickly muttered at the other end of the line.

"Hello"

"Abe, it's Jake."

"Jake. How is life in the Peaks? It is good to hear from you."

Jake chose not to inform Abe about the current problems in his love life and of the supernatural environment he appeared to be living in.

"I've got a great new song; the hook line is awesome; it just takes your head over after only one hearing. Forget the new album, get me in the studio and we'll rush a single out. This is the rebirth of Jake Zennor. I'm back"

"I'm glad to hear it. Okay, Jake, I'll set it up."

CHAPTER 21

Jake couldn't sleep. Suffering from insomnia was becoming increasingly irritating to Jake, and whenever he did manage to sleep he was either plagued by bad dreams or awoken by the haunting melody from the old piano. Still, he knew he should be grateful for the introduction of the music into his life however unlikely the source of inspiration, as it had ensured that he had crafted a new song. A damn good song too, one of Jake's finest in fact – an achievement that appeared very unlikely in recent months.

In actual fact, Jake realised that his lack of sleep tonight was not completely due to the usual reasons of his mind dwelling on his break up with Lucy and the fact that he was missing her more than he would care to admit. For the first time in a long time, pure adrenaline was keeping him awake due to the feelings of satisfaction and excitement regarding his music. The kind of excitement that he had experienced as a child on Christmas Eve waiting for Father Christmas to come down the chimney and deliver his Christmas presents. The kind of excitement that he had experienced when signing his first record contract with Blossom of Eden and then subsequently achieving their first Number 1 soon after. The rush of adrenaline was intense, knowing that he would soon be recording his latest song "Love Lives Forever." In his mind's ear, he was playing out all the various instrumental parts and arrangements, he already knew how the song was going to turn out – and it was pretty good.

One of the villages near to Abba Manor was Monyash. Like many of the Peak District villages, it was built around a grassy green. It was to some degree a typical peakland market village and it was like so many others a former lead mining village too. Jake had always been intrigued by its connections to the Quaker religion. The farmhouse at the head of the beautiful Lathkill Dale was used as a Quaker centre for a time.

St Leonard's Church in Monyash was founded as early as 1198. As a child, Jake had been impressed by the church's paragon asset of a 10ft long chest with wrought iron decoration. His imaginative child-like mind would often imagine it to be more as a coffin, harbouring a 10ft giant inside. This he knew could be true as another favourite place to visit in the Peak District was allegedly the grave of Little John, the trusted right-hand man and friend to Sherwood Forest's legendary Robin Hood buried in the churchyard's grounds of the more northern Peak village of Hathersage. Jake would stare for what seemed like hours at the massive grave amazed that a man could ever have stood so tall.

A plate that was used as a chalice is also harboured in St Leonard's Church in Monyash. Jake's youthful vivid imagination would allow this chalice to be none other than the Holy Grail used by Jesus Christ himself at the last supper, but when he eventually learnt that it dated back to only 1726 he realised that it was an impossible scenario.

Monyash sits 300 metres above sea level and possesses a definitive crossroads at the heart of the village.

As he couldn't sleep Jake decided that he should get up and venture into the village. He ditched his pyjama bottoms and traded them for a clean pair of boxer shorts and indigo coloured jeans, and then covered his already naked upper torso with a cotton and polyester mixed fleecy top before going downstairs to finalise his attire with walking boots and a hooded outdoor jacket. He had left Elgar fast asleep on the bed and smiled as he amiably envied his pet's natural ability to snooze at the drop of a hat. Jake hoped that the long walk ahead and night air might have a soporific effect on him.

The nip of the cold night further awakened Jake if anything; although Jake reflected on how rewarding it was to be out at such an hour when the majority of the population were tucked up in their beds. Armed with a torch he ventured up his driveway and once reaching the top, for the first time turned to take real notice of the stone sign, or now he realised signs, that informed folk that they had reached Abba Manor.

There were two signs present, one for the etching of the two words required: *Manor* on the second sign and of course the preceding sign housed the word *Abba*. But Jake noticed that the sign housing the word *Abba* was jagged after the final *a* of the word and off kilter with the positioning of the *Manor* sign. Jake hadn't thought about it before but he now realised that the word *Abba* was either meant to be a longer and different word altogether or it perhaps originally had other words following it. The stone had clearly been broken away to spell the word *Abba* – either on purpose or perhaps the missing letters had crumbled away by the years of erosion caused by the bleak Peak District winters?

Jake surmised that the stone signs were likely to be as old as the house so that meant the word *Abba* was unlikely to have been the original intention of the house's name. Abba was a nonsensical invented word derived from the initials of the four members of the Swedish pop band. As Agnetha, Benny, Bjorn and Anna-Frid had not been around in the 17th Century Jake pondered that an enthusiastic fan could have perhaps broken the sign in the seventies but the fact remained that this house had never really simply been called Abba Manor. It had actually been called Abba – something – Manor. Jake was now curious to know what the correct name should actually be.

Puzzled, he continued his walk into the dark night. Within the first five minutes, he forgot about the name of his house as he had spotted a barn owl in flight dancing in the light of the silvery moon above the cornfields and also a fox safely crossing the country road only about 15 metres ahead of him. The tranquillity was an enriching experience as Jake walked along the silent roads towards the village.

Eventually, Jake could see the dotting of limited street lighting informing him that he had reached the village centre. Just as the rest of the walk had been, the village was peaceful as its residents slept into the night. However, Jake became surprised as he began to hear something in the near vicinity. As he got closer and closer to the village centre the noise became clearer. It sounded like music. Jake defined the music as having a kind of bluesy edge to it. The melody had an infectious quality but at the same time sounded slightly unnerving. It wasn't a song that Jake was familiar with. He concluded that a couple of lovers must have pulled up close to the village green and simply had their car stereo playing. He soon reached the crossroads at the village centre but he didn't notice a parked car anywhere in sight.

With the exception of the natural light cast by the full moon in the dark sky above, the only light that fell onto the village green was the faint illumination provided by the signs of the village pub and the historic blacksmith's workshop that had since been converted into a bistro. Jake refrained from walking any further as the dim light revealed a silhouette sitting on the bench. Jake was too far away at this stage to be able to make out any facial features, but one thing was for sure, whoever the silhouette belonged to it was definitely responsible for the sound of music that penetrated the quiet night. Jake was able to see that the figure had an acoustic guitar astride its knee and was blithely plucking at it as he sang along.

Jake took stock of himself. Why should a stranger playing the blues in the middle of the night unnerve him? The poor fellow was probably a fellow insomniac who ventures down to the village green every now and again for a bit of musical exercise, that's all. It suddenly crossed Jake's mind that it may be good to discuss musical preferences and stuff. This could be the very guy he needed to meet on a night when he was void of sleep.

But Jake sensed something chilling about the stranger. There was something *unexplained* that Jake couldn't quite put his finger on but the sighting was revving up a whirlwind of uncertainty in his gut. Jake's inner-self cried out for him to turn around and return to Abba Manor before the stranger noticed his presence. However, Jake ignored his own request as curiosity tempted him to walk closer towards the stranger.

The guitar riffs seemed to almost hypnotise Jake's steps as he edged closer to the musician.

"Hi, friend." It seemed a good start. The stranger spoke first, not lifting his head and continuing to thrash out expert guitar riffs.

"Hello," replied Jake. "You play well."

"Thanks very much, although I don't believe that I am quite in your league Mr Zennor."

Jake was a little taken aback that the stranger had recognised him so quickly in the darkness of the night, especially as he still hadn't raised his head in order to make eye contact. Jake was still unable to see the stranger's face, although he could now make out the unusual hairstyle. It seemed very matted, almost dreadlocks but not quite, and Jake thought it was similar to that of a surf boy but far more unkempt – yet it still looked cool! There was just about enough light to determine that there was not any sun-kissed blond highlights to suggest a lifestyle of hanging about on the beach. Besides this was the Peak District in the Heart of England, it had no coastline; a surfer would certainly be lost in these parts.

"I don't recognise the tune; did you compose it yourself?"

The stranger gave a sinister laugh; Jake felt he was mocking him.

"Yes, I am responsible for this tune. Tell me, do you like it, Jake?"

"Very much so. It seems very hypnotic."

"Is it something that you wished that you had composed yourself, Jake?" The stranger's head was still hanging down, the face concealed by the drooping matted hair. The continual plucking of the guitar rudely interfering with the dialogue was now becoming an irritation for Jake.

"Yes, I guess so. It's a good tune."

Just then, for the first time, the stranger raised his head to look directly at Jake. Simultaneously he abruptly ceased to play the guitar in mid-chord. It was not a natural cadence to finish on and the disharmony rang out uncomfortably into the dark night. The unusual face was gaunt and looked lived in and old before its time. It was hard for Jake to pitch an age. The darkness still concealed the stranger's eyes under the safeguard of the matted hair. Curiously his skin was neither dark or light, he appeared to belong to no obvious race of people in particular.

"Well tell me, Jake, what would you give for me to let you have this song?"

"What do you mean?"

"Well, maybe we could come to some arrangement." The stranger's tone was sinister.

"You want money from me?"

The stranger cackled loudly. "No, no my dear boy. Don't you know that money is the root of all *evil?*"

Jake could detect a hint of irony but did not yet know why.

"Well to be honest mate, I like your song but I don't like it that much. To be perfectly frank you can keep the song."

"Ok Jake, I guess you don't want my song. Why would you when you have just composed such a fascinating song of your own?"

Jake was puzzled, how could this stranger possibly know about "Love Lives Forever"?

"Do you know Abe?"

"I know of him, but unfortunately, he is quite a good man in life so I don't have much call to spend time with him. Besides, he is still alive and kicking for now. There's still hope for him I guess, perhaps there remains time for some form of corruption to come his way in order to tarnish his good name. You may be interested in learning that I do know an old sparring partner of yours by the name of Nick Santini, although I am not here to talk about him even though he has been quite a loyal servant. Some people actually call *me* Nick you know, amongst other things. My own personal favourite is Lucifer. It's a small world, don't you think so Jake?"

With the stranger's words things began to become uneasily clearer to Jake. He realised the poignancy of his meeting place with the stranger, and worse still he now realised whom the stranger was. He subconsciously touched at the gold cross that hung from his neck.

"I get it. Here I am a rock star, standing at a crossroads in the middle of the night under the light of a full moon. This is the part where I sell you my soul and in return, you ensure that I have the most glittering musical career that I could ever possibly wish for. Oh, and when I die I just happen to live out my eternal life in the depths of hell. I didn't think a crossroads in the Peak District was your usual thing, though, what happened to the southern states of America where you pick off the souls of Blues musicians?" Jake's use of sarcasm even surprised himself.

"Very astute Jake, well done. Well, what did you expect horns and a tail? Perhaps you should have been a detective and not a musician all these years. Maybe I could help you with a career change."

"In return for my soul."

"Of course," smiled the Devil. "I can make dreams come true."

"I'm happy as a musician thanks."

"I was only jesting Jake. I know that music has always been your destiny and that is why I want something else from you as well as your soul."

"And what's that?"

"Your song. Although I would obviously change the ghastly title of 'Love Lives Forever.'"

"Thanks for the offer but I don't need your help. When I record the song, I am confident that my career will be resurrected anyway."

"Resurrected, fine choice of wording Jake. Maybe you are right but how can you be sure? Whereas, I can guarantee your success."

"Look no offence, but I don't want to give you my song and I don't want to give you my soul either. Anyway, if you are who you say you are why can't you just steal my song?"

"I am afraid rules are rules Jake, and sometimes even I have to abide by them. If I try to pick out the notes on my guitar my hands simply freeze, it is an impossible task. I need you to willingly give it to me because the inspiration that you received for this song was very clearly protected by all that is good."

"Then I shall keep my faith in all that is good, and I believe that will help me in my career and the success of my new song. I am truly thankful for the inspiration I have already received in composing "Love Lives Forever"."

Satan cackled out another mocking bout of laughter. "Don't make me laugh Jake, since when have you been so religious. I know that even as a child you had to be dragged to *his* so-called church by your mommy. She was the only reason you attended, not because you believed in all that claptrap that they rambled on about on a Sunday."

"I've always believed in the power of good over evil but not necessarily the way it has always been presented. Anyhow, now that you, the fallen angel has chosen to show himself to me I guess I now have proof that God really does exist after all."

The Devil was losing his patience with Jake and didn't appreciate his bravery and audacity. For the first time, Satan allowed Jake to look into his eyes and Jake was intimidated as the burning red eyes stared at him like two balls of menacing fire. The Devil's voice changed and began to talk in tongues as he almost roared his words of anger at Jake. "You know nothing, Zennor. Now I warn you, do not mess me around. Give me your soul and I promise to make you the most successful musical artist that has ever lived...or died for that matter. Believe me, you will not have been the first to have entered into such a deal with me."

Jake was now frightened at his surreal situation and regretted his previous cockiness. He looked over to St Leonard's church which sat only about 200 yards away or so. If he made a run for it would he make it to its safe haven? He then noticed the eerie sight of the slanted gravestones in the churchyard and wondered if any of the Devil's disciples had been buried there over the years and could be conjured out of the earth to stop him in his tracks – a casualty of Jake's studying of Michael Jackson's "Thriller" video over the years. It was very likely that the church door was locked anyway, a shameful necessity these days due to the vandalism and thefts suffered by the houses of God.

"I'm very sorry if I have offended you, Mr err Devil?" Jake cringed at his clumsy words.

The Devil returned his voice to its original tone and dimmed his fiery eyes. "Please, call me Lucifer. Don't cower Jake. It doesn't suit you. It is not my intention to frighten you. I will ask you one last time. In return for your soul, I will promise you success for the remainder of your career. The soul will be mine to claim on your final day upon this Earth and you have breathed your last breath, which I can assure you will be a long time coming. If you grant me your song now as well as your soul I will ensure that you become the most successful musical artist of all time and for any time to come. This is a wonderful offer Jake; you should consider it very seriously."

For a split-second Jake seriously contemplated the Devil's offer, but then he quickly got a grasp on reality. He summed up that life on Earth may not always be that great, but he was damned if he was going to have an eternal life of hell - quite literally.

"What will happen if I don't take your offer, as generous as it is?" Jake prayed that the Devil couldn't notice his bluff on the inclusion of the word generous.

The Devil smiled. "Don't worry Jake I will cause you no harm. You shouldn't believe all that you read about me you know. I'm not a monster! You of all people know how the written word can sometimes paint an incorrect picture of a person's character."

Jake was forced to agree based on his own experiences regarding the proportion of blame aimed at him for Alannah's death.

"It's your choice, Jake. You can take what I am offering and have guaranteed success beyond your wildest dreams or you can take your chances doing things your way. But let's be honest, things ain't too rosy for you at the moment, are they? How many records did your last album sell again?"

Jake pulled off an Oscar-winning performance making believe that he was giving the matter a lot of thought before finally turning down the Devil's offer once and for all.

"I'm sorry, sir. I'm extremely grateful for the offer but I will have to decline."

"Ok. Too bad. It's your loss, Jake."

"Well, that remains to be seen. I guess for the moment it looks like my soul is destined for someplace else when my time comes or you wouldn't have offered me this deal."

The Devil gave a strangely reassuring smile. "My, you're a clever one, Zennor. It is safe to assume that your soul is destined elsewhere as we speak, Jake, but who knows what naughtiness you may get up to in the future. I may still have a claim on you one day. You can never say never."

Somehow Jake found himself smiling but then he quickly turned thoughtful. "Do you mind if I ask you something? I understand if you don't wish to answer, you are certainly not obligated to under the circumstances."

"Go ahead."

"Well, I do not necessarily share the same opinion, but I was always taught that the act of suicide was a sin, and I just wondered if that meant that Alannah was with you and your world."

"That is some question, Jake. I do practice client confidentiality you know."

Jake feared the worst although he knew how lovely and caring Alannah had been. If she were in the depths of hell with people like Nick Santini then it simply wouldn't be fair. "Please."

"You refuse my offer and then ask me a question like that. You have a nerve, Zennor."

Jake winced but then was shocked as the Devil spoke again. "Don't worry Jake, she isn't with me. You must remember that the other guy has the first refusal on souls and he is partial to doing a lot of forgiving."

"Thank you."

The Devil reached out his hand to offer a handshake. Jake was unsure.

"Go ahead, there is no hidden agenda," smiled the Devil.

Jake cautiously took the offer of the handshake, concluding there would have been a far worse fate had he decided not to shake hands with the Devil and subsequently ending up snubbing and offending him. But placing his trust in Satan was not something that he thought he would ever have to do.

Surprisingly the Devil was true to his word. It appeared to be a simple handshake.

"I'll, err, be on my way then," said Jake

The Devil nodded.

"It was nice meeting you," Jake couldn't believe his own words.

The Devil nodded again.

Jake began to walk away and return homewards towards Abba Manor.

He heard the Devil's voice call out to him.

"Hey Jake, if you change your mind about my offer give me a call. Even I have a phone you know. You'll reach me on 666."

Jake waved goodbye after experiencing yet another incredible unforeseen event and continued his homeward journey as he heard the sound of blues guitar starting up.

He concluded that his venture outdoors was in no way going to aid with his difficulty in sleeping tonight.

CHAPTER 22

It was a cold and rainy day in Sheffield but the recording studio possessed familiar warmth for Jake. He was always content in the environment of what he did best. Music was unquestionably a labour of love for Jake, a world to get lost in and a safety net to save him from any unwanted distractions.

Jake had remarkably recorded the haunting piano melody for "Love Lives Forever" in a single take as if guided on an ocean of serene inspiration. He quickly added the necessary musical arrangements and additional instruments to complement the track. It all sounded wonderful.

The only other musician that appeared on the record was Saul Jackson, the drummer from Jake's previous band Blossom of Eden. Saul was a cheeky individual who had an infectious sense of humour and he and Jake had remained good friends in spite of the band's split. His smouldering good looks had always resulted in him never being short of female admirers. The other band members used to tease him about how the drummer always seemed to end up with the girl, but it was fair to say that the other members of Blossom of Eden had also had their pick off the menu of groupies that would readily be on offer, even the least attractive member of the band: bass player Fergus Sutcliffe. Saul was of mixed race and had a sharp dress sense, though today he was dressed casually in a stripy long sleeved T-shirt and a pair of self-styled cut-off jeans.

Jake had entrusted the help of Bjorn and Joey to help engineer and produce the song. These two long-time professional friends of Jake's were as respected and recognised in the music business for their work from behind the mixing desk as Jake was for his creativity in the spotlight. Jake also valued their input and judgement. They would pull no punches and would give constructive criticism when justified. Jake felt it important to have an objective sounding board for his work. However, on this occasion of recording "Love Lives Forever," their verbal input was virtually non-existent. The eerie hook of the piano melody was infectious and addictive to anyone who had the pleasure to hear it, and this included Bjorn and Joey as they listened with pure admiration. The song coupled with Jake's ability to play and sing it so completely and so proficiently blew them away. The musical notes seemed to flow out of his fingertips like small fountains of sparkling melodic spring water and the lyrics beautifully entered the air in the haven of Jake's perfectly suited voice. This would be a very easy piece of musical engineering for Bjorn and Joey.

The vocal track was typically going to be recorded separate to the music, although Jake's guide vocal as he played would have proved more than sufficient for the final mix.

Jake entered the singing booth and proceeded to perch on the tall stool. He took a sip of mineral water to assist his vocal chords and then placed the headphones on his ears. He signalled a thumb sign to Bjorn and Joey through the thick glass shield of the booth to indicate that he was ready to sing a 'take'. Bjorn began to relay the backing music to the headphones in order for Jake to continue and record the main vocal.

The song began with the piano melody as the perfect introduction and undemanding prompt for Jake to begin to sing, but Jake raised his hand to halt the recording session.

"What's wrong?" enquired Bjorn, his voice appearing directly into Jake's headphones.

"I'm not sure, it's weird," came Jake's reply. "I can hear interference through the headphones. It sounds like a woman's voice faintly speaking, but I can't make the words out."

"That's impossible Jake," stated Joey. "We are using a brand-new reel; the tape is virgin. Try it again."

The music was played again. "Ok Jake, take 2," instructed Bjorn.

"No, no. I can still fucking hear it," there was an annoyance in his voice carried over from Joey's remark insinuating that Jake had been mistaken, coupled with the fact that the woman's voice was preventing the nearly completed song from being a finalised recording.

Bjorn spoke, attempting to be diplomatic. "Jake, mate, we really can't hear anything out here except the music that has been put down."

"I'm not imagining it," replied Jake, unimpressed by the situation.

Joey spoke again, "Perhaps the phones are just picking up a freak radio signal or something? The tape is definitely clear." Joey knew his offer of an explanation was unlikely as the studio had soundproof walls and extremely efficient equipment.

"Well whatever it is, it sounds fucking spooky… It is still going on…SHIT." Jake then unexpectedly threw off the headphones with alarming speed and force. He put his hands to his ears indicating that they had encountered some pain. Something had visibly unnerved him.

"What is it, Jake?" enquired a startled Bjorn nearly falling off his chair.

"A scream," stated Jake, obviously disturbed. "I swear to God I heard a woman screaming followed by some sort of animal noises or something. I tell you there is some weird fucking recording on that tape, or I'm picking up something awful going on from somewhere."

Saul and Bjorn exchanged a concerned look.

Joey entered the booth and put on the headphones himself, powered by a mixture of morbid curiosity and a genuine desire to try and resolve exactly what was going on here. He heard nothing.

"Jake whatever it was has stopped. Honestly, mate, there is nothing coming through these headphones now. Let's try the take again."

Jake cautiously put on the headphones once more. Joey was right, it seemed okay. "Okay, we'll go again."

Bjorn pressed the relevant buttons once more. "Take 3."

There was no further interference.

The adrenaline that had ensued due to the mysterious voice and scream seemed to enhance Jake's vocal performance and he immediately put down a superb vocal for "Love Lives Forever."

"That was great," said Joey who had returned to the mixing desk.

"Yeah, that was bang on," said Bjorn, "It's a wrap."

"Do you have to be so fucking clichéd," joked Jake.

"It really did sound great mate," said Saul.

"Cheers," acknowledged Jake.

"Listen, it's been a long day. I'll mix this down tomorrow after we have all slept on it," said Bjorn. "We have definitely got a hit single here though Jake, well done mate."

"Cheers," said Jake accepting the compliment. "I want this in the shops a.s.a.p. Now, does anyone fancy a drink? I think this calls for a celebration." Jake was so pleased with the way things had ultimately gone with the song, he soon forgot the mysterious happenings that had voiced themselves through the headphones.

"Any excuse for a piss up, aye, Jake," joked Joey. "I could definitely do with a night cap; I think *I've* deserved it."

"*You've* deserved it?" laughed Jake. "Fuck me you only twiddle a few knobs, it's me who does all the hard work."

Bjorn felt compelled to join in the banter and fall on the side of his production colleague, "Hey Jake, it's me and Joey that make you sound good. You couldn't do it without us."

Jake laughed at his friend's remark, purely taken in the spirit that it was meant. "Well if I really need you that much, the least I can do is buy you a drink. Come on let's go, my palate's getting drier by the second."

"Actually guys, you're all wrong. I think you will find that it is my rhythm section which is holding that song together. I think that it is me who deserves a drink the most," said Saul typically wanting to join in the banter.

Joey and Jake looked at one another before answering in perfect unison. "Bollocks!"

"I'll catch up with you in a while," said Bjorn. "I'll just finish off here and make sure everything's saved to the computer and disks before I turn everything off."

"Okay, we'll catch you in a bit."

Jake, Saul and Joey then promptly got up and headed for the pub after a hard day's night.

It was a lengthy process to competently save the day's work and to shut down the various machinery of the studio. It was a process that Bjorn had done many times before being the true professional of his craft. Engineering and producing music were as much a labour of love for him as it was for Jake to provide it. A competent musician himself he had never craved to be in the foreground of the business, but to be fair he didn't possess the charisma or star appeal that is required to be a legendary artist anyhow.

Bjorn's strength belongs in his inquisitive mind, which is always working overtime to come up with new musical sounds and various ways to mix tracks. He loved to experiment and he loved working with Jake as he recognised the uncanny ability of Jake to come up with prolific good music time and time again. Personally, he couldn't understand why Jake's career had taken a nosedive since he had become a solo artist. Jake's music was a pleasure to work with and carried such depth and originality. Bjorn could become totally enthralled in Jake's work and with each new piece a new door always seemed to open. Although Bjorn was arguably the best at what he done, when working on Jake's music he always seemed to be learning and discovering new things and ideas such was the channelling of Jake's automatic inspiration. Jake was infectious in many ways. To put it simply, in Bjorn's mind Jake was a musical genius.

Bjorn gave the machines one last check and was satisfied that all the power was shut down. He smiled to himself, pleased with the day's work and was now looking forward to joining his three drinking buddies down the pub. As he turned to exit the studio he reached to turn out the light and put the place into complete darkness. It was then that his blood unexpectedly ran cold.

Bjorn heard a voice. This alarmed him enough believing he was the only one left in the building, but what really freaked him out was that the voice distinctly seemed to be coming through the equipment that he knew he had personally only moments earlier completely shut down. It was a voice that seemed much deeper than humanly possible, yet a high-pitched screaming voice could just about be detected accompanying it in perfect unison giving the impression that although there were two sounds to the voice, it definitely could only belong to one entity. The voice was distorted and almost inaudible as it came through the speakers, but it repeated a single message over and over again, like an old vinyl record stuck in a groove.

The words would register with Bjorn forever.

"Be true to this music and the music will be true to you... Be true to this music and the music will be true to you…."

The hair stood up on the back of Bjorn's neck.

What did this message mean? Was it a warning or simply a piece of advice?

It seemed an unnecessary message to make to Bjorn who was always *true* to any music he worked on, after all, he loved music. But the haunting voice repeated the message again and again, and Bjorn sensed the emphasis of being true to *this* music. Did the voice mean Jake's music in general or the latest composition of "Love Lives Forever"?

One of Bjorn's favourite pastimes was researching the paranormal. He remembered learning about this sort of phenomena when unexplained contact is made via electrical tapes and equipment. He remembered it being referred to as *white noise*. Is *white noise* what he and Jake had experienced tonight?

Frozen to the spot, Bjorn felt compelled to make sense of the voice he was hearing in spite of his fear. Was he rooted to the spot because of terror or because the voice was so hypnotising he was being forced to listen to it?

"Be true to this music and the music will be true to you."

Be true to *this* music. *This music* must be of reference to "Love Lives Forever" contemplated Bjorn. *And the music will be true to you*, Bjorn began to interpret this as a positive message. He believed that he might be hearing a prophecy via some kind of electronic voice phenomena that the song was destined to become a hit. *Okay so if we respect this particular piece of music it will reward us*. Bjorn was happy now that Jake's suggestions of using classical arrangements as opposed to a lot of electronic sounds were an even better idea than he had at first envisaged. How was there a better way to be truer to a piece of music than to use the tried and tested sound of classical instruments? Now he came to think of it, Bjorn recognised that the catchy, haunting hook line of the song did seem to be a timeless piece of music, that would not appear out of place if heard in any given era, a magic ingredient that always seemed evident in all the great classic songs of years gone by.

The voice then suddenly ceased to speak its cryptic message as abruptly as it had begun.

A short eerie silence followed but was interrupted by the unplugged equipment now being used as a vehicle for the terrorising sound of a piercing scream of a woman clearly in distress.

Bjorn was so shaken that he skipped the pub and headed straight home.

The next day, after very little sleep, Bjorn composed himself and decided to tell Jake of his strange experience.

"If you had told me this a few months ago Bjorn, I would have advised you to seek medical help, but I have come to learn that nothing seems impossible anymore. I'm not sure what reality means these days, but I do believe my own eyes and ears for sure. If you're telling me, Bjorn, that you heard a ghostly voice speak through musical equipment and speakers that were clearly turned off and had no power source whatsoever, then I for one fucking believe you."

"That's not all Jake," said Bjorn relieved that Jake didn't think that he had turned into a nutcase overnight. "Listen to this CD of what I hope is to be the final mix of "Love Lives Forever"."

Jake took the CD from Bjorn and placed it into the CD player. Just as the piano melody climaxed on the second phrase of the introduction a woman's scream could be heard, ironically in perfect tune and giving the brilliant song an even greater edge.

"That's the scream I heard after the voice had finished speaking Jake. Fuck knows how it got into the mix. None of us heard it when we were recording."

"Fucking hell Bjorn, what's going on?"

"I don't know Jake, but that eerie scream definitely needs to be on the song. It sounds fucking amazing."

CHAPTER 23

Jake rebooted his laptop. It annoyed him every time he needed to do this due to the screen freezing or the computer running slow. Sometimes Jake was convinced that computers had a mind of their own and enjoyed toying with their user's sanity, mischievously choosing to crash at the most inopportune moment.

Jake liked to use his laptop as a means to safely store his song lyrics but initially, he would always approach his lyric writing using the traditional method of pen to paper. His main use of the computer these days was to access the Internet where he extensively researched information on paranormal activity and the history of the Peak District in an attempt to make some sense of the hauntings that he had been experiencing. The internet was a fairly new phenomenon in terms of widespread use in the 1990s, but of course Jake had the financial means to experiment with emerging technology. Inadvertently he had become rather informed about his local area in his quest to understand the hauntings.

Another necessity for Jake to possess a laptop was so that he could access his emails in order to keep himself in touch with family and friends. Abe always managed to send him quite inventive e-mails, not always connected with work, and usually with the inclusion of a peculiar and comical attachment that he had downloaded from the Internet. It was only certain privileged individuals that had access to Jake's personal e-mail address, his sisters Blanche and Toni dutifully filtered many external e-mails for him that came through a public e-mail address in return for a generous financial allowance that he gladly paid them. His sisters had better business sense than Jake, so he left them to manage most things that didn't fall into Abe's remit.

The laptop began to beep as the various menu screens came and went during the reboot.

Jake was pleased and relieved that the reboot appeared to have been successful. On so many previous occasions it could take him three or four attempts to reboot the system into working with success.

He clicked on his inbox in order to access his e-mails. He had only received three new ones in total and he quickly opened them to reveal their contents. The first was just a 'hello, how are you doing?' e-mail from Fergus and the second was from his Internet provider offering a various amount of deals that Jake would usually not bother to take them up on.

Jake's heart sank when he realised that none of the e-mails had come from Lucy. He really missed her. He opened the third and final e-mail and it cheered him up when he realised that it was from Saul to say that he had really enjoyed participating on the "Love Lives Forever" recording. He went on to state that he also enjoyed the subsequent piss up afterwards. Saul also confirmed in quite graphic detail his success in bedding the barmaid at the end of the night's frivolity. Saul had enquired as to whether Jake had managed to catch the name of the willing participant, as he couldn't quite remember it himself. Typically, it had not been her name that had interested Saul.

Jake was just about poised to reply to Saul's e-mail when a pop-up window appeared on the screen stating "You have got mail; do you wish to read it now?"

Hoping that it was Lucy, Jake instantly clicked on the "yes" box to access the latest message, but he became confused and disturbed at what appeared next on his laptop screen.

HELP US! HELP US! HELP US! HELP US! HELP US! HELP US!

The two-word message appeared over and over again resulting in the screen becoming totally covered.

Jake manoeuvred the e-mail upwards using the arrows on the sidebar but the unnerving plea still kept repeating. HELP US! HELP US! HELP US!

There appeared to be no end to the e-mail, the two words simply kept repeating into infinity.

Who are *us*? Jake thought.

He looked at the "sender" box on the e-mail; it revealed that the desperate message had been sent by "The Lovers".

Who the fuck are the Lovers? He thought. *And how have they got hold of my email address!*

He clicked on the cross in the top right-hand corner of the screen in an attempt to close the e-mail down, but he found it impossible to ignore such a heartrending plea.

Jake looked around the room anxiously as if he may find some answers to who the Lovers could be, but of course, he didn't find any clues at all. He ran his fingers through his hair not knowing quite what to do.

I've got to help them, he thought, assuming the message was genuine. But where are they?

HELP US! They had said. HELP US!

He returned his eyes back to the screen in desperation and noticed that his in-box had received another new e-mail.

He hesitated to open it as it was from another sender whom he did not recognise: "The Man of the House."

Curiosity compelled him to open it.

This latest e-mail didn't repeat itself over and over again; instead, it just gave four words in total to deliver a far more chilling message.

DON'T YOU FUCKING DARE!

CHAPTER 24

Residence of Lucy Ives, Kensington, London

Lucy lay on her bed staring up at the brilliant white ceiling as her hands played with her bunch of keys. It was a habit that Lucy unconsciously carried out on a regular basis, her hands would work overtime therapeutically working through each key in turn and then back again as the troubled thoughts in her mind worked even harder. Lucy was the sort of person that kept every key she needed or didn't need, in a single bunch. The keys to the front and back doors of her quaint Georgian residence, the keys to her silver Mazda, the keys to her pedestal and drawers at the office and about half a dozen keys which she had clean forgotten what their purpose had been were all evident. The playing with the keys was more poignant at present as the bunch was being held together by a clump of wood taken from the oak staircase at Abba Manor. The wood had literally broken away during a spontaneous and robust moment of passion between Lucy and Jake. They had both seen the funny side and Jake had arranged for a local wood turner to shape it into a heart and to include an entwined carving of Jake's and Lucy's initials upon it. Lucy loved it and it instantly became her key ring on receipt of the unexpected gift. Jake would often tease her on how she was unable to use a dainty handbag as the key ring and keys were responsible for a considerable occupancy of space. Jake himself always chose to travel light and his modest set of keys would easily fit into his jeans or jacket pocket.

Lucy ceased staring at the ceiling and fixed her eyes on the key ring. She stroked the carved image of Jake's initials with the same care and attention as if she was stroking his face.

"You bastard, Jake. Why do I miss you so much?"

She broke her tear-filled eyes away from the key ring and glanced at the time on her bedside clock. The red LED display showed 17:30. It was time to run a bath and begin to get ready for the evening. She had reluctantly agreed to go to a work's bash. At least Patsy would be there. She was a good and loyal friend but above all, she was a right good laugh. Patsy was of a persuasive nature and had left Lucy little alternative but to attend tonight's event.

Battling against a lack of motivation and enthusiasm, Lucy wrenched herself off the bed and took the short walk down the landing into her bathroom. She took the keys in with her and lay them down on the marble sink unit surround, with the carving of the initials positioned so that they could be viewed when she would ultimately take her position of relaxation in the bath. Lucy had amazed herself at how soppy and sentimental she had become. She was almost ashamed at caving in from her usually prided persona as a tough cookie! However, Lucy was also a highly intelligent woman, and she realised that finding true love for perhaps the first time in her life was a much more appreciative state of existence to be in than simply being a stubborn bitch! She had an enlightening realisation that her time with Jake had proved that it was far more rewarding to "work to live" rather than her previously unconscious ethos of "living to work". Up until now, she had been career mad! She conceded that she actually liked being in love, though she didn't appreciate the emotions of melancholy at present being apart from Jake. In spite of her misery, Lucy did, however, feel totally justified in her actions to orchestrate the split. She believed that Jake simply wasn't yet over Alannah and she wanted to respect that situation even if it meant heartache for herself.

Lucy reached over to run the bath turning the large brass hot tap on a full flurry and then suitably following with a quarter turn of the cold tap which produced a much smaller trickle of cold water. Momentarily her mind raced back to when she had been convinced that she had seen blood spouting out of the taps at Abba Manor. She managed to push the thought from her mind, as her own bath water was appearing more and more inviting. She glanced at her impressive range of bath oils; Lucy enjoyed collecting these even more than her gathering of keys. There was no contest, tonight's state of mind demanded Lavender with Ylang-Ylang. Lucy wished to relax, Patsy wasn't due to collect her in the taxi until 20.30, which meant that there was ample time to indulge in the comfort of a hot soothing bath even before the obligatory ritual of applying makeup, ironing tonight's yet-to-be decided outfit and perfecting and styling one's hair.

Lucy had just begun to unscrew the bottle top to the bath oil when the phone rang.

Slightly annoyed, Lucy tutted and left the bathroom to answer the phone which was positioned on her landing. Her annoyance soon left her when she realised who it was.

"Hi, Lucy, how are you?" Spoke the cheeky Liverpool accent, with a now slightly developed twist of an East London invasion due to years of living in the capital.

"Oh, hi Patsy, I'm fine."

"Mmmm, you say you're fine but I can tell that you're still feeling low."

"You know me too well."

"You are still beating yourself up over that glorified pub singer, aren't you?"

"Patsy, Jake is a very competent musician."

"Okay, okay. If you're defending him then I know it must be true love."

"Stop twisting my melon, girl," laughed Lucy.

"See, I bet that is the first time that you have creased your face today with a smile."

"Probably, I wish I didn't miss the bastard so much."

"He hasn't called yet?"

"Not a word."

"It's his loss baby. I tell you what. Tonight, you are going to put Jake Zennor to the back of your mind and we are going to have a good old-fashioned girl's night out. I've got a bottle of gin in my handbag to liven things up, if anyone notices the bulge I'll just say that I'm carrying your extensive collection of keys for you."

Lucy laughed again, "You're nuts, Patsy."

"At least you're laughing again, I'll pick you up about half past eight as arranged."

"Yeah, okay. I still haven't decided what to wear."

"Do what the song says, come as you are."

"Not likely."

"I thought I needed to phone you. I thought that you were going to back out and spend the rest of your days as a hermit moping about the place."

"I did consider cancelling but what the hell, I'll be ready at 8.30."

Just then Lucy noticed a small stream of water seep under the bathroom door.

"Shit I've left the bath running; I'll see you later Patsy."

"See y…"

Lucy placed down the receiver and quickly entered the bathroom to turn off the taps. She threw two nearby bath towels onto the floor in an attempt to mop up the excess water and released the plug in order to get the bath water to a reasonable level. Panic over.

Or was it.

She waved her arms about to compromise the steamy environment and glanced towards the mirror.

The mirror was naturally steamed up, but Lucy felt a shiver run up her spine as she read the chilling words that had been scrawled in the condensation.

Love may live forever but you will not.

Lucy called out in vain. "Who is in here? Where are you? Who are you?"

Of course, no one answered. Lucy knew that both her front and back door were both currently locked from the inside.

She grabbed her bunch of keys and darted downstairs. She reached her front door and began to fumble with the locks in a state of panic. She was convinced that she could hear footsteps slowly coming down the stairs but was too terrified to look back.

She managed to compose herself for a second, took a deep breath and successfully opened the door. As she did so she let out a scream for she was sure that she had felt a hand touch her shoulder. There was nobody about in the street to hear her scream. And when she turned around there was no one there either.

Come on Ives get a grip! She thought to herself.

But then she heard the footsteps again, this time, accompanied by an eerie cackle that gave the weird impression that the voice was both right upon her but also somewhere in the distance. She didn't hang around to debate whatever was happening and she ran for all she was worth to her Mazda which was parked in the permitted residents' space on the road, freeing the central locking as she approached it. It was a good sound to hear the doors open by the car electrics and to see the lights flash as it always did when successfully opened.

But then as she went to open the car door the locks somehow shut down again.

Lucy pressed the key fob again to attempt to free the locks.

It would not open.

She could sense that whatever was following her was getting nearer and nearer.

She tried the fob again.

The locks opened.

Lucy reached down to the handle. The locks sprung shut.

Lucy quickly decided to open the car via the old tried and trusted method of using the key in the lock.

Again, like at her front door she fumbled in a state of anxiety. She could hear the voice cackling and could now sense hot breath at her neck.

This time, the door opened. Lucy got inside as quickly as she could.

As she looked up she could see that there was not a soul in sight.

A momentary feeling of relief swept through her sweating body.

Then she saw her front door slowly swing open, but not enough to reveal if something was behind it.

She fumbled with the keys once again, cursing herself for hosting so many of them, until finally, she attempted to start the ignition.

The engine turned over but then died.

This had never happened before in the 3 years that Lucy had owned the car. She had always been delighted at how reliable the vehicle had served her and it had chosen now of all occasions to let her down!

She turned the key again.

The engine was making some sort of strained noise as if almost making a connection but then ultimately failing.

Lucy punched the steering wheel in frustration.

Then as she looked up she could see a figure approaching her.

She had only seen movies depicting the stereotypical image of the Grim Reaper, but Lucy could not conjure up any other description for the tall figure approaching her which was shrouded in a deep black tunic that hooded its head and face.

A long bony hand reached out towards Lucy with the index finger beckoning a "come to me" motion.

In desperation, Lucy turned the key in the ignition again.

The engine died but the car was sounding healthier.

The long bony hand reached out and was about to grab the car door handle when all of a sudden the engine shot into life and Lucy was soon off breaking the thirty-mph speed restriction in the making.

Lucy looked into the rear-view mirror and she could see the figure standing at the side of the road, and then it slowly disappeared as if it was evaporating just like the steam that it had seemed to materialise from in Lucy's bathroom.

Lucy drove as if her life depended on it to no place in particular, she was simply glad to be away from the Grim Reaper or whatever it was back at her house and roadside.

Eventually, she found that her unplanned journey had taken her close to Craven Cottage, the home of Fulham Football Club, and concluding that she was now safe parked adjacent to the River Thames.

She rested her head on the steering wheel glad that her ordeal seemed finally over.

After a short while, Lucy raised her head again and then it happened.

Every driver in the world has at one time or another felt a presence on the backseat and quickly checked to discover that actually there was nothing there, but for some strange reason, their imagination had demanded that they take a look.

But as Lucy peered in the rearview mirror she could see that the back seat of her car was indeed occupied.

She froze as she saw the same figure that she had left at the kerbside about 3 miles before sitting on her back seat, grinning a bony grin from its skeletal face. There were no eyes in the sockets to gauge an emotion but she could sense its delight in toying with her.

She turned away hoping this could not be happening and caught sight of the treasured wooden heart key ring. The carving of the entwined initials had disappeared; instead, the skeletal face of the unwelcome stranger that had appeared on the back seat had replaced it. Then the inanimate wooden face came to life and began to distort and cackle.

Without hesitation, Lucy yanked the key ring from her keys and got out the car. She threw the wooden heart with its distorted face to the ground and began to stamp on it shouting and swearing through her violent actions.

"Fuck off you bastard, leave me alone," she frantically shouted over and over again as the cars sped past her, her actions inspiring some curious looks from the drivers.

"Fuck you!" The key ring eventually broke in two and Lucy picked up both pieces and threw them into the cold and murky water of the River Thames.

She heard a scream come from the wood as it hit the water, had she really defeated the stranger so easily?

She looked in the car and it was empty.

Lucy then caught sight of a young couple sitting on a bench, who had obviously halted their petting session to witness this crazy woman stamping on a piece of wood and swearing at the top of her voice. Lucy gave an apologetic wave but was then further embarrassed when she noticed a grandmother with her hands over her grandson's ears, their trip to watch the boats gently move up and down the River Thames taking an unexpected pause when the crazy woman appeared swearing at the top of her voice.

This embarrassment had quickly brought Lucy back into the world of reality and she was able to get in the car and complete the return journey to her home with a little more focus.

She cautiously went up her path and into the house; the front door had been left slightly ajar.

Lucy went up the stairs and into her bedroom. Everything appeared fine.

Now for the moment of truth.

Lucy entered the bathroom.

Lucy was amazed to see that the mirror was crystal clear showing no trace of the awful message that had previously been there.

She slipped off her clothes and dipped her toe in the bath. The temperature was perfect.

Whatever had happened seemed to be over. She concluded somehow she must have imagined it. But it had seemed so real.

Then she thought of Abba Manor with all its hauntings and happenings. Then she thought of that key ring made from the wood of the staircase at Abba Manor.

Oh well, the key ring was gone now, and she lived in a small Georgian terrace in Kensington and *not* that damned sprawling creepy place known as Abba Manor.

Lucy enjoyed her bath and prepared for the night ahead.

CHAPTER 25

When Jake climbed the three concrete steps and entered the Barley Mow through the yellow painted door the pub was already in full swing. It was Saturday night and that meant the Barley Mow in Bonsall was hosting live entertainment at the west end of its single rectangular room. The small holding was typically packed to the rafters and the mass body heat added to the humidity of the pub's climate. When the entertainment was being hosted here it often made Jake think of The Beatles playing at The Cavern in Mathew Street, Liverpool. The Cavern was a converted underground cellar where again swarms of people squeezed in to watch the entertainment. Such humidity was generated in The Cavern that condensation would literally run down the heavily disinfected walls of the dwelling causing by all accounts a very distinctive smell. Quite apt then really that when Jake entered the pub, the gentleman with a good head of grey-streaked hair was performing a reasonable rendition of the White Album's "Blackbird".

With the majority of the crowd viewing the night's entertainment, Jake had remarkably entered the Barley Mow fairly unnoticed, apart from the people that were packed together whom he inevitably had to snake through in order to get to the bar. Each time he said 'Excuse me' in order to gain another few steps, people would turn to one another whispering things like "was that really him?"

Jake ordered a guest ale from the welcoming barmaid, paid his money and turned to face the entertainment on offer. Leaning on the bar, Jake was impressed with what he heard.

The modest space available in the Barley Mow dictated that most of the entertainment was delivered by solo artists or duos. Any rhythm section was usually on a bongo or a single snare drum. Tonight's entertainment was simply a singer with an electro-acoustic guitar and a single microphone. He played well and sang well. Jake could decipher that this guy had a wealth of experience behind him, most likely playing in the countless pubs and clubs of Derbyshire for perhaps the past thirty years or more. No doubt just as Jake had done, he would have played in a band, or bands, at some point and he was one of a long line of talented and competent musicians who for one reason or another just didn't get that break to make the big time.

"Who is this guy?" Jake asked the barmaid.

"Do you want his stage name or real name?"

"The name he goes by when he entertains as well as this."

"Donny Ramon. He's pretty good huh?"

"Yeah, his finger picking is exceptional"

Then as Donny Ramon waited for the applause to calm down following his rendition of The Eagles' "Lyin' Eyes" it happened.

Donny Ramon had looked beyond the sea of heads before him and spotted Jake Zennor standing at the far end of the room.

"Thank you, you're a great crowd. Now then Ladies and Gentleman for the next song I'd like to invite a very special guest onto the floor. Put your hands together for one of the great sons of Bonsall, the one and only Jake Zennor."

The crowd could hardly believe what they were hearing. Jake Zennor was a household name and he was in this very pub!

Jake acknowledged Donny with a wave. "It's your show mate, you crack on. You're doing a sterling job." It wasn't difficult for Donny to hear Jake's raised voice over the compact room.

"I insist Jake. I could do with a break anyway."

"Come on Jake," said one chap not far from him and similar requests echoed around the room.

Jake placed down his pint of ale, threw up his hands and conceded defeat. "Okay, okay." He made his way towards Donny amongst cheers and many pats on the back. In spite of his relative unpopularity at present with British society, when a bonafide pop star walks into a local pub and is about to entertain you for free it's very difficult not to get excited.

Jake shook Donny's hand before taking the shiny black Kramer Ferrington guitar from him.

"Nice guitar, mate," said Jake.

"Thanks. I purchased it in '88 in Memphis, Tennessee, whilst doing a tour that way."

"Impressive."

Jake sat on the stool and the crowd quietened waiting for this unexpected treat to unfold. He quickly got comfortable with the guitar's action by doing a few tuning exercises and then followed this with that iconic opening chord to "A Hard Day's Night." He was ready.

"Ok, ready?"

The crowd responded positively. It crossed several minds in the audience that in effect they were watching a Jake Zennor performance similar to the televised *Unplugged* sessions which had become a trademark of 1990s music. In years to come, Nirvana's *Unplugged* session in particular would become a very defining and legendary performance.

What a shame that there were no TV cameras present in The Barley Mow tonight.

Instinctively Jake began to pick out the opening notes to Bob Marley's "Redemption Song". He hadn't planned it; it just came to mind. The song was a favourite of Jake's which he always liked to jam privately using an acoustic guitar but this was the first time he had ever played the song in public. This unique song of Marley's was his final single before his untimely death in 1981. Ironically the epitome of reggae music had chosen to craft this wonderful song in more of a folk style and it seemed to suit the ambience of the Barley Mow pub. Nevertheless, the message in the song was typically Marley.

"Why had Jake chosen to play it?" Great songs can always mean different things to different people. What chimes with them may not be the original intent of the songwriter but time and time again the best songwriters in the world have stated how unconcerned they were at how their songs were often interpreted. Subconsciously was Jake seeking freedom from the paranormal happenings at Abba Manor? Was he seeking redemption for Alannah and the Summers brothers? Whatever the inspiration for Jake to perform "Redemption Song" the crowd enjoyed the rendition and once Jake had finished performing the applause was gratifying.

"Thank you, you're a wonderful audience. You know what you guys. I've played to stadiums filled with heaps and heaps of people but doing an intimate little gig off the cuff like this one is pretty nerve-wracking, I can tell you. I take my hat off to Donny. Anyway, would you like to hear another one?"

The crowd expressed their affirmative response and Jake promptly provided a rendition of John Lennon's "Working Class Hero."

When Jake finished that song to another resounding round of applause a pretty girl in her mid-twenties who was fortunate enough to be near the front asked aloud a very pertinent question. "Jake. Why don't you do one of your songs?"

The room fell silent as Jake considered the question. Why wasn't he performing any of his own songs? Instinctively he had belted out a couple of covers but any pop star in this position would have naturally offered up some of their own hits, wouldn't they? Had he chosen "Working Class Hero" in an attempt to connect with the audience of that ilk? The truth was Jake was so affected by the rejection of society of his most recent music following Alannah's death he was actually scared to play his own music. Finally, he spoke.

"Do you really want me to perform one of my songs?"

The crowd cheered amongst cries of "You bet," and "Of course, Jake."

The feeling was reassuring. "Okay, would you like to hear something new?"

The crowd cheered even louder.

"Okay give me a second." Jake quickly placed his fingers over the frets as he quickly worked out the notes of the piano that now had to be transposed onto a guitar. He was ready.

"Okay, you guys and girls. For a very special audience in the Barley Mow pub in my hometown of Bonsall, especially for you here is a world exclusive. I hope you like it."

The opening bars captured the crowd immediately. The melody was as beautiful on the guitar as it was on the piano. Transfixed and mesmerised the crowd watched attentively as Jake performed an acoustic version of 'Love Lives Forever.'

As Jake sung out the last note the applause was deafening. He was beyond pleased.

Outside someone had gone unnoticed as all the focus had taken place inside the four walls of the pub. The stranger was peering through the sash window of the Barley Mow and they too had admired Jake's performance of the world exclusive. The acoustics and compact infrastructure of the pub enabled the music to easily be heard outside.

In spite of the humidity, the Devil ran his icy fingers through his matted hair quite unsure of what his next move would be regarding Jake Zennor.

CHAPTER 26

It was Sunday morning. Jake took a tranquil stroll to the village shop to purchase a Sunday newspaper. It was a luxury he enjoyed whenever his busy lifestyle permitted. In truth, he never really wanted a newspaper due to the distrust and contempt he held for the journalistic industry, but collecting one from the shop was as good an excuse as any to walk through the peaceful countryside.

Jake loved to connect with Mother Nature as he walked. The birds singing, cows grazing, buzzards or hawks flying above the trees and even the stillness and damp atmosphere of an early English morning, a feeling that Jake found priceless as the cool air enveloped and embraced him. A stroll in the countryside gave as much pleasure to Jake as the sanctuary of a whisky glass, and the whisky was beginning to flow on a more regular basis since paranormal activity had entered his life. He was also still missing Lucy, another reason that encouraged him to hit the bottle.

The countryside was a place that was good for both Jake's soul and sanity, which was often compromised by the ruthlessness of the music industry. In many ways, Jake belonged on the showbiz merry-go-round due to his unique talent, but his sensitive side including his honesty and integrity did not belong in the cutthroat world of the rich and famous, hence his need for a "get out clause" fashioned by his decision to retreat to the glorious Peak District.

The tranquil stroll was compromised when Jake stumbled upon a gatepost which curiously had the lifeless corpse of a black crow cruelly nailed to it.

Who could do such a thing? Pondered Jake, genuinely disgusted.

Just to the left of the crow and a little further behind, actually concealed by the wheat in the field, Jake could make out what appeared to be two small legs protruding from the crop. Instantly he feared that he had stumbled upon the victim of a child sacrifice carried out by the Devil worshippers who had so abruptly invaded his Halloween evening with Lucy. He feared that this time, the sacrifice had been successful for the psychopathic Satanists.

Jake looked around before climbing the gate. There was no one in sight and the air was suddenly eerily still. Even the birds had stopped singing.

He slowly moved towards to what appeared to be the legs and crouched amongst the wheat and long grass. Slowly he reached his hand towards the body, terrified of exactly what he might touch.

His finding brought a huge sigh of relief but equally threw up an element of disturbed curiosity.

Jake had discovered what was known as a corn dolly, an item crafted from a once popular pastime linked with rural life and dating back as far as pagan times. In most instances the creation of the corn dolly was an innocent venture, simply crafting a dolly from the last sheaf of harvest in passed down tradition, but Jake was also aware of evidence linking the corn dolly to more sinister happenings such as the absence of facial features to intimidate those of a beautiful nature or as to act as a symbol of a cult – he had also read Stephen King's

Children of the Corn. He also believed that the majority of sinister rumours of superstition had been circulated by those of compromising Faiths in the UK and the USA as a desperate attempt to unfairly tarnish the reputation of Paganism. However, he was convinced that this particular dolly's location close to the nailed crow could be no coincidence. This particular corn dolly was also oddly larger in size than usual, hence Jake's initial belief that he had found a child.

Jake then looked beyond the corn dolly a little further and spotted a dead fox hanging from a tree as if it had been a convicted criminal in life. The image was very disturbing and Jake's heart went out to the poor creature. Jake had always opposed the practice of Fox Hunting in spite of his love of the countryside, but this act before him seemed particularly sick and unnecessary.

Jake realised that the crow, the corn dolly and the fox were all situated in a perfect diagonal line. He understood that their placings must have been deliberate and wondered if they had been placed along a lay line, a natural line of energy conducted from the earth that could often be associated with acts of evil. In addition to the books that he had purchased from the bookstore on the A515 Roman road, Jake had recently felt compelled to learn more about the paranormal and the occult, and in doing so had read evidence of cemeteries and houses inadvertently being created on lay lines, which resulted in no end of paranormal activity. He was becoming quite an educated man regarding the happenings of the paranormal.

With this bizarre discovery, one thing seemed for sure. Regardless of the capture on Hallow's eve of the Devil worshippers, it appeared that the net was still required to be cast further afield. It appeared that Satanism or at least some other type of sick practice was alive and kicking in the Peak District. Jake feared that Devil worshipping was a cancer that could never be totally combated. He feared that evil people, or indeed even perhaps the *Undead* were destined to always walk the Earth.

Jake had inadvertently discovered this site of what appeared to be satanic activity, or perhaps it was just the act of a lone nut? He knew farmers often shot and hung up foxes as a warning to others, but that didn't account for the crow and the dolly. But in reality, what could he do on discovering this random and bizarre activity?

For now, he intended to leave well alone. He refused to have his tranquil stroll to the village shop so crudely interrupted. He was putting up with enough unexplained goings-on at Abba Manor and he was determined not to let this latest encounter compromise his mood. He never did find out who "The Lovers" or "The Man of the House" were, but thankfully his e-mail inbox had not become invaded since. He concluded or rather he *hoped* that the messages were just a cruel hoax. It was unclear however how whoever was behind the messages could have gotten hold of his personal e-mail address, as it was so well protected usually.

Jake continued with his walk and was determined to continue to enjoy doing so. He decided that he would inform the police on his return home about his findings in the field and leave it to them to investigate.

After collecting his paper, Jake would possibly favour the longer route home under the circumstances.

Although Jake firmly believed in the essence of living for the day he had always been attracted to the feeling of nostalgia, hence part of the reason for his wanting to return to the Peak District. The Peak District had inspired much of his work. It seemed that you could take the boy out of the Peak District but the Peak District could not be taken out of the boy. He reminisced as he continued with his stroll, but now able to fully appreciate the history connected to the area following his extensive research to try and understand what was conjuring up the supernatural activity that he had experienced. Jake figured that the more he researched the history of the Peak District, both its supernatural and natural historic events, then the more he could appreciate why things were happening. Jake already possessed some decent knowledge of the area but he had now inadvertently educated himself to a very commendable level, mainly using the books that he had purchased from the bookstore but also using the recently introduced internet and various records on offer at the libraries of the Peak District's towns and villages.

And so, Jake let his mind fondly roam back in time as he continued his country stroll armed with an extensive knowledge of the Peak District.

Jake enjoyed a happy childhood, in spite of the family's lack of financial resources. His Father, Cyril Zennor, worked as a bus driver, which enabled the young Jake to stowaway and explore the Peak District to his heart's content. Jake considered his dad's occupation to be cool as George Harrison's father had also been a bus driver. Jake's dad would allow him to travel on the bus for free and dropped him off at various places across the Derbyshire Dales along the routes that he was travelling. Following his only son's day of adventure, he would then pick him up again on the return journey so that he was able to arrive home for teatime. Jake always hoped that his mother had prepared his favourite meal of egg and chips for tea, followed by the local delicacy of Bakewell pudding. If his mother had enjoyed a small win on the bingo he would occasionally enjoy the luxury of *double* egg and chips.

Jake grew up in a 3 up and 2 down mid terraced ex-miner's cottage in Bonsall. The kitchen and living room were one, whilst the bathroom was also situated downstairs. As his only siblings were 2 older sisters Blanche and Toni, Jake was fortunate enough to have the privacy of his own bedroom while his two squabbling sisters were forced to share a bedroom. Jake never could understand the arguments that developed between his sisters over such trivial matters as borrowing a blouse or make-up without permission. While the squabbling brewed, Jake was able to lock himself away within the sanctuary of his poster-clad walls featuring The Doors, The Beatles and other musical influences who were not necessarily icons of his generation but ones whose musical creativity had stood the test of time. There were so many posters on view that the wood-chipped covered walls that had been coated with magnolia emulsion could barely be seen. Of course, provision of space was also allowed for the Page 3 girls and pretty TV actresses of the day, the term 'political correctness' had never been invented in these very different times. Another inclusion was that iconic Athena poster of a cheeky female tennis player whose back is to the camera so that her face could not be seen, but her extremely shapely backside was in full view. Jake's hormones were raging as hard as his composed guitar riffs from inside that 8ft by 6ft bedroom. Discovering the art of masturbation during his teen years became almost as fulfilling as perfecting the most challenging of lead guitar solos.

His mother Polly would often nag at Jake to tidy his bedroom, but the endless amounts of half-written song lyrics on random bits of paper, which included disused envelopes and brown paper bags, were sacred to Jake and he would just look at his mother and attempt to reassure her by saying "Don't worry Mom, it may look a mess, but really it is just organised chaos." That phrase actually later inspired one of Blossom of Eden's greatest hits. "Organised Chaos" became a platinum selling single reaching number 1 in a staggering seventeen countries, crucially including the USA. He begged his mother to keep hold of the scraps of paper claiming that they would be worth millions one day when he was famous!

These days Blanche and Toni have grown out of their adolescent quarrelling. Working side by side they are responsible for the running of Jake's fan club and the maintenance of his website, but initially, they both trained to work in the nursing profession, following in the tradition of Matlock's most famous daughter Florence Nightingale who had left an amazing legacy following her death in 1910. Florence had lived at Lea Hall on the edge of the parish until the age of 5 when she then moved to Leahurst, a home which had been built by her father. Impressively, Florence became the first woman to receive the Order of Merit for her valiant medical efforts during the Crimean War of 1854 to 1856. By attending the wounded of the British Army at night she became affectionately known as "The Lady of the Lamp." This phrase once again inspired Jake to pen a song for Blossom of Eden. Although never released as a single "The Lady of the Lamp" became a cult album track on the band's third album simply entitled "Peak", a reference to their established musical achievements and of course the band's native homeland. Florence returned to her native Derbyshire in August 1856. Florence was so taken to the hearts of the British people that she appeared on British Sterling banknotes.

Jake loved his time growing up in that small, but homely cottage, in spite of his sisters' quarrelling. He also loved growing up in Bonsall and near the surrounding towns and villages, Cromford and Matlock being the closest.

Matlock is a very magical place for children and the young Jake Zennor was no exception, for although it is within the Heart of England it has a very definite seaside feel to it with an abundance of Fish and Chip shops, Ice Cream parlours and a sprinkling of amusement arcades. Matlock even hosts a promenade and a bandstand!

It is thought that even as far back as the Romans lead was mined in Matlock. It was not until the early 19th century that the town's importance took hold when it was rapidly developed as a spa. Today the town is used as the headquarters for The Derbyshire Council.

From a hill nearby the ruins of a castle look down on Matlock and neighbouring Matlock Bath. It is within the grounds of Riber Castle built by John Smedley that Jake would sometimes bunk off school, often with Nick Santini before he grew up into the form of the Devil. Smedley had also been responsible for the construction of six churches within the area including the one that Polly and Cyril Zennor had married in. The grounds of Riber Castle were to Jake as was Strawberry Fields to John Lennon, the Liverpool orphanage that Lennon would escape to as a child to play and explore, which he immortalised in song. Jake himself often included autobiographical experiences into his own songs. Jake considered John Lennon to be a genius and to be one of his greatest influences, although the Beatle seemed to have played little part in the inspiration of "Love Lives Forever." It was still a nagging mystery just who had inspired this tune for Jake and who was in control of playing those piano keys at Abba Manor. Jake would not dare to contemplate that it could possibly be the spirit of John Lennon guiding him with the melody of "Love Lives Forever" – that thought was far too mind blowing. The tune was contemporary yet classical at the same time which gave it a unique quality. "Love Lives Forever" was in no doubt a fantastic musical masterpiece and it seemed that a force from the other side was responsible for continually playing out the primary tune at Abba Manor, but who?

At the age of 17, John Lennon had tragically lost his mother Julia when she was knocked down and killed by a drunken off-duty police officer. At the same age, Jake had lost both his parents in a Road Traffic Accident one frosty night. Now that Alannah was also dead; death was an unwanted theme that occurred and inevitably shaped Jake's life. The deaths of the Summers brothers had also affected him deeply. It explained his struggle with alcohol and his notion of living for the day. It was one of the reasons why he also reminisced and looked back on his life with great affection for those first seventeen years. Jake had a happy life in the Peak District, and although he ultimately achieved his ambition of becoming a successful songwriter and artist, and enjoyed all the financial rewards that came with it, he would swap it all to have his parents alive with him today. Barely in their forties, both Cyril and Polly were cruelly cheated of seeing their only son achieve his musical success and fame. Jake had penned one of his most beautiful and successful songs following this tragedy, simply entitled "Why?"

One of the key reasons for Jake returning to the Peak District was the feeling of always being close to his parents here. He sensed that they were a part of every peakland breeze and within the roots of the trees and blades of grass that grew across the dales. In short, the Peak District could provide some small comfort for his tragic loss.

Jake began to think of some of the places that his dad would take him to on his bus or where he freely roamed and made his own way – even hitching the odd lift from lorry drivers or quarry workers. Folk seemed more trusting and carefree in yesteryear concerning the welfare of their children and Jake's parents were no exception. It was not felt that such a tight rein was required and the belief that a child could be snatched was not as prominent as today. For Jake, his parent's attitude enabled him to discover a wonderful childhood while fortunately avoiding danger or anything sinister. Cyril and Polly dearly loved him, as they did Toni and Blanche.

Cromford is often referred to as the cradle of the industrial revolution and it was Sir Richard Arkwright who put the village on the map in the late 18th century. With the decline of the lead mining industry, Arkwright was able to utilise the ready supply of cheap labour in Cromford and bring employment into his world of textile manufacture. In Cromford, he recognised that it was an ideal setting to generate power with the plentiful amount of water available. He, therefore, built the world's first successful cotton spinning mill in 1771. The Cromford mill was so successful that he went on to build further mills in the area: Haarlem Mill in Wirksworth and Masson Mill in Matlock Bath. Arkwright's water-powered cotton spinning mills were so revolutionary they were soon adopted in Europe and America. Masson Mill has since been converted into a shopping complex and recently Jake visited there with Lucy treating her to some expensive authentic peakland perfume whilst he treated himself to one of the sought-after Scotch whiskies on sale there. How he would love to smell that perfume on her soft skin again, he missed her so much.

The industrial revolution in England was the catalyst of the developing transport network and in Cromford, the young Jake delighted in playing up and down the canal towpath and the disused railway line, now known as the High Peak Trail. Cromford's North Street built in 1776 and its terraced 3 storey buildings, which were used to house the mill workers, always intrigued him as this was the first planned street in Derbyshire.

Curiously when Jake and Nick would bunk off school they found church graveyards an ideal place to loiter due to their quietness and inconspicuous environment. St Mary's Church, which stood just below the mill, was a favourite haunt. It mattered not to Jake if his truancy and fun occurred on Church of England or Catholic soil. He had never been religious, even though his mother had ensured he had been baptised Catholic. His father had actually been of Church of England faith. Jake and his sisters had therefore decided to have their parents cremated and scattered peacefully together across the River Derwent resolving the headache of where to bury them if they were to remain together for evermore.

St Mary's church contains Arkwright's tomb. Now that Jake's mind had been opened to the possibility of the existence of paranormal activity, he often concluded that a man that so heavily dominated an area in life could easily return to walk there again in death. Surely the great man's spirit would be comfortable moving around the streets of Cromford or sitting in one of the three Cromford pubs.

Travelling out of Cromford, although it was necessary to climb the hill to Middleton Top, Jake would find himself in Wirksworth. Often he would delay his journey by stopping off at Black Rocks where the view was simply breath taking across the Derwent Valley. He had often climbed Black Rocks with Roland and Che and it now saddened him to think that he could never share such good times with them again.

Jake's own childhood village of Bonsall was extremely picturesque with its random chocolate box cottages and tranquil atmosphere. Since his recent return to the Peaks, Jake had often frequented the two public houses in Bonsall lapping up the quality of their real ale, and of course their fine selection of whisky. He particularly loved the atmosphere of The Barley Mow pub where he had showcased an acoustic version of "Love Lives Forever".

Like Cromford and Bonsall, Wirksworth was once a lead mining village and indeed was able to boast being the most important lead mining centre in the country, including as far back as Roman times. There was a local rumour that a ghostly Roman army had often been seen on certain nights marching along what is now known as the B5035 road. Jake of course also now knew that such a ghostly army definitely marched along a certain stretch of the nearby A515. By swotting up on the Roman's involvement in the Peak District, Jake was able to make some sense of his Roman ghostly occurrences. But what he hadn't worked out yet was if the Roman happenings were connected to the paranormal activity at Abba Manor or if they were simply a separate stream of hauntings?

Like so many peakland villages, Wirksworth is centred around a market square and as you move away from the centre there are delightful narrow alleys and clusters of cottages. Jake once used it as a setting in one of his music videos.

Wirksworth also has a St Mary's Church. Built in the 13th century the 152-ft. church is, without a doubt, the jewel in the Wirksworth crown and it also featured in the music video. It curiously hosts 2 fonts, one originating from Norman times. The young Jake had hours of fun simply meandering around its circular pathway. The most impressive possession of the church is arguably the Saxon Coffin lid, dated roughly 800ad. It was found accidentally in 1820 when a slab was removed in front of the altar. Its carvings depict the life of Christ. Blossom of Eden used a picture of this coffin lid on one of their album covers.

Like many other Derbyshire villages, Wirksworth participates in the Dressing of Wells, which originated from Pagan times when thanksgiving was conducted for the gift of water. Jake was pleased that such Pagan traditions were still being practised in his beloved Peak District, it made perfect sense to him to respect and give thanks for what Mother Earth had provided, especially in the Peaks. However, he hoped that the evidence he now knew of regarding Devil Worshippers in the area hadn't somehow twisted the Pagan beliefs for their own gain. He was aware how Paganism was misunderstood by most contemporary folk without their misconception receiving a helping hand from Satanists.

Forever possessing a sense of fair play and regardless of his own baptism into the Catholic Faith as an infant in line with the wishes of his mother, Jake disapproved of the way Christianity had usurped traditional pagan days of importance and festivities with their own celebratory dates as an attempt to destroy the Pagan way of life. Nevertheless, he had to concede that his own beliefs on doubting religion and rebelling against his baptism had been thrown into confusion recently following his meeting with the Devil, his sightings of ghosts and his knowledge of exorcisms that had been performed by the Catholic

Church as told to him by Father Irwin. The icy cynicism that he had felt about his faith since the unjust deaths of Alannah, his parents, the Summers brothers and even Nanette's husband in a mining accident was possibly beginning to show signs of thawing.

Extremely close to Wirksworth is the delightful village of Middleton. The writer D.H Lawrence lived here for a year in a small dwelling called Mountain Cottage. The writer used Middleton in his book "The Virgin and the Gypsy" where it bore the pseudonym Woodlinkin. On learning this Jake chuckled at how he was not alone in drawing experience from the Peak District and introducing it into his creative work.

One of Jake's favourite haunts as a child was Carsington Water, a man-made lake used to supply water to the homes of the Midlands. Although made by man its beauty is akin with most waters of the Lake District in the English county of Cumbria. Jake used to love lazing on the bank, staring up at the sky making shapes from cloud formations. He would stare for hours forming such shapes of a bear or large bird in magnificent flight. His creative imagination, which had produced such prolific songwriting, was exercised from a very early age.

Further south still from Carsington stands the impressive town of Ashbourne. It is possibly as south as one can travel whilst still remaining in the Peak District, indeed the Derbyshire town, which borders Staffordshire is often referred to as the "Gateway to the Peaks." Traditionally a Market town, Ashbourne has boasted such famous visitors as Bonnie Prince Charlie, King Charles I and Dr Johnson who was a friend of Ashbourne's respected native Reverend John Taylor.

Ashbourne was a town that Jake liked to visit beyond his pre-pubescent years. Prior to their fame he and Nick enjoyed being willing participants in the bizarre ritual of an annual football game, which only just warrants that description. Each year on Shrove Tuesday and Ash

Wednesday, Ashbourne is host to the largest and roughest version of the game in the world when two teams in their hundreds commence battle on a 3-mile-long playing field by 2 miles wide! Ashbourne simply becomes a glorified centre circle as the game begins each day at 2pm from the town's centre in the Shaw Croft Car Park. The game lasts no further than 10:00pm unless a goal is scored after 6.00pm. In 1928 the Prince of Wales, who later became Edward VII released the ball for kick off, thus giving the game a Royal seal of approval and the game is actually believed to date from Elizabethan times. Jake's paternal grandfather played and fought in this particular game, earning many a Zennor boast and talking point for years to come. The sets of goals are 3 miles apart and were originally mill wheels at two local mills. These days the goals are purpose built structures, and today's large ball is also purpose made.

Jake and Nick would latch on to the team represented by those born North of the Henmore River, known as the Up'ards. The aim was to beat the Down'ards from South of the River. Strictly speaking, only Ashburnians were meant to participate but nobody seemed to mind Jake and Nick pitching in. Although often described as a football game the ball is seldom kicked and the pitched battle often spills into the river with both grown men, and women wrestling for ownership of the ball.

There are very little rules of safety in this bizarre game, bones get broken, teeth get knocked out and if you manage to grab hold of the ball you would hang on for dear life in the name of honour regardless of the pasting that you would most likely receive. Amazingly it is all taken in good spirits in spite of the appearance of a battlefield. Shops and banks are closed for the day and sensibly boarded up for protection. Only a lunatic would park their car in the vicinity. Now a rock star, Jake wondered if his fame would compromise his return to play once more in the game because he always had loved the competitive element. Jealous individuals wishing to make a name for themselves could quite possibly single him out and become overzealous in the customary rough nature of the game. He was resigned to the fact that even though his life seemed less demanding now that he lived outside of London he could never perhaps fully escape the negative aspects of his fame.

In ironic contrast to the rowdy Shrovetide games, Ashbourne paves a gateway to the beautiful and tranquil countryside known as Dovedale. Here Jake would prolifically soak up inspiration for his creative songwriting. He adored Dovedale and its rolling hills dotted with sheep and peakland stone. He loved to walk along the river Dove that cuts through the valley and skim a stone across its surface. His personal best was 5 skips achieved at the tender age of thirteen.

For Jake, the A515 that ultimately stretched from Ashbourne to the market town of Buxton cut through some beautiful scenery that caught the appreciative and inspirational eye of the young Jake and Abba Manor was positioned not too far away either. Naturally, he had taken this route home the night when he and Lucy had witnessed the Roman Battalion of ghosts. He had wanted to share with Lucy the road that had been so affectionate for him as a child, but he would never have guessed that he was going to end up sharing a supernatural Roman experience with Lucy in addition to its stunning beauty. The road bypassed Dovedale and the Arbor Low stone circle. In these recent days of apparent paranormal activity, Jake was beginning to wonder if the Arbor Low stone circle had been used for any Devil cult activity. As a boy, he innocently marvelled at its very existence. Unlike the world-renowned Stonehenge, the stones at Arbor Low all lay flat and Jake now realised that they would be perfect to use as sacrificial stones. His mind harped back to the Satanists who had invaded his Halloween's evening with Lucy. Had they ever been to Arbor Low to practice their unearthly activities? Equally, he knew that the isolated farms around nearby Hartington were of medieval origin and wondered what activity had occurred there over the centuries and perhaps even more recent years. He remembered the words of the policeman that Devil worshipping was widespread in Derbyshire. Jake was beginning to suspect any strange face he came across, almost becoming obsessed with the speculation.

Jake had educated himself about the tors and hills in the Peak District. They were undeniably beautiful but he had analysed their origin and the dark secrets that they held. He knew that ancient burial mounds caused many of the bumps in the landscape and it was not inconceivable to now believe that the hills and fields of the Peak District could be rife with spirits. Jake thought of Halloween and how it gave licence to allow all the ghosts to walk the earth for one night only. With the literally hundreds of bodies buried across this land it didn't bare to think about how many could rise and walk the earth again. His mind jumped back again to his own Halloween experience when the congregation of Devil worshippers had invaded his own land at Abba Manor. Michael Jackson's ground-breaking video for his song "Thriller" had been responsible for creating a strong visual image of what roaming ghouls could look like for everyone and these images were currently in Jake's mind's eye.

Forcing his mind back to more pleasant thoughts, both the young and adult Jake Zennor liked Hartington for its cheese factory at the edge of the village. Their Derby Sage was second to none. And no one could make Derby Sage sandwiches like Polly Zennor, cutting farmhouse bread thick enough to be reminiscent of a doorstop.

Not far away is Bakewell, famous for the Bakewell Pudding, a dish containing almonds and jam that was another successful home cooking rendition of Polly Zennor. Recently he had relived his youth by taking Lucy to feed the ducks and geese as they strolled along the river that runs at the back of the development of shops in Bakewell. It had been a wonderful day.

Jake's intense but fond reminiscing ceased when he eventually reached the shop. There was no doubt in Jake's mind that he had definitely made the right decision in returning to his beloved peaks. The countryside and villages were simply adorable. With each breath of fresh country air, he was cleansing his mind of the supernatural happenings that had compromised his return so far.

As Jake entered the shop he even took pleasure from the sound of the old bell, which gave a ring to let the shopkeeper know someone had entered the shop as it must have done thousands of times before over the years. Jake loved the unspoilt characteristics of English Village life, characteristics that seemed to have a mind of their own and refused to compromise with so-called progress and movement towards the 21st century.

"Good morning, Jake," came a welcoming voice from behind the counter. The shopkeeper was a jovial fellow of stout appearance, who favoured combing his hair across his forehead in a failed attempt to cover his baldness. His cheeks were as scarlet as strawberries served at Wimbledon, and Jake noticed how his upper clothing always seemed to be peppered with food stains, this morning's decoration mainly consisting of egg yolk. Jake liked him.

"Good morning, Arthur. How's the wife?"

"Fine thanks, Jake, she's having a rest though because the family are coming over for lunch. Cooking for six adults and seven grandchildren can be a challenging but rewarding operation for her. That's why I'm holding the fort in here; I'm under strict orders to keep out of the way, probably because I can't resist dipping a finger in the Apple and Rhubarb pie before it's even baked. Actually, Jake, one of our granddaughter's thinks that you are great. She's a bit of a fan. I don't like to ask but do you think she could have an autograph?"

"Only the one granddaughter?" joked Jake. "Of course, she can. What's her name?"

"Meredith," answered Arthur.

"Nice name."

"American I think. You know these youngsters have all their funny new age names these days, what's wrong with a bit of tradition aye?"

Jake just laughed and duly obliged with the autograph, speaking aloud the words he was writing down. "To Meredith, the one and only, love Jake Zennor." On completion, Jake handed the autograph to Arthur.

"I tell you what Arthur. I'm going to be refurbishing part of Abba Manor into a recording studio soon, so when it is up and running why not bring Meredith along to take a look around?"

Arthur was delighted. "Jake you are a true gentleman; it would be an honour for Meredith. She'd absolutely love to do that. I'll let her know. Now then, have you come to purchase anything from my humble abode or has this just been a social call?"

"What's in the papers today?"

"I don't know; I haven't had time to look at them yet with me being on my own today."

"I'll just take the usual then. I only have it for the football results really. I'm not a fan of the press. How much is it again?"

"Jake don't insult me. You sign an autograph and invite my granddaughter and myself to your home and you still think that I will charge you for a lousy Sunday newspaper? Go on lad, pick one up on your way out. They're on the bottom shelf by the door, just behind the milk crate."

"Cheers Arthur. I'll see you soon."

Jake bent down, collected the paper and left the shop, causing the bell to ring once more. As he strolled back home he began to search for the sports supplement, carrying out his Sunday morning ritual of reading the paper backwards from the rear and momentarily glancing up from the pages to ensure that he wasn't about to bump into a street lamp or something. His lack of faith in journalism always dictated his selective reading in the newspapers.

Suddenly a wood pigeon swooped over Jake's head causing him to startle. He accidentally dropped the newspaper on the pavement, and as he retrieved it he could hardly believe his eyes. Roughly between the third and sixth page a picture of himself and Alannah stared back at him. For a moment, he felt numb, not sure to be angry at the newspaper or at himself for failing to notice the picture and article at first sight. He had no choice, he had to read the article to see what had been written, but inside he knew that it would be inevitable that it would cause him distress. A flurry of emotions ran through Jake as the article unfolded to reveal Alannah's child abuse from her father. His worst fears had been confirmed. Who could do this to him? He was confused and angry. Nick was dead, himself disgraced by association with child pornography and surely Alannah's father was too much of a coward following his beating (Jake did not know of Archie's intervention to erase Alannah's dad from the equation!) *It had to be Lucy? How could she do this to me? How could she betray me in this way?* Jake pondered momentarily. *She wouldn't…would she?*

But Jake knew that he had upset her.

And Jake could not place anyone else in the frame.

The last thing Jake Zennor thought he'd be doing today was planning a trip to London.

CHAPTER 27

Residence of Lucy Ives, Kensington, London

"How could you? How could you do this to me you bitch? I thought you loved me. You swore to me that the secret was safe. I trusted you but I should have known better. Once a journalist from the gutter, always a journalist from the gutter. You're a fucking parasite."

"Jake, will you please calm down and tell me what the hell you're talking about."

"This!" came Jake's reply as he threw the newspaper at Lucy.

Lucy rubbed her eyes before fixing them on the newsprint. Jake had disturbed her attempt to recover from a drink-fuelled night out with Patsy and some mutual girlfriends. As such she had not had any TV or radio on at all today. She read the article and it had an instant sobering influence. Lucy sat down and ran her free hand through her hair and she then began to shake her head. Her facial expression showed confusion as her mind tried to search for an explanation of the article. No explanation came, only a feeling of disbelief as the previous night's cocktails also conspired to add to her confusion.

"Oh my God, Jake. This is terrible. I don't understand. Who else have you told about Alannah's past?" Lucy guessed what Jake's answer would be but she felt compelled to ask the question to divert suspicion from herself, especially as she had no immediate answer on how to prove her innocence.

"You and only you," raged Jake. "More fool me. I trusted you."

"Jake, I thought you knew me better than that. I would never betray you like this."

"That's just it, isn't it? I do know you and I know what your lowlife occupation is. You work for the scum who use the pseudonym 'press'. Why did I ever think you'd be any different, deep down you're all the same? It's in your DNA. And as you took the decision to storm out of my life, I guess you feel you don't owe me an ounce of loyalty."

"Jake, I work for magazines now, you know that. And whether we are together or not, I am not a person capable of doing this shitty piece of reporting, especially to someone I care about. Although from the barrage of abuse I've taken from you these past few minutes I'm seriously doubting my judgement on ever caring for you."

"You've got friends all over that parasitic industry. I know that you are not stupid enough to write this yourself, so who is your fucking ghost writer? Did you get any money from this garbage or was it simply a chance to teach me a lesson?"

A penny dropped with Lucy, or rather the feeling of a knife being driven straight through her heart. She felt sick. Her mouth fell open and she then put her head in her hands.

"Oh, Shit. No, no, no, no, no. I think I know what could have happened."

"Yeah, you took the hump over that song I was writing and so you decided to ruin my career and the memory of the girl that you thought the song was about. You are one sick and twisted…."

Lucy intercepted with a rage that almost matched Jake's, but hers was born out of frustration. She raised her voice to make her point.

"Jake, will you listen to me for a second and cease acting like a fucking Neanderthal. I am not that petty to do this to you or to Alannah. I care about you, and I even still fucking love you but do not be so self-indulgent to believe that I would totally compromise my own self-respect in some sort of game just to hurt you. Get fucking real and grow up!"

Lucy paused a moment and composed herself. "It must have been Niall."

"Who the fuck is Niall?"

"Please, Jake sit down. Let's calmly discuss this and *together* we will work a way out of it. Trust me."

In spite of his anger Jake sensed the sincerity in Lucy's voice and took a deep breath before sitting down. He looked into Lucy's eyes and could see a genuine torture she seemed to be experiencing. "Go on then, and this had better be good."

"Niall is Niall Jennings. A scumbag and lowlife of the highest degree. He also happens to be my boss and like a lot of bosses he is an arrogant nasty piece of work. When you and I broke up it hit me harder than I care to admit. It was not an emotion I was used to and in an attempt to reclaim my usual persona and dare I say happiness, I went to a party held for the company to entertain clients and create some networking opportunities. All the magazine staff were there and my girlfriends thought I could do with a night out, as I haven't been a barrel of laughs to be around lately. However, all night I ached for you to be by my side with me. I just could not get into the partying mood, and I sat down all night feeling sorry for myself, sinking any alcoholic beverage on offer. I wouldn't get up and dance and it was clearly obvious that I didn't really want to be there. I really did drink much too much. I thought it was the only thing I could do to get through the evening and to try and dull some of the pain I was feeling."

"I guess I can relate to that," said Jake.

"Jake, I have been so upset since our argument and my mind has been torturing me. I'm hardly sleeping or eating and this isn't like me, I've always prided myself on being a tough cookie. I keep replaying the words that were said and wonder if I could have expressed my feelings better. I do not resent Alannah, I really don't, she was good for you and I really do get that. But I did feel as though I was competing with her memory. I've felt so lousy and the night of the party was no different from any other since our split in beating myself up, wishing I hadn't been so clumsy with my words to you. Niall, forever the predator, spotted me at my weakest point and came over to me. I was drunk, upset and he offered me a shoulder to cry on. I had so much that I needed to say and so much bottled up emotion that just had to be released. I was drunk, vulnerable and…he seemed kind for once and listened to me."

"You told him about Alannah?" enquired Jake, remarkably controlled by his standards.

Lucy nodded, a single tear rolling down her cheek.

"He kept ordering drinks for me as he let me ramble. He promised that the stuff about Alannah would stay secret with him. I let my guard down. He said that I could confide in him as a friend and to forget he was my boss. I really thought he was being kind. I should have known better; he hasn't got a compassionate bone in his body. How could I have been so bloody stupid? He was prepared to listen for a while, but after paying for my drinks he finally took exception to me only talking about you Jake and how I wished we were still together. He turned pretty nasty and insisted that I go off into one of the hotel rooms with him, he said that he hadn't wasted his night listening to my sob story without his reward. He wanted something in return. I told him to get lost but he ignored me. He got physical and grabbed me so I slapped him and he eventually stormed off. I then left in a taxi, calling it an early night and wishing that I hadn't even bothered to turn up for the party at all. This story in the newspaper is obviously his revenge. Jake, I am so very, very sorry. How could I have been so stupid? I guess you are right to blame me and yes I did break a confidence, I've made a catastrophic misjudgement. Like Niall, his friends are reptiles too and Billy Blue who writes the Showbiz column is a good friend of his. I guess sleaze balls help each other out and that's how this Billy Blue exclusive has transpired. How can you ever forgive me, Jake?"

Jake looked at Lucy, he was still angry inside but he remained calm for her sake. He realised that she had been stupid but could also just about understand why. He felt ashamed of the initial onslaught of verbal abuse that he had scornfully bombarded upon her. Seeing her again, even in these circumstances, made him realise that deep down he still loved her, but he strongly felt that Lucy had nevertheless betrayed him no matter how you viewed what had happened with Jennings and no matter how inadvertently. At this moment in time loving Lucy just wasn't enough, he doubted that he could ever forgive her. He failed to see how their relationship could ever recover from this.

"So where do I find this Jennings? I'll fucking kill him."

"No Jake. If you track him down I know that you are capable of doing him some serious damage. I'm not saying that he doesn't deserve it but just think of the bad publicity he will ensure gets put into the media, not to mention involving the police. He could ruin your career and your life with his contacts. He will personally see to it that the press has a field day with you. He is not worth dirtying your hands on. Please don't do anything silly, Jake. You are worth ten of him."

Lucy moved closer to Jake and lifted his sunken head in her hands. Their faces were close and they looked into one another's eyes. "Jake, I miss you."

"I miss you too."

The magnetism between them was too strong and within seconds they were kissing one another. Soon after, their lower garments had been stripped away as they engaged in passionate and intense lovemaking. It was over almost as quickly as it had happened and during the pants of breath, Jake found some words. "I'm sorry Lucy, we shouldn't have done that."

"Why not? It's a bit late to find a conscience now."

"It's obvious I want you but I just don't know if we can survive all of this Niall stuff. I can't help feeling betrayed somehow."

"Stay the night, Jake. I've said I'm sorry for what's happened. Do you want me to beg or something?"

Jake calmly stood up, resigned to the fact that the story was out there, the secret he had kept protected for Alannah's sake all this time was a secret no more. In truth, what could he do about it now? He realised that chastising Lucy wasn't the answer, she'd made a mistake but he could see she was in pain for what had happened and he certainly had no desire to hurt her any further. But he couldn't be with a woman who had released this most sacred of secrets, a woman he now felt that he could never trust no matter how much he truly loved her. He simply had to leave.

Jake's words were softly spoken to Lucy but they still managed to cut like a knife. "Perhaps it was wrong of me to have fucked you just then, but in truth, it's a bit late to show how much you care now, Lucy. I love you, and perhaps I'll always love you but you betrayed me and that's just something I can't forgive. I'm truly sorry it's ended like this. I'll see myself out."

Lucy put her head in her hands and began to sob.

CHAPTER 28

Jake had a disturbed night of sleep as Lucy broke into every dream. Even the half bottle of scotch did little to relax him. He must have dozed off at some point as he was suddenly awoken by the sound of his bedside phone ringing. Jake managed to reach out and grab the receiver without raising his head from the pillow. He waited to see if a voice would follow.

"Hello, is that Jake Zennor."

"It could be, it depends on who is asking," replied Jake with some hostility. He was not in the mood to get involved in a conversation with anyone, especially not a total stranger. He also feared that any stranger making contact could only mean one thing: the press.

"I'm sorry to disturb you Mr Zennor, allow me to introduce myself. My name is Bridget Prosser and I am the Managing Director for a newly founded charity called CAVES."

"CAVES?"

"Child Abuse Victims Everyday Support. Please, may I express on behalf of the organisation how you have our every sympathy following the revelations of your late fiancée's ordeal. It must have been very gratifying for her to know that you were by her side helping her as much as you could. Unfortunately, most of the victims I have contact with simply have no one to turn to except our charity."

Jake began to stir from his slumber. "Err, thanks. But I feel I let her down in the end."

"A natural reaction Mr Zennor which I know only too well, but you shouldn't blame yourself. I realise how difficult it must have been for you living your life in a goldfish bowl, I'm amazed Alannah's story hadn't surfaced earlier."

"I tried to keep what happened to her out of the public eye as much as I could."

"But there was no need for either of you to be ashamed of what happened to her."

"You know; I guess for the first time ever I can see that now."

"With your fame, both yours and Alannah's, I believe a message of great awareness has been sent across the world of what child abuse really is like for millions of people. Since the recent publications about your experience, the helplines have been red hot with victims now contacting us with the courage to step forward. I believe you have given the victims a whole new platform to step forward from, and a warning has been sent out to the pitiful human beings who think they can commit these dreadful acts of cruelty. You have shown that child abuse is not something to be buried under the carpet. Society can now be shaken into confronting child abuse and doing much more to eradicate it. Forgive me Mr Zennor for going on, but as you can tell I am very passionate about my work. You see, my daughter, like Alannah, also committed suicide following sexual abuse from her father. Well, to be precise in Dana's case it was her stepfather. I never had a clue what was happening right under my nose. I felt the guilt then much as you do now I should imagine, but by doing the charity work I am trying to repay her for my unintentional yet devastating negligence. I also know that with each victim I help my little girl did not take her life in vain. I served five years for that bastard but it was worth it just to begin to repay what he had done to my little girl. I also ensured that he could not interfere with anyone else again."

"What did you do? Kill him?" asked Jake intrigued.

"Almost, but that would have been too good for him. Instead, I effectively used a kitchen knife to ensure that he was no longer in working order if you know what I mean. The bastard has to sit down to pee now."

"Way to go! You are making my eyes water, but I would definitely call that poetic justice. They should have given you a medal, not a five-year prison sentence. I am sorry to hear about your daughter, though."

"Thank you. Your no-nonsense approach to child abusers is akin to my own thinking. But you have also proven through your relationship with Alannah that you can be sensitive to the needs of the victim. All through your relationship with her you never faltered or turned your back on her. Ok so you played away sometimes according to the newspaper exclusive, but there is no way the finger can still be pointed at you for Alannah's decision to take her own life. It is clear that she must have been tormented from an early age. She was with you for many years and chose to be engaged to you, the public understands the dynamics of her decision to end it all a little better now I should imagine. And as I said before, your fame has now opened a door for our work to reach even further afield. We can touch even more lives and help many more victims."

Jake was taken aback by the essence of the phone call; this was not the reaction he was expecting from the revelations in the media. They may not have intended it but Niall Jennings and Billy Blue seemed to have inadvertently done him a favour. "Well thank you for your kind words, Bridget. I'm glad that my position in life carries some advantages."

"Jake, I wondered if you would like to become the patron for our charity. We would really welcome someone of your stature on board with us. You have the intellect, sensitivity and even ruthlessness when required to help our cause. I know that you will have the public support to help us with our work and campaigning. I think this is a great opportunity for both of us. What do you say?"

"Well I could certainly do with a shift in how the public perceives me, I guess. And if my helping others also works as some sort of tribute to my love for Alannah that can only be a good thing, right? It is very nice of you to consider me for such a prestigious position, Bridget. In fact, I have not felt being of such value for a long time. It would be a pleasure to be the charity's patron. I accept, thank you very much."

"No thank you, Jake. It is a pleasure to have you on board. Oh, by the way, congratulations on your number 1 single. I should have mentioned that earlier in our conversation. I'll be in touch with dates of meetings and charity procedures etcetera. I'm happy for you to have a solicitor look over things if you wish."

"Err, okay, no problem. I'll look forward to your next contact. Take care. Bye."

Jake put down the phone then immediately retrieved it again and punched in a series of familiar numbers. Abe answered after three rings.

"Abe, is it true?"

"You bet Jake. Number fucking one in the hit parade. You were right to release "Love Lives Forever" as a prequel to the album. It's the fastest-selling single of the year. It's gone straight into number 1. And everyone is talking about that scream on the track too. I don't know how you achieved that scream but it's great. You're back, Jake. By the way, I've arranged a one hour special with chat show king, Marty Rodgerson. It's to be screened in a couple of weeks. You are the only guest, Jake. A one-hour special devoted to the living legend that is Jake Zennor; forget sharing the couch with a couple of B-grade celebrities. I'm afraid I need you down in London, Jake."

"Steady on Abe, you'll make my head swell even further. Okay, I'll be there tomorrow, book me into the usual hotel."

"I've already done it. Under the pseudonym Mr Peak. See you soon friend."

"See you soon."

"Oh Jake, I almost forgot. I have also sorted out something to get to the bottom of the weird things going on at Abba Manor as well. I'll explain in more detail another time. We'll get the Marty Rodgerson show out of the way first."

"Righty-ho! See you soon."

"Bye buddy."

Jake replaced the telephone receiver before punching the air in a cocktail of delight and excitement. He was back.

CHAPTER 29

Jake could easily cut the mustard when it came to performing live. As part of the one-hour special with Marty Rodgerson, he gave a perfect rendition of "Love Lives Forever" singing and playing his heart out at the piano. The live studio audience gave a standing ovation and Jake returned to his seat amongst the applause to resume the interview with the chat show host.

"That is a truly wonderful song, Jake, you must be thrilled with it."

"I'm very pleased with it, thanks, Marty. It is a very inspired song."

"About anybody in particular?" Rodgerson delivered the question that was on the lips of the whole viewing nation. The show was also to be repeated in the States in about a week's time.

"Well, Marty, the generic sentiment of the song is obviously *love* in the universal sense of the word. To me "Love Lives Forever" is sending out the message that 'all we need is love', a sentiment that dominated the music and vibe of the late sixties of course, however, the song is also very personal to me and is homing in on autobiographic experiences. In the verse, I am singing the lines "everybody needs a dream to chase, everybody needs a resting place." So, I'm still chasing *my dream* of true love as unfortunately I can't spend the rest of my years with Alannah, and I have found *a resting place* in my home up in the Peak District and of course Alannah is now at peace in her resting place. So, in a way I'm saying I loved Alannah, she's now safe from harm, but I recognise that life for Jake Zennor moves on and I need to find a way to be happy with my life. My resting place, my home, is my choice, but the house that I live in can be a big and lonely place without someone to share it with."

"Please elaborate, Jake."

"Well, I guess I am singing about everyone in my life that I've loved, including the past and most definitely the present."

"We of course now know of the tragic circumstances that Alannah had to endure through her life, and also the support and love that you gave to her, but it sounds as though that you have inevitably had to move on from the whole painful experience and no-one would hold that against you, Jake. Tell me, is there a new lady in the life of Jake Zennor?"

Jake gave a smile. "I thought that you might ask me that question, Marty."

"Well, I wouldn't be doing my job properly if I was not asking about your happiness, Jake."

The rapport was excellent between the two men. Rodgerson forever the professional and forever the gentleman was obviously fishing, but with a respect that Jake recognised. The audience were hooked.

"Well, there is a special lady whom I would very much like back in my life. I've been a bit of a Jackass and I'm afraid letting my macho pride rule my heart may have scared her away. That is all I'm prepared to say at the moment but watch this space should she be able to forgive me."

"Come on Jake, we are all in suspense here. Can't you tell us her name?"

"No, sorry. It wouldn't be fair while we are not technically together at present, as much as I'd like us to be. I hope that you will all know about her soon enough but let's just say that some creases need ironing out first. I just hope that I haven't let this wonderful lady slip through my fingers."

"Okay Jake, I know when to give up. I sincerely hope that it works out with the mystery lady as you surely deserve some happiness, my friend."

"Thank you, Marty."

Miraculously Jake's association with Lucy had not managed to enter the public domain as the time that they had spent together had been spent largely unnoticed out of view in the Peak District. Both Lucy and Jake had friends who respected their privacy and wouldn't blab, not that Jake and Lucy had particularly wished to keep their relationship secret, it had just turned out that way. Even Billy Blue had ceased to use Lucy's name in his newspaper article, instead concentrating wholly on spilling the beans on Jake's previous relationship with Alannah and her tragic experience at the hands of her father. The irony being that Blue's actions had inadvertently helped Jake's career progress and altered the negative public perception of him.

At present, Jake thought that if their attachment were truly over he wouldn't wholeheartedly reveal Lucy's identification in case it would embarrass her. But if she was watching this interview he hoped that she could read between the lines and see that he was prepared to offer a plea on national television if it resulted in them hooking up again. Keeping her name out of the equation, Jake ceased the opportunity with both hands.

Like all good interviewers, Rodgerson changed direction with the conversation and again did not shy away from asking the questions that the public were interested to know the answers.

"Jake, obviously, you have been inadvertently touched by the horrific practice of child abuse through Alannah's experiences and the once secret sordid life of Nick Santini, do you wish to comment any further at all? It must be difficult to deal with such matters that you would not have ever chosen to be a part of your own life."

"Well, Marty, none of us can ever really choose what enters our lives from time to time, after all life is what happens to you while you are busy making other plans as a great man once said, but I do believe that for every negative that we encounter we must try and produce a positive from it. Life is a constant learning experience. I realise that I am in a far more privileged position than a lot of people and I am grateful that I have never been a direct victim of any kind of child abuse, but I have come to understand the pain such atrocities bring to the loved ones in addition to that of the victims. But there are people out there who can help and who understand. That is why Marty, I would like to announce that from next Monday all royalties from "Love Lives Forever" will go directly to the charity CAVES whom I have agreed to be a patron for. CAVES work extremely hard to help victims of child abuse including those who need support by association.

"That's a wonderful thing, Jake" and with those words, Rodgerson led the overwhelming applause in the studio.

Jake had to wait a while for the applause to die down before continuing to speak. "Thank you, you're all very kind. I'd also like to announce that my forthcoming album will be dedicated to the memory of Alannah Ashe who was a very special lady in my life and whom I will never forget. I miss her but take some comfort that she can finally rest in peace. Alannah is symbolic of all the victims of child abuse across the world."

Spontaneous applause rang out again.

"That is truly wonderful, Jake. What will the new album be called?"

"Well if I return to your previous line of questioning, there is a clue in the album title regarding the special lady who has recently touched my life in a big, big way."

"A clue! You are really teasing us Jake. Okay, Jake let's hear it."

"The album is called *The Road To St. Ives*." Jake then politely turned away from Marty and looked straight into the television camera before continuing. "Because the road to St. Ives is the road that will lead me to where my heart, my happiness and my future lies." His romantic cryptic message was intended for one person only until she was back by his side once more and then he didn't care if the whole world knew of his love for Lucy Ives. He hoped that his romantic gesture to her would pay off.

"Well, there is the clue folks! Does this mean that the mystery lady is from the West Country of Cornwall?"

Jake simply smiled.

"He's clearly giving nothing away ladies and gentlemen," laughed Rodgerson.

Lucy Ives was sitting at home watching the show unfold, dabbing her teary eyes from a box of tissues and listening attentively at the amazing revelations from the one man that she had only ever truly loved. With a tear running down her cheek, she, of course, understood Jake's cryptic message cemented in the title of his forthcoming album.

CHAPTER 30

"Have you prepared the candles as I requested Mr Zennor?" spoke a deep and droning East European accent.

"Yes, they are all in position and ready to be lighted, just as you instructed."

"Very good, may I just powder my nose before we begin?"

"Err certainly, you can use the downstairs bathroom if you like. Just go down the hallway and it is the second door on your left. After you have err, powdered your nose, you need to turn left when you come out of the door and then turn into the second entrance on your right where you will enter the room that I think we should use. I have a table in there and the candles are all set up nicely."

"Very good, Mr Zennor. I shall meet you in there with the others."

When the lady was out of earshot Jake turned to Abe.

"So this is your idea of getting to the bottom of things at Abba Manor, is it? Hiring a crackpot who thinks she can talk to the dead!"

"Now come on Jake, I've known Imelda for many years now. I used to promote her shows before I concentrated on musical careers."

"Yes, phoney and fraudulent shows. You used to tell me how she had people planted in the audience, claiming that she was talking to their dead relatives while the remainder of the unsuspecting audience lapped it all up open -mouthed. If only they had known the truth."

"Come on Jake give the woman a chance. She's not a complete charlatan. What have you got to lose?"

Jake just sighed and led Abe into the room keen to get this farce over and done with as quickly as possible. The two friends sat around the big oak table and waited for Imelda. Already seated were Fergus Sutcliffe who was always keen to become involved in things of a spiritual nature, accompanied by his Japanese wife Naoko and Jake's sisters Blanche and Toni.

"Hey Jake, do you think she will be able to contact Mom and Dad?" enquired Blanche.

"I doubt it," replied Jake. "The woman's a fake."

"You can't be sure of that," said Blanche.

"Should be a right giggle," said Toni, who had always taken life less serious than her sister. She was a happy go lucky socialite who could match Jake drink for drink if they were ever out partying together.

"You should take this more serious, Toni. You shouldn't mock the occult, you never know what could happen," said Blanche.

Toni's response was to laugh at her sister's remarks.

Imelda graced into the room full of self-importance and Toni instantly switched a look to Jake and they both mischievously sniggered at the plastered-on foundation, extreme bright red lipstick and tasteless over-applied blue eye shadow that she was wearing. Luckily Imelda hadn't noticed their frivolity.

Abe got up from his own chair and like the old-fashioned gentleman that he was pulled a chair out for

Imelda before ensuring that she was sitting comfortably. She thanked him for his efforts but her nose remained aloft in the air snootily and it was easy to tell that she held a very high opinion of herself.

"Mr Zennor, would you please dim the lights and light the candles," she ordered.

Jake went along with her request. The sooner this was over with the better.

"Before we start I must stress that at all times we must ensure that our hands remained joined together. This will ensure that the energy of the spirit world is at its maximum capacity in their attempt to connect with us. If you break the circle, then the séance will possibly also break." Jake couldn't help but wonder if the deep and seductive East European accent was as phoney as Imelda's shows.

"Now please join hands, close your eyes and the séance can begin."

With a mixture of cynicism and optimism, everyone obediently carried out Imelda's request.

Fergus and Naoko were both spiritual people and had come to the séance with an open mind and a sense of curiosity, as had Blanche who had often enjoyed watching this sort of thing on TV shows and believed that genuinely contact could at times be made with the spirit world. She was no means a lady of a totally gullible disposition but she always became interested when the medium was able to focus on something that they couldn't possibly have known beforehand, such as the name of a favourite teddy bear as a child or an unobvious part of the body where a birthmark rested. This evening Blanche genuinely wanted to make contact with her parents and Jake knowing this was concerned that Imelda may callously play on her hopes. Due to Jake's fame, of course, there was plenty of information about the Zennor family already in the public domain for Imelda to draw from.

The séance began with various requests from Imelda urging the spirit world to make contact.

"Is there anybody there," she said in her deep drone.

Very original thought Jake catching a glimpse of Toni who was really finding it hard to contain her giggles. This made him want to laugh too until his mind jumped back to when he and Lucy had played with the Ouija board.

Imelda requested the spirit world to come forward once more. "Is there anybody there?"

Just then Jake, who again had disobediently opened his eyes for a few seconds, noticed the candles flicker in unison. He was a little more startled than he would have imagined because the candles seemed to actually extinguish and relight again. He closed his eyes tight shut again, pretending that the phenomena had not happened.

"I have made contact," Imelda announced. "I have a small oriental lady with me. She wishes to make contact with someone on this table."

"I guess that would be me then," said Naoko cynically.

"Yes. It is you that she seeks."

Surprise, surprise, thought Jake along with the majority of the group.

"She is a lady who is always close by you. She is never far away and she wants you to know that she is happy where she is."

"Is Jojo happy too?" enquired Naoko.

"Yes, your father is happy as well."

"Jojo was my dog as a child."

Toni couldn't help but snigger aloud as everyone instantly opened their eyes.

"Sometimes the spirit world can send me mixed messages. Ah yes, Jojo your dog. I see him clearer now. Yes, he is fine also."

Everyone closed his or her eyes again.

"I have another lady with me now. She was a very kind lady, but her life was tragically cut short much too soon. It feels as though the time of her passing was not what was planned for her."

"It's Mom," said Blanche.

Jake cringed.

"Yes," continued Imelda. "I can see the letter P. Her name is associated with the letter P."

"Mom's name was Polly," said Toni.

"Polly, yes I see it more clearly now."

"I bet you do," said Jake who was still unconvinced. It was well documented in many biographies about Blossom of Eden that his mother's name was Polly and how she and Cyril had been killed in a car crash.

It was Abe's turn to cringe at Jake's unconcealed attitude towards what he thought of Imelda's talents.

"Polly says hello to her three children and she wants you to know that she is safe with your father also. Jake, she particularly wants you to know how proud both she and your father are of your musical success. They are delighted for you."

Imelda had partially won over some of Jake's attention. He couldn't help but hope that his parents were somehow making contact. He had always hated the fact that they had been killed before his rise to fame. If they really did know of his success, then his feeling of unjust regarding their death could be a little more contently balanced. But is this what self-professed mediums do, prey on the vulnerable emotions of those left behind to reel them into their charade?

"Toni and Blanche, your mother is pleased with the way that you and your brother have all supported one another since the accident that claimed their lives, and Toni, your mother tells me that your father has always been pleased that you have managed to maintain your sense of humour for all these years. Blanche, they are both delighted with the two beautiful grandchildren that you have provided for them."

Just as Jake had felt about his parents not knowing of his fame due to their untimely death, Blanche had always been saddened that they had not been able to know their grandchildren.

Toni was delighted at her father's message if indeed he had truly made contact with them and Imelda was not performing a cruel deception. Toni's reaction to her parent's premature death had been with a determination to live life to the full as her parent's passing had highlighted the fact that no one can ever really be sure when it is their time to die. Toni always lived for the day.

"Your mother is leaving us now. She leaves her love with you, her three children."

Jake opened his eyes again to see a single tear roll down Blanche's face. His heart went out to his elder sister.

There was silence for a few seconds before Imelda spoke again.

"Now I am walking across a luscious green dale," spoke the East European voice. "It is full of beautiful scenery and a beautiful blue sky, but strangely the feeling is not good."

Imelda paused before continuing.

"I am finding it hard to breathe... It is getting worse. I am very short of breath…As if I am suffocating"

Jake and Fergus looked at one another. They instantly thought of the day that Roland Summers sank into the bog and died. Jake knew that both Roland's and his brother Che's deaths had in the main escaped any major press coverage, except maybe some local reporting in the Derbyshire Newspapers and TV News. Jake's connection to the brothers had thankfully never taken flight with the media. It could be possible that Imelda had some form of gift after all. It was not wholly inconceivable that she was feeling the tragic symptoms of Roland's death. Jake did consider the possibility that Imelda may have unsuspectingly tapped up Abe for some information beforehand, but he doubted that his shrewd manager would have proved so naïve.

"I'm getting a name now. Ralph or Ronald perhaps? Definitely the letter 'R' is prominent."

"Roland," offered Fergus.

"Yes, that is it. Roland. He asks if you ever did get to the pub following the strenuous walk you did with him."

Jake, now slightly more impressed smiled and answered, "No we didn't make it. It didn't seem appropriate under the circumstances."

"Roland says he is sure that you've made up for it since anyway. He now says goodbye and I leave his love with you."

The next few minutes passed uneventfully. Jake secretly hoped that Alannah may come through to him, but he still wasn't altogether convinced that Imelda was genuine.

Suddenly Abe began to shake. His shaking became so apparent that everyone opened his or her eyes, including Imelda and they all looked at him.

Abe began to speak as if hypnotised or in a trance. The strange thing was it wasn't his voice that was coming out of his mouth. It was that of a woman!

CHAPTER 31

"Help me, please help me!" begged *Abe* in a female voice.

"He has picked up a spirit. Abe has picked up a spirit," said Imelda, strangely appearing very unnerved considering her line of work. "They are using him as a channel to communicate. What is your name?"

Alannah? Hoped Jake, but his heart soon sank.

"Ruth, my name is Ruth," answered Abe still violently shaking. Blanche and Jake had sat either side of Abe and they were having difficulty holding the chain of energy together.

"Does anyone here know of a Ruth?" asked Imelda. The others all shook their heads.

"What is it you want Ruth? Can we help you at all?" Asked Imelda.

"You can't help us. Nobody can. It's too late." *Abe* began to sob.

"Us? Who are *us*, Ruth? Who is there with you?"

Suddenly Abe's demeanour changed again. He looked enraged and his voice turned into a much harsher and deeper tone of a man, again a voice that was alien to Abe's persona.

"Mind your own fucking business. Who the hell are you lot to come here asking questions?"

"We mean no harm," offered Jake.

"Ah, Jake Zennor. The music man of the house. Don't make me laugh. I am the musical genius and this will always be my house. You are an imposter Zennor. I am the MUSIC and I am the MAN. Not you or anybody else."

"What is your problem dude?" asked Jake, possibly unwisely as the look from Imelda suggested.

"I can kill you just like I killed them," snorted *Abe*.

"Killed who?" enquired Imelda. "Who are you?

"Yeah, big man. What is your name then?" Mocked Jake.

"Be careful Jake," warned Imelda. "Abe seems to have connected with a very bad spirit."

The other three ladies Naoko, Blanche and even Toni began to look very frightened. Elgar had been snoozing on a nearby armchair and following a troubled meow; he had shot out of the room to avoid the unnerving supernatural occurrence.

"You should be afraid of me Zennor," said *Abe* using a sinister tone that could never belong to him.

"Fuck you," came Jake's reply.

Suddenly Abe stood up breaking the chain of hands and began to beat his chest like a rabid ape snarling and growling.

Jake was regretting his mocking now, not because of any fear for himself but because he was frightened for his friend and manager. Something seemed to have possessed Abe and it didn't look good.

Abe then leapt at Jake and grabbed him around the neck. "I'll kill you, you peasant bastard."

Jake refused to fight back because he couldn't bring himself to hit Abe even if it was someone or something else driving his rage. Fergus attempted to pull Abe off Jake, but whatever was controlling Abe caused him to lash out with his arm, hitting Fergus into the face and subsequently knocking him across the room. This was no mean feat considering the size of Fergus, and Abe seemed to be displaying a strength that seemed to belie his own small frame.

Then suddenly Imelda began to sing the words of "Love Lives Forever." Her voice had also changed. She was actually singing with two voices, one male and one female beautifully harmonising one another. The female's voice sounded as if it could have belonged to Ruth considering her earlier connection.

Everyone turned to look at Imelda and she simply shrugged as she sang, as if to indicate that she did not understand why she was singing or where the words were coming from.

Then the old piano in the nearby room began to accompany her singing, playing that same haunting piano melody that had inspired Jake to compose his greatest ever hit.

Abe released Jake's neck and then fell to the floor before suffering what appeared to be some sort of seizure.

Imelda stopped singing and ran over to Abe to take the manager's head in her arms.

Jake crouched down by them and recognised the change on Abe's face to that of a more peaceful look as his convulsing began to stop.

"He is going to be okay," said Imelda in her usual East European drone. It seemed her accent was genuine after all. "The bad spirit has left his body."

"I guess I owe you an apology," offered Jake. "I didn't actually believe that you were capable of contacting the dead. But you have certainly proved you're worth now. You obviously do have *the gift*, as they call it."

"Don't apologise Mr Zennor, I am as surprised as you are."

"What do you mean?" asked a confused Jake.

"In over thirty years of doing readings, shows and séances, this is the first time that my powers have actually worked!"

CHAPTER 32

Abe was back to being Abe again and he had trouble believing the story of the séance and his possession during it. He had no recollection of his experience, but with a consistent set of witnesses to corroborate what had happened he had to accept that it had actually happened.

Meanwhile, the unexpected characters that had appeared at the séance gave some indication to Jake of who was responsible for sending him the unexplained e-mails that he had received. He concluded that Ruth must have been one of "The Lovers" who had pleaded for HELP! And whoever had manifested himself by using Abe's body as a channel in order to subsequently threaten to kill Jake, could well have been the same evil bastard who had stated, "Don't you fucking Dare!" Just who was he? He had referred to himself as being both *the* man and *the* musical genius of the house as if to dismiss Jake's own notable achievements of composition and the fact that Abba Manor was now his home. Was he insinuating that Jake had somehow attempted to usurp him at Abba Manor, and musically as well? But it didn't make sense. This nasty character could surely not be responsible for the haunting and beautiful piano music that had inspired Jake to compose "Love Lives Forever?" Even Father Irwin had suggested on the day that he came to bless the house that there was nothing of evil about the music that transpired from the old piano.

Delighted with the way his career was developing and his acceptance back into society, Jake was able to utilise his drinking habits for pleasure once again, instead of requiring the endless bottles of scotch to numb the pain and prevent his mind from torturing him. He still missed Lucy, but he was able to view her absence on a more philosophical level these days. Whether she had witnessed his coded message to her on the Marty Rodgerson TV special or not, Jake realised that she could not have escaped the imminent whispers following his TV appearance being echoed in the very industry that she worked for. Jake figured that she would contact him if she felt the need and pressuring her would be unwise, and if she didn't contact him then he simply hoped that she was happy in her life. Yes, he missed her and even ached for her, but his outlook on life these days was to live with no regrets.

Jake also felt comfortable that Alannah could finally rest in peace, and although a part of him would always miss her too, he knew he need not blame himself for her tragic death and was comforted by the thought that she was at least free from the pain that she had undoubtedly felt whilst alive. One thing that living at Abba Manor had convinced him of was *yes* there was most definitely life after death. He was sure that the kind and sweet Alannah could only have been destined for a better place.

Tonight, he had decided to drive to Knockerdown Inn, a welcoming Public House made of peakland stone based near Carsington water. A family-friendly pub, Knockerdown Inn could boast a collection of animals that live happily at the pub's rear and Jake liked the friendly ambience, albeit tonight was a night when he was happy to entertain his own company and reflect on the progress of his musical career with a small intimate drink of celebration.

Jake pulled his Ferrari into an empty space in the car park of the pub, safe in the knowledge that it wouldn't be harmed in spite of its worth. Knockerdown Inn never encouraged the likes of rowdy troublemakers; in fact, on a weeknight such as tonight with the hour fairly late, its clientele would usually only boast a handful of local middle-aged folk who largely kept their business to themselves except for a polite greeting or farewell. Ironic really that in Jake they had a wealthy superstar as one of their regular drinkers, but it was the sort of place that Jake could comfortably relax in. In contrast, he did of course often enjoy painting the town when socialising with his buddies or Toni, but tonight Knockerdown Inn more than fitted the bill for a quiet reflection on life whilst being in a state of contentment.

Jake ordered a pint of real ale with a double whisky chaser, a bit naughty really considering he was driving, but he vowed to himself that he would have no more alcohol thereafter. He sat by the diamond leaded window amongst the vast amount of hanging brass ornaments and dark wood and looked out onto the extensive beer garden. As he took the first mouthful of creamy nectar from his pint glass, he couldn't help but compare the comfortable atmosphere of Knockerdown Inn to that first night on his return to the Peak District when the mysterious taxi driver named Archie had taken him to The World's End. It had been a good thing that Nanette had been there that night to save him from an unwelcome evening of social disaster.

As Jake had entered Knockerdown Inn tonight there had been no evil stares from the locals or a display of resentment at his presence. The World's End was probably the only pub in the local Peak District vicinity that Jake had decided not to become fully accustomed to. Indeed, he never went there again after that initial encounter, and he often wondered why a person as lovely as Nanette should frequent such a hostile and miserable place. Nanette had remained a loyal and valued if somewhat unlikely friend to Jake since their meeting in the otherwise hostile World's End.

He took his time drinking his pint of real ale wanting to savour every last drop of the thick and creamy liquid. In contrast, he quickly downed his single malt whisky. The ale was that good he wanted to return to the bar for a second pint but sensibly opted for an orange juice and lemonade. For once, a second whisky was not necessary.

Jake paid the barman, an elderly gentleman of very few but polite words. He wasn't sure who actually ran Knockerdown Inn but whoever was responsible for the home cooked food on offer on the pub menu he would gladly shake their hand. Jake had tasted the food before now and had been very impressed with the traditional cuisine, it was as good as the ale on offer. The food had stopped being served some time earlier this evening before Jake's arrival so he made do with a packet of roasted peanuts to complement his soft drink.

Jake returned to his seat and took his time drinking his pint of non-alcoholic beverage as he scanned the environment. He spotted a log fire that pleasantly smouldered away radiating comfortable heat. Jake was positioned not too far away from the fireplace. The carpet was multi-patterned with a random tile-effect giving a warm and welcoming feeling to the eye of any would-be customer. The carpet was of a high quality and hard wearing nature, a necessary requirement to cope with the multitude of walking that crossed its surface. The pub was shrouded with a lot of dark timber including panelling along the bottom half of the walls and ceiling beams. Behind the bar, Jake was impressed by the selection of many different types of whisky, some unusual and hard to come by just like the real ales on offer in the casks.

When stood at the bar, Jake had noticed a couple sitting in the corner, almost in hiding it would seem. Their body language suggested to him that they were having an affair. He guessed they had arrived in separate cars, him most likely in the dark-blue BMW series and her in the sporty Peugeot with the convertible roof, both of which Jake had spotted in the car park. It was not the sort of weather to have the hood down on the Peugeot, indeed it was a very chilly and typical winter's night in the Peak District with the biting wind howling around the stone walls of the pub. Pretty soon the fog would be coming down and Jake was mindful not to leave it too much longer before he returned to Abba Manor. Besides Elgar would inevitably want to be fed by now. That cat could eat for England!

Turning his gaze from the alleged *adulterous* couple, although Jake did find the lady's dark red hair and somewhat plump and almost fully exposed breasts difficult to ignore, he witnessed an old boy sitting on a stool at the far end of the bar. He was supping his ale out of a silver tankard. It seemed obvious to Jake that this gentleman had found great pleasure in spending many years sitting in that very same seat, supping his favourite beverage in his favourite pub. But then again was his face hiding a much sadder story? Was the pub the only place he could feel comfortable in, a sort of retreat from a life of tragedy or loneliness?

As he scanned the remainder of the pub he noticed that there was only about a dozen or so people present who, it has to be said, did not have anything much to take notice of.

He finished the remainder of his drink and decided it was time to go home, even though the earlier ale had tasted so good he could quite happily have stayed there until closing time and beyond!

Jake was conscious that he might have strayed over the legal driving limit of alcohol. He looked at his watch, one real ale at 4.7 percent proof and a double whisky drank over a period of 1 hour and 40 minutes with a packet of peanuts to soak and combat the alcohol. Jake momentarily wrestled with his conscious but figured if he went for a slash to pee some of the alcohol away he would be all right. He felt totally sober anyway and besides, he knew that he did possess a high resistance level of being able to handle his booze. Years of practice had seen to that.

The air had chilled further since Jake's arrival at Knockerdown Inn and as he left through the oak door into the car park he felt the wind instantly claw at his face. His prediction of fog had also proved correct, but by squinting slightly he could still make out the public-house sign with its artistic inscription of Knockerdown Inn, slowly swinging away accompanied by the noise of its creaking hinges which sang out eerily through the quiet night.

Jake shuddered with the cold and realised that there was little point in standing in a chilled state staring at a pub sign. He walked over to his Ferrari unlocking the central locking system via the key fob and the red lights signalling the unlocking of the car's doors penetrated the fog. The noise of the car's alarm being released caused a nearby fox to run to shelter.

Jake got into the car and although it cut out the bite of the wind it was still an icy temperature inside. He started the engine and quickly turned on the car's heating system. The windscreen quickly demisted and Jake was soon leaving Knockerdown Inn behind and meandering homewards through the fog on the country lanes and roads of the Peak District.

The fog was creating an eerie atmosphere and Jake's animated imagination was becoming extremely active. The moonlight merging with the fog gave the impression that the trees were tall dark figures, and their branches appeared as long twisted arms reaching out to try and drag their victims into the pits of hell.

Despite the ever-increasing dense fog, Jake could still clearly see the full moon shining above the evil dark figures, confirming the concept that the night-time gave consent for all that was not living to have their time upon the earth.

Then he saw it.

The fog falling upon winding country lanes had forced Jake to compromise the speed of the Ferrari, in spite of his desire to get home as quickly as possible. Therefore because of the relatively slow speed of Jake's driving, he was able to see it clearly, the fog providing no shield to the apparition. In fact, what Jake had seen seemed to have its shape illuminated by a surrounding glow.

Jake slammed his brakes on causing the car to skid to an abrupt halt.

Had he really just seen it?

Had he really just passed such a dreadful sight?

Hanging from one of the branches (a good thick and sturdy branch not one of the long evil twisting arms) seemed to be a figure of a man.

Jake was convinced that he had definitely seen the swinging corpse.

The figure of a man hanging, totally void of life and swinging slowly in the cold night.

Jake searched his mind for an explanation. Perhaps he shouldn't have driven on a bellyful of alcohol after all. Perhaps he was hallucinating. But he felt cold stone sober. Especially now!

Then he heard the sound of the creaking of the branch carry on the eerie breeze, caused by the weight of the unfortunate individual. Even from the haven of his Ferrari, he could hear the rope rubbing against the bark of the thick branch.

He didn't want to turn around. The sounds had convinced him that he had indeed seen a figure hanging from the tree.

He plucked up the courage to look in his rearview mirror. Jake could see the glow illuminating but needed to slightly adjust the mirror in order to bring the tragic sight into full view.

The figure was still there, hanging, swinging and totally void of life. The eyes were bulging from their sockets and the tongue was protruding from the corner of the man's mouth. A thick rope noose surrounded the broken neck, the head cocked to the right.

Jake was disturbed at the seemingly young age of the tragic individual; he guessed his age to be no more than early twenties. Jake reflected on such a waste of a youthful life. He wondered what could have driven this young man to take his own life in this way.

Then Jake noticed the clothing draped on the hanging corpse. It did not appear to be any contemporary fashion. The feet were totally exposed not supporting a single trace of footwear and the trousers were dishevelled and much too short for the length of the dead man's legs. The shirt and trousers were made of a much thicker and uncomfortable looking material than anybody would wear of today, it was almost sack like.

And what was causing the glow around the body?

By now used to the notion that paranormal activity existed, basing his assumptions on his experiences at Abba Manor, Jake concluded that perhaps he had seen the ghost of a hanging man. Ironically he found some small comfort from this conclusion, he didn't relish the fact of stumbling upon a recent suicide and having to involve the police and a possible grieving family.

Jake plucked up the courage to turn around and face the vision once more without the fragile protection of the mirror.

He turned his head slowly.

But by the time he had turned around the body had vanished. All that remained was the large, thick branch of the tree but there was no hanging corpse swinging from it.

Jake shivered and wrestled to clear his thoughts. He quickly began to drive away from the spot of the ghostly apparition.

Not entirely shaken but definitely feeling a distinct sense of unease, Jake decided that he no longer wanted to return immediately to Abba Manor. He was ashamed to admit to himself that he didn't want to be alone. Jake remembered that Nanette lived not far from here and so made a slight detour to call upon her.

It was a good and reassuring feeling to drive into the small hamlet where Nanette lived. It felt safe to be back amongst the *living* and the odd shining indoor light from the cottages. The smell of burning coal fires from within was a welcoming environment to Jake.

He pulled up outside Nanette's cottage and walked up the short pathway to her front door. He knocked hoping that she was in. It was always hard to tell at night as she and her daughter Bethany preferred to generally live in the rooms at the rear of the cottage.

As Jake waited anxiously for the door to be answered, he admired the peakland stone brickwork of the cottage and the display of Nanette's hanging basket consisting mainly of winter pansies. Due to the fog and natural darkness, Jake could not make out the colour of the flowers.

Jake felt a sense of relief as Nanette cautiously opened the door and peeked from the small opening behind the safety chain.

"Jake! Hello, how are you?" She was genuinely glad to see him if a little surprised. "You gave me a bit of fright; I don't usually get visitors after dark."

"I'm sorry to disturb you, Nanette. I just felt like a bit of company. I hope you don't mind me calling."

"Not at all you daft beggar. It is always a pleasure to see you, Jake, you know that. Let me take the safety chain off and I'll let you in."

Nanette momentarily closed the door to release the safety chain and reopened it again to welcome her guest.

"Do you fancy a drink at all, Jake? I'm just about to have a cocoa actually. I'm sorry I haven't got any booze in at present."

"A black coffee would be fine, Nanette. Thanks."

"Sounds serious." Nanette had been a good confidant to Jake over the months, providing a wise ear to all his troubles regarding Alannah and Lucy. Curiously though he had hardly mentioned to her the supernatural activity at Abba Manor, possibly because of his fear of being ridiculed, but deep down he knew that having a friend like Nanette placed him in the fortunate position to be able to tell her anything he wanted without derision or judgement.

But he needed to tell her about the sighting of the hanging corpse and once he did the floodgates opened. Jake told Nanette there and then every little detail of what had occurred at Abba Manor. It puzzled Jake why none of the information seemed to shock her!

"Let me guess the exact location of where you witnessed this unfortunate individual hanging from the tree Jake." Nanette's large hoop earrings swayed as she spoke. "About 1 mile past the derelict unused Farm House coming north from Knockerdown Inn the road twists and dips slightly, around the Brown Ale Bay area of the lake. Well, it is pretty much in this dip in the nearside field to your vehicle that the young man was swinging from the big thick branch."

Jake was taken aback by Nanette's accuracy. "Nanette, that's amazing. How could you possibly know that?"

Nanette smiled. "Let me grab my coat. Come on we are going to go back to that very spot this instant. There is something I want to show you."

"What right now?"

"Yes now."

"I'm not so sure I want to Nanette; it wasn't a very nice experience the first time."

"Don't worry you'll be fine."

Nanette grabbed her coat and locked the door behind her as Jake reached his Ferrari.

"I'll turn the heater on to warm the car inside."

"Thanks, Jake." Nanette sat down snugly into the leather interior and fixed her seat belt. "Okay, Ghostbuster. Let's go."

Not too much conversation was exchanged between the two friends as they returned to the spot where Jake had witnessed the hanging corpse. Jake was too apprehensive about seeing the disturbing apparition all over again to engage his mind into producing any constructive dialogue. Finally, he reached the spot that they were destined for and slowly parked the car into a safe position.

"It was there Nanette; I swear clear as day it was. I don't know why it's not there now."

"Yeah, it's not as though he was in a state to walk away now is it," joked Nanette.

Jake turned his head to face Nanette. "You don't believe me, do you?"

"Oh, I believe you all right Jake. Come on get out of the car."

Jake was a little astonished to see Nanette steaming ahead of him and then beginning to climb the hedgerow in order to get into the field so that she could get closer to the tree that had earlier supported the hanging corpse.

"Come on slowcoach," she shouted casually.

Jake increased his pace in order to catch up with Nanette. The grass beneath them was somewhat sodden, but they still reached the tree with relative ease. The fog was becoming denser but visibility was still achievable.

"Okay, Jake, up you go."

"Are you mad? I'm not climbing that tree."

"Well, I can't Jake. For me to show you what you need to see you will have to climb up to that thick branch. You are twice as fit as me."

"But that branch is where the rope was tied that had some creepy guy swinging from it."

"It's okay, Jake. Don't worry. Trust me."

"Oh, Bloody hell. Okay, if you insist," and with that Jake carefully climbed the tree until he was sitting astride the thick branch, a leg hanging on either side. The branch was more than capable of supporting his weight.

"That's great Jake, now shift along about another couple of feet and feel the bark with your fingers."

Jake once again obeyed Nanette's curious instructions.

"Can you feel anything yet?"

"Yes," shouted Jake in reply. "There are grooves present which are entirely circling the circumference of the branch."

"That's right, Jake. So, what do you think caused those grooves?"

"Well, I guess they could be rope marks."

"You've got it, Jake. You weren't imagining what you saw earlier at all. Those grooves are there as proof and testimony to what this tree was used for many years ago. This was a *hanging tree* Jake, where criminals of the day were hanged for their crimes. The markings are caused by the weight of many a hanging corpse swinging in the noose of the rope."

"So I did see a ghost of someone who was once hanged here."

"You certainly did Jake. You're not going mad and you're not the first to have witnessed something eerie here."

"Fuck me, I'm coming down. I suddenly don't like being up here."

Nanette laughed.

Jake retreated down the tree and returned to Nanette's side.

"I wonder who it was that I exactly laid eyes on Nanette?"

"Ghosts are usually hanging around, no pun intended, because they are restless spirits, so my guess is that it was perhaps one of the victims of many a miscarriage of justice. Someone who didn't actually deserve to die and passed over before their time was rightly due. Mind you this one looks like young Billy Chubb. He was hanged for taking advantage of the farmer's daughter if you catch my drift. He deserved to hang all right. If you ask me, it's a crying shame that you can't still hang bad'uns like him of today."

"You can see something," inquired Jake.

"Of course."

"But why can't I see anything now?"

"You are only just beginning to develop your third eye, Jake. You need to open that part of the brain that can see paranormal activity. Sometimes people only see a ghost once in a lifetime. Sometimes, usually the narrow-minded cynics of this world, never get to see life from the other side at all. Your third eye, or inner eye if you prefer, is like any part of your body, it needs exercise. Some of us are born lucky or unlucky, depending on which way you look at it."

"What do you mean?"

"I see dead people. I always have done since a small child. I used to think that it was perfectly normal that people were walking around with part of their heads missing or having their body parts falling off. Then I realised that I have a gift. Some days I think it's a curse mind. People like me never get to switch off you see. I constantly see things, hear voices and communicate with the dead."

"Nanette I had no idea."

"Well, I don't share this information with people of the living too often. I also learnt early on what it was like to suffer ridicule and prejudice. But as you have seen a ghost yourself tonight Jake, and I consider you a good friend I don't mind telling you."

"I'm glad you have told me, Nanette. Perhaps you should come over to Abba Manor. I think that you may be able to help me out with that shit load of stuff I told you about earlier. I definitely wish that you had been at the séance"

"Okay, Jake. I'll come over, but I must admit with the rumours connected to that place, like what I told you that night at our first meeting at The World's End, the chances are if I do see something it may not be very pleasant. Then again you live there and you are okay, aren't you? Ghosts usually still walk this earth if they feel that they have unfinished business. They sometimes feel that they need to get a message to the living; it can be very frustrating for them actually. Some ghosts, on the other hand, do not even realise that they are dead, I suspect like Billy here, and some just appear for the sheer hell of it finding great satisfaction in scaring the shit out of people."

"I have to ask you something Nanette; something I've been intrigued about for some time. Why do you drink at The World's End?"

"Well, I never like to drink alone."

"What do you mean, you always go on your own, minding your own business. That first night I met you, you were on your own."

"Have you not being listening to me, Jake. The World's End is my husband's favourite pub. I don't like it too much myself but it keeps him happy if we go there."

"But Nanette, your husband is dea-." Then Jake realised what he was saying and the penny dropped.

Nanette gave a reassuring smile. "You often find my Tommy sitting in The World's End in the very same seat that he has always occupied."

Jake stood open mouthed.

"Come on let's get back to the car, I'm freezing."

Nanette linked Jake's arm and guided him back to the Ferrari.

"By the way, Jake, Alannah likes the new curtains that you have chosen, but she still finds it annoying the way that you leave half-cut onions in the fridge causing a stink to high heaven on opening the fridge door."

"You can see Alannah?"

"Yes I can Jake, and she found the sight of you nervously spread-eagled over that branch just now very amusing."

"Nanette, I'm amazed."

"Oh, and Jake she wants you to know that she likes Lucy. She thinks she is good for you and maybe sometimes you shouldn't be such a stubborn ass."

Jake smiled as they reached the car. He looked up into the foggy sky. "Bless you, Alannah."

Nanette continued as they got into the Ferrari. "Jake, your mother is a little worried about your drinking habits although Roland and Che Summers are finding her concerns highly amusing as they continue to drink the bars dry where they are. Your father admires your choice of car; he says it wins hands down compared to the old bus that he used to drive."

She was still continuing as Jake started the car and began to drive away. "…And do you remember your grandmother on your father's side who really liked Al Jolson and the big band stuff? Well, she is wondering if you could do some music similar to that, she doesn't care much for this modern stuff and do you remember…."

Nanette continued relaying her messages from beyond the grave all the way home.

CHAPTER 33

Now that Jake's career was firmly back on track he decided that it was necessary to incorporate a fully equipped music studio within the structure of Abba Manor. Jake was settled at the old house, and in spite of the various supernatural happenings that occurred he was happy to have Abba Manor as his home. Jake had accepted that the house was haunted but he didn't particularly feel in any danger. And he was successfully managing to balance his musical career outside of London with the desire to live in the tranquility of the Peak District, after all, the new lease of inspiration that Jake held for his songwriting in his chosen location could not be denied. "Love Lives Forever" was proof of that.

Jake's drinking habits had decreased to a reasonable moderation; he rarely drank in the house now except for the occasional *reward* for working hard at the piano composing his music.

Gone were the days of having to drink to numb the pain from the challenges of life. Of course, he still thought of Alannah, but with a lot less guilt and with the knowledge that she was now safe wherever she was. The public support that he had received for the tragic situation concerning Alannah had proved very reassuring, and it enabled him to move on with his life with the appropriate amount of memories that he would always have for his deceased fiancée.

He still missed Lucy, though. Almost three weeks had passed since his revelations of a mystery woman on The Marty Rodgerson Special. Perhaps his clues had been too cryptic even for Lucy? Perhaps she hadn't even seen the TV show or hadn't heard about what was said? These days it would be splattered all over social media and electronic newspapers, but social media was only an emerging force in the 90s and word of mouth was still the primary gossip spreader.

Jake contemplated that he had simply blown things with her. He knew he had difficulty in controlling his temper and although a woman would never have to fear a physical assault from him, his verbal wrath that day on their last meeting could not have been pleasant for Lucy. He accepted that she could even have justifiably construed his outburst as being totally unforgivable. And then after they had made love he had simply walked out. How would that have left her feeling? Used no doubt at the very least. He had screwed her and then simply walked out the door. *Oh, Jake you can be such a prick sometimes.*

Still, he always had Elgar to keep him company, and Jake never felt that he was totally alone in the house with the sound of creaking floorboards, the unexplained moving of objects or furniture and the occasional presence of a definite entity standing behind him. He had simply got used to the things that once instilled fear and alarm into him. Jake always felt safe and content these days in Abba Manor and had simply grown used to the *sharing* of his home. After all, for the length of time that he had been living there, and with all the supernatural encounters that had occurred, not once had Jake actually been harmed.

Nanette had remained a loyal confidant for Jake and she had recommended a team of local builders to tastefully construct the alterations to Abba Manor. He was hoping that Nanette might show up herself today in an attempt to interpret the supernatural happenings that had been going on in his home. Jake was delighted to be able to utilise people from the local community. He would be able to pay them an amount of money for their work that they would previously only have dreamed of. Jake had suggested the price himself, realising that he was being generous but he felt it important to contribute and show his support for local talent. Being a philanthropist gave him pleasure and he intended to invest a lot more money into the local community as the years roll by.

Jake had designed the plans himself for the additional building work in line with the limited planning permission granted for a listed building. Extra bricks of peakland stone were to be bonded into the ancient brickwork of the house and built outwards from the west side of the property. A bricked-up wall that curiously seemed to partition a small part of the house, and was not an obvious addition from inside the property, was to be demolished to gain access to the soon-to-be music studio. This had only been a recent discovery by Basil the chief builder during the process of expertly assessing the structure.

Jake was currently stood on the lawn with Basil who was a weighty man in his fifties who always seemed to have a scarlet complexion to his face and a demand for endless cups of tea. He was a man of few words, yet the word *fuck* seemed the most used word in his vocabulary, but he was undeniably an expert in his field. The two men were going over the finer details of the forthcoming construction when they were interrupted by the noise of a car entering the driveway. The yellow coloured Mazda parked up and Jake's heart fluttered as he immediately realised who it must be. His smile broadened like a Cheshire cat as Lucy stepped out of the car looking as beautiful as ever. He was surprised but delighted that she had turned up.

"I see that you are having some building work done," enquired Lucy nonchalantly.

"Yeah," replied Jake. "As I'm too lazy to travel to various recording studios around the British Isles and beyond, I thought that I might as well have my own built and do some homemade productions from now on."

"Well, that sounds great Jake, but are you sure that it is a recording studio that you want?"

"Well I am a musician," replied Jake looking puzzled.

"What about a nursery instead, that would be nice."

Jake looked baffled at Lucy's suggestion. "Lucy, what are you going on about? I've just told you I'm a musician, not a flaming nursery worker."

Lucy smiled. "Yes you are a musician Jake, but you are also going to be something else."

"Sorry, I don't follow."

"A father."

Jake was genuinely stunned at Lucy's revelation and his jaw dropped open.

Lucy broke the silence with a giggle.

"Jake close your mouth before a train drives into it."

"B…but. How?"

"Do you need me to draw you a picture, Zennor?"

"Tell me again. I think I might be dreaming."

"I'm pregnant Jake Zennor you clown, and if you are shocked by that news perhaps I shouldn't tell you that we are actually expecting twins. It seems that making love whilst you're in an acute state of anger makes you more fertile, Stud."

Lucy's candidness caused Basil to feel more than a little awkward.

"Twins? Twins! Wow! That's great!" said Jake. "That's really great, I'm so happy."

Jake couldn't contain his delight as he immediately embraced Lucy, kissed her and lifted her from the floor spinning her around. His genuine joy at being told he was going to be a father was plain to see.

"Steady, Jake. You have to be careful with a woman in her fucking condition," said Basil, appearing even redder in the face than usual. "Err, pardon the language ma'am. Congratulations to you both."

"I'm so glad that you are happy Jake, I wasn't sure how you would take the news."

"It's the best news ever Lucy. My career's back on track, I'm going to have a family and the woman I love is hopefully going to share this big lonely house with me." Jake's face suddenly dropped. "Sorry. I'm being a bit presumptuous, but surely this proves more than anything that we should be together, Lucy. But what about your career? You won't want to live here; you will feel that you need to be in London."

"Oh no I won't," said Lucy firmly. "I plan on living here and being a kept woman for a few years. I've got all my life to be writing articles and I can write them at home if needs be. I'm looking forward to just being a mom. Anyway, I got fired from Lynx Magazine."

"The independent Lucy Ives is going to be a kept woman; I've heard it all now. That has shocked me more than knowing that I am going to be a dad to twins. And what do you mean you got fired?"

"Well, I was officially told that due to efficiencies that needed to be reached in the budget I became surplus to requirements. However, I reckon that bloody nose I gave Niall had something to do with it."

"You hit him again?"

"I know I should be more careful in my condition, but I've never felt so satisfied hitting another human being in all my life. I'm afraid he pissed me off just a little too much when I confronted him about leaking the stuff about you like that. He is such an arrogant twat. The best thing is I received a round of applause when I socked him one, let's just say he is not the most popular guy in the world. I've received plenty of good wishes too when I announced that I was moving to Derbyshire. A bit presumptuous of me I know, but I figured things out after seeing you on The Marty Rodgerson show. I just had to be sure I was doing the right thing, after all, it wasn't just me I had to consider anymore, was it? Once I'd decided what to do I needed to tie up a few loose ends in London, I didn't want anything to get in the way of us being reunited, Jake. It's funny, Niall didn't congratulate me. I expect he probably felt embarrassed lying on the floor bleeding everywhere."

Jake and Lucy hugged each other once again.

"You're my Wonderwall, Lucy."

"Don't get too cocky Mr Zennor, girl power is strong at the moment even if yours truly is taking some time out. It looks like this new all-girl band the Spice Girls are going to give you a run for your money."

"Well, they offer something different to the Madchester scene I guess. That's the beauty of British music, Lucy. It just keeps evolving. Perhaps to truly secure my place as an evergreen artist I should perform a duet with Ginger Spice?"

"Nah, Scary Spice is more appropriate, especially with the scary things that have gone on here at Abba Manor."

Just then the cheery mood was altered when a labourer ran from inside the house. He appeared ghostly white and clearly troubled. He collapsed on the lawn and promptly threw up the contents of his packed lunch.

"What's wrong, Greg? Enquired Basil.

Greg wiped his mouth with the back of his hand and spluttered his reply. "I don't mean to break up the happy party Mr Zennor, but I really think that you should come and take a look at something."

The labourer led them all to the unexplained wall that he had been demolishing. A sufficient amount of destruction had taken place to reveal an opening large enough to peer through, but it was only with the aid of Greg's torch that the true shocking revelation could be realised. They all found it hard to believe their own eyes, and Lucy confirmed her shock by letting out a scream, for there before them lay two skeletons, their hands entwined giving the impression that they must have died together holding hands. The clothes they wore were obviously from a distant period and were eerily in a good condition compared to the frame that they enveloped. It was also peculiar that the usual stench of death and decay was not evident with such a finding, especially as the wall had held everything in for what appeared to be such a long time. The clothing also suggested that one skeleton had been a male in its living years and the other a female. The free hand of the female skeleton was clutching a book of some description, the whiteness of the bony fingers strangely complementing the dusty black cover. The state of the book appeared to mirror the good condition of the clothing.

Despite the gruesome discovery and her initial terror, Lucy's curiosity got the better of her and with a long stretch, she was just about able to reach for the book and retrieve it to the hands of the living. She wiped away centuries of dust and turned the delicate pages. The language was written in the hand of old English, but Lucy had been educated enough to understand such literature.

"It's a diary," she stated. She began to scan the words before relaying them to Jake and the builders, who listened attentively and with an excited sense of eagerness. Lucy was about to unlock a story that had remained buried for centuries.

As Lucy read aloud, it came to light that a wealthy aristocrat once owned Abbadon Manor in the eighteenth century. The aristocrat also happened to be a talented musician who had composed music for the gentry of the day and had hosted a number of garden parties in the grounds of his house. His name was Joshua Bleak. The diary revealed that he was an unpleasant and very wicked man who married the unfortunate lady who now seemingly lay as a skeleton before them when he was in his fifties.

She was thirty years his junior and her name had been Ruth. It seemed obvious that the diary belonged to her.

Tears began to roll down Lucy's face as Ruth Bleak's tragic story unfolded. Ruth's father had practically sold her to Joshua Bleak in exchange for a patch of land that he could use for farming.

The diary revealed years of physical abuse that Ruth had suffered at the hands of Joshua, graphically detailing beating after beating as if putting her experiences down on paper resulted in some kind of therapy for her. Either that or perhaps Ruth had a notion that at some point, no matter when, the truth would eventually be revealed about Joshua Bleak.

Jake couldn't help but recognise the parallels in his own life. He was a musician and Alannah had suffered aspects of abuse from an older man, albeit the abuser had been her own father in Alannah's case. Nevertheless, Jake found the similarities uncanny and in truth a little disturbing.

It was clear that Ruth had been unhappy in her marriage, but the diary went on to reveal how a young musical understudy to Bleak had given her a lifeline of hope. His name had been Charles Trott, and it became apparent that Charles was the skeletal corpse that lay beside her. Jake found some comfort in the fact that if Abba Manor could attract musicians, it didn't necessarily attract evil men and he chose too akin himself to the unfortunate Charles Trott rather than the wicked Joshua Bleak.

The relationship of Charles and Ruth began with love at first sight, and although the beatings continued from Bleak, Ruth admirably learned how to cope by indulging in many a secret rendezvous with Charles. Charles soon became a tremendous composer in his own right and was earning a sound reputation amongst the necessary circles, this was also beginning to compromise the limelight of Bleak who began to resent the young prodigy rather than celebrate the product of his tuition.

The diary was more like an autobiography than a simple diary, the language used was passionate and full of emotion. The words went on to reveal that Ruth and Charles had planned to flee to America in order to start a new life together, away from the brute known as Joshua Bleak. They were confident that they could survive on Charles' earnings as a musician, and indeed he already had some work lined up across the Atlantic. Ruth would be free from the monstrous hands of Bleak forever and she could live out the rest of her life with the one man she herself had chosen to love. A man who loved her in equal measure and a man who actually took pleasure from showing her the respect she deserved.

Then disaster struck.

Bleak discovered the affair and his jealousy for Charles' musical ability now became dangerously entwined with the knowledge that the young prodigy was sleeping with his wife. Bleak also managed to discover the plan to escape to America so he hired a mob of corruptible villagers, who could be easily bought, to force the couple into the room, and to brick them in behind a wall away from the rest of the world. They were beaten and had their ankles tied to a beam so they had no means of escape. It must have been unbearable as Ruth and Charles could only painfully look on as the wall was built brick by brick right before their very eyes. Bleak simply stood by laughing hysterically, totally satisfied with the evil act that he had orchestrated being realised. The doomed couple had been granted the light of a single slow burning candle, but once that had faded their final moments together were destined to end in darkness.

Unknown to Bleak and the unscrupulous mob, Ruth was able to salvage one last piece of dignity for herself. For safely tucked beneath her flamboyant clothing had been her diary. Ruth was able to update the memoir almost right up until her final breath it seemed. Her diary seemed complete and she had had the time to finish her memoirs before the light of the candle had finally ceased.

Ruth had managed to capture her belief that she and Charles would always be together as they were about to pass over into the afterlife simultaneously. Ironically, Bleak had pushed the couple into a beautiful last few days together in spite of his cruel intentions. Lucy read aloud Ruth's final words:

"As I physically grow weaker, my spirit grows stronger knowing that my final breath will be with my darling Charles. I would not exchange these final days together for a single day living a life behind the other side of the wall, for I have never been free whilst married to my beast of a husband, Joshua Bleak.

"I am convinced that Charles and I shall live happily together as we pass over into eternal life. God, please bless us both and welcome us into your kingdom away from the cruelty of the days that we have had to endure on earth. We share great pleasure knowing that we can stroll hand in hand through the gardens of heaven, never again suffering at the hands of Joshua Bleak, as when he shall finally pass his final breath he will surely be tossed into the burning fires of hell to languish in all his evil and misery for eternity. As for Charles and myself, we both know that Love Lives Forever…"

Jake could hardly believe that Ruth had used those very same words that had inspired his own successful lyrical content: *Love Lives Forever.* He and Lucy exchanged glances of amazement; their eyes spoke a thousand words that their tongues could not.

Greg then began to shine the torch further into the darkened room. It appeared that using a sharp piece of stone, Charles too had managed to etch the same words onto one of the walls. *Love Lives Forever.* A deliberate and final defiant statement awaiting Bleak should he have ever re-entered the room. Charles' intention most likely being to prove to Bleak that his attempt to separate them could not even be achieved in death.

"It's incredible," said Jake. "What a tragic and moving story. And to think it all happened here in Abbadon

Manor. And at last, I now know what the full name of this place finally is."

"Do you know what the word Abbadon means Jake?" asked Lucy. Jake could see Lucy was a little disturbed.

"No, what does it mean?"

"The word Abbadon is a Hebrew word. It can also be spelt with a single b and double d. The word appears in the Bible to describe a place of destruction. Quite apt considering Joshua Bleak once owned this place."

"It seems that this house has been harvesting a power struggle between love and evil for centuries," said Jake.

"Well it seems that love has finally won," said Lucy.

"I'll make sure it does. Those old stone signs at the top of my drive will be smashed off the wall and from today onwards this place will no longer be known as Abbadon Manor or even Abba Manor. This house will never again be a place of destruction. From this day forward our home will be known as Senara Manor."

"*Senara Manor.* That sounds nice what does it mean?"

"What? I finally have the opportunity to educate the knowledge filled award-winning journalist Lucy Ives?"

"Just get on with telling me, Zennor."

"Senara was one of the ancient Cornish saints and Saint Senara gives her name to the village of Zennor. Zennor is the Cornish name for Senara. It makes sense in so many ways. She is thought of as divine by the fishermen of Cornwall, so she is a clear symbol of good. However, she also had some bad press for falling pregnant out of wedlock, so that reminds me a little of your situation now Miss Ives."

"You cheeky thing. But Senara Manor, it makes sense, it sounds nice. I like it."

"Senara Manor it is then."

Jake then felt something unexplainable rush through his whole being. He felt an amazing compulsion to run across to the piano and dismantle the lower wooden casing. He grabbed one of the builder's abandoned screwdrivers and headed for the piano that had been such a vital inspiration for his return to success. Everyone followed, concerned that the recent findings must have freaked him out. Jake slowly removed the lower panel of the piano taking care not to damage the antique wood. Masses and masses of paper fell from the base of the piano now that it was exposed. Jake took a handful and quickly scanned their contents.

"Most of these seem to be letters of love sent in secret between Charles and Ruth. When Bleak wasn't around this would indeed have been an ideal hiding place. Jake then stumbled upon something even more intriguing. The paper had a series of staves and notes jotted on it.

"What is it?" asked Lucy noticing the euphoric expression on Jake's face.

"I don't believe it. It's a partially completed music score composed by the hand of Charles Trott, it clearly shows his signature and name." Jake simply could not contain his excitement.

"Look Lucy. Look at this."

"I see the notes Jake, but I can't read music. Why are you so excited?"

"Because of this phrase of notes here," said Jake pointing at the paper. "Look at this bunch of notes, can you see how the pattern keeps repeating through the piece?"

"Yeah, I can see that, but the score isn't complete, is it? It looks a bit short."

"It clearly isn't finished Babe, but that repeating phrase is the chorus to "Love Lives Forever.""

"What!" Said Lucy. "That's impossible!"

"It all makes sense now Lucy. This piano inspired me to finish the ultimate love song. Charles finished his song for Lucy from the grave. Somehow, someway he did it through this piano…. and through me."

Suddenly a new voice spoke. "It sounds as though you don't need my help after all Sherlock."

"Nanette. Hi, how are you? We've made quite a discovery."

"So I see."

The jigsaw was complete. A cloud formation altered in the sky above Senara Manor that revealed a strong beam of sunlight. For the first time in centuries, daylight reached into the forgotten room as it traded places with a hoard of bricked up secrets. Jake and Lucy hugged each other, safe in the knowledge that love really can live forever.

EPILOGUE

There was a standing ovation and robust hand-clapping as Jake gladly accepted the award for "Lifetime Achievement and Services to Music" even though he intended his career to have plenty of time to run yet. True, he had slowed down in his output of work these days, but then again he had already achieved so much. And besides, he was now a grandfather!

In the years that followed the success of "Love Lives Forever" and *The Road to St Ives* album, both worldwide platinum selling masterpieces, Jake had picked up countless music awards, including both at the Grammys and the Brits. His impressive record-breaking achievements had included both Best British Male Artist and Best International Male Artist, and every time that he had released an album or chart single more often than not he would scoop the awards that were created for these accolades. Sometimes he would also win the award for best music video too.

The "Best Male" awards had amazingly all been won in consecutive years, proving that no matter what new talent came along, Jake could not be dethroned from his undisputed status as the greatest achieving British Solo

Music Artist of all time. The consistency of his achievements had been phenomenal. His solo career had indeed surpassed anything that he had achieved with Blossom of Eden, no mean feat, as the band had inevitably only ever been outshone by the achievements of The Beatles.

Jake had even been inducted into the prestigious Rock and Roll Hall of Fame, recognised as a credible performing artist and for his extraordinary achievements in songwriting.

He could have been Sir Jake Zennor but he had respectfully declined the knighthood for reasons he said he would always keep private, but many suspected it didn't align to his wish to just be one of the ordinary people. Bowie had made the same decision years earlier. Jake's decision had no negative impact on his ongoing success.

Jake had progressed into writing songs for other artists and had even produced highly acclaimed film scores and penned a couple of musicals that had literally enabled his name to be seen up in lights on Broadway and London's West End. He viewed being asked to provide a song for a James Bond film as one of the pinnacles of his career. Jake also enjoyed being involved in a series of charity work and had remained a patron and campaigner of CAVES.

But to Jake his greatest achievement in life had been his family. He had remained happily married to Lucy, who herself was now a successful novelist having shifted her literary skills away from the world of journalism. She too had achieved many awards for her work, successfully being able to juggle her valued family life with her creativity, although she had waited until the twin girls, Ruth and Charlie, were out of nappies before embarking on her *new* literary career. In addition to the twins, Jake and Lucy had produced another two children making four in total. Pagan had inherited her mother's natural blond hair and greatly resembled her, whereas Elton, named after the Derbyshire village near Matlock and not the piano playing rock star, was the spitting image of Jake. It was Pagan who had so far produced the only grandchild, a boy named Jake after his famous grandfather. Jake and Lucy both doted on him.

On the night that he had witnessed the spirit of the criminal Billy Chubb hanging from the tree, Nanette had suggested that Jake may have been developing his inner eye for connecting with the supernatural, but he never did see a ghost again. Nanette suggested that this could be because his mind was in such a content state now, with his settled family life and musical achievements that his mind had no wish to develop further into this field. The demons of guilt and grief that had once tortured Jake's mind had quite rightly subsided into occasional flickers of cherished memories.

Jake and Lucy seldom spoke about the ghostly encounters that they had once experienced and the grim yet productive findings of the two skeletons and its journal in the bricked-up room. After all, it was only Jake, Elton and the twins that ever played on the piano these days, it never plays on its own anymore and Senara Manor is a happy family home to the Zennor dynasty, never occurring any supernatural activity again since the day that the secret wall had been knocked down.

There had never been a need to tell the children. Lucy had even omitted to include the experience in an acclaimed biography that she had penned about Jake. This part of *their* story would have undoubtedly reaped in financial rewards and various spin-offs such as film rights, but the protection of the family was to them far more important. In light of everything that had happened, Jake and Lucy still believed that some things were best kept secret.

Jake and Lucy ensured that the remains of Ruth and Charles had received a proper dignified funeral even if it did come centuries after their tragic death. They were buried together in a plot in the village graveyard so that they could finally rest in peace together having suffered death together in their quest for love and happiness.

Father Irwin had kindly agreed to conduct the service and Jake had gladly paid for the expenses of the funeral and headstone. Lucy ensured that fresh flowers were always to be placed upon the grave.

Jake had always felt grateful and privileged that he had been *chosen* to complete the composition of "Love Lives Forever" and was satisfied that he was able to release the tragic clandestine of Charles and Ruth so that they could finally rest in peace. He guessed that the scream captured on the recording of the track most likely belonged to Ruth and if that were true she had remarkably managed to secure her voice onto a multi-selling record centuries later, providing a unique dynamic to an already great song. Jake's only regret was that Joshua Bleak had literally got away with murder all those years ago, but then again he surely must have died a lonely and unhappy man. One thing was for sure, he could never have grown old with Ruth. Jake found comfort in his own belief, based on his spiritual journey since his return to the Peak District, that Joshua Bleak was indeed burning in the fires of hell for all eternity.

Of all his musical achievements, it was "Love Lives Forever," that had undoubtedly produced the most success. Jake had won the prestigious Ivor Novello songwriting award for the composition and in any musical poll it was always doing battle with John Lennon's "Imagine" and Queen's "Bohemian Rhapsody".

On accepting this latest award for "Lifetime Achievement and Services to Music" Jake felt compelled to share with the audience how much he valued this song and how it was responsible for kick-starting his career again following the split of Blossom of Eden. As he spoke, every now and then he would run his fingers through his grey mane and his infectious smile melted most female hearts before him even though the wrinkles around the eyes were a little more obvious these days. The song had set the path for Jake's place in musical history to become secure and he spoke fondly of the song that had been "good to him".

Following his speech, the audience were once again moved to a standing ovation to congratulate the evergreen Jake Zennor for his extraordinary achievements.

It was now understood by all, first came Elvis, then The Beatles and then Jake Zennor.

As the crowd whistled and cheered one individual clapped slowly with a wry smile of acceptance. He hadn't engaged in conversation with anyone all night and his unkempt hair was matted and hung down over his face, concealing his features from any would-be prying eyes.

For once the stranger was gracious in defeat, for even he had to admire Jake's remarkable success and recognise that in the end, the man before him who was adored by millions, had simply not needed his help.

For Jake Zennor had achieved all of this without selling his soul.

AUTHOR'S NOTE

I've always considered the Peak District to be a very special place. It has a magnetic quality and I often feel drawn to the area.

I first discovered its beauty as a young boy when I was taken to the lush green hills of Dovedale. Countless trips to places like Ashbourne, Cromford and Matlock followed over the years and we've holidayed in Bonsall, Carsington, Holymoorside and Monyash. At the time of writing, the most recent trip to Bonsall was a pre-Christmas break in December 2015 and I was reminded just how gorgeous this village is with its inviting pubs and haphazard yet inspiring cottages. It's a delight to walk up and down its unpaved roads and the village always seems so peaceful– except perhaps in The Barley Mow of course where satisfied folk pack into the single rectangular room for its warm welcome, entertainment, ale and good food. Our first trip to Bonsall, in the late 90s actually while Jake Zennor's solo career was gaining speed, still survives on videotape where a very young Paige (who turns 21 this year) can be heard referring to a picture of a Flutterby! Possibly a more accurate description for the creature than the traditional word of Butterfly?

A weekend with a few of my mates in 2010 found us staying in the Hostel in Castleton. We climbed Mam Tor on a blistering hot day before supping at each and every pub between Edale and the return journey on foot to Castleton. The ale was pure nectar. It was also one of the great lad's trips I had taken with Brian, one of two friends I sadly lost this year and who this book is dedicated to. RIP.

And why did I write this book? I actually began to write this novel under the working title of *Divine Inspiration* in the late 90s, therefore before *Beneath the Floodlights* and while I was still active in the music industry. Entity Fair, the band I was in at that time had not long recorded their one and only demo at a studio in Cheltenham (Damo the guitarist was at Uni there). The singer Scott, to this day, is still my loyal companion for going to Molineux and frequenting the pubs of Wolverhampton before and after the matches we attend.

So, I loved music and didn't want to detach myself from that part of my existence as I moved into my augmentation of storytelling from songs to novels, hence the creation of Jake Zennor and the story that you've just read. It also made sense to set it in the Peak District, the area I love so much, especially as at the time of initial scribing I was hooked on the TV series Peak Practice, just one of my guilty pleasures. Peak Practice had me dragging the family to Crich, the village where it was largely filmed trying to spot locations that had appeared in the series. *Things They'll Never See* may well be the one and only book I set outside of Birmingham, but one thing I've learned over the years is to never say never!

For some reason, I never quite felt pleased enough with the story to have it published and it obviously took a back seat as my two other books found their way into print. But now after reworking the book, the launch of the ghost story feels right and I hope you agree. The injection of the music of the day was only written on the latest rework some 20 years later, so although much of what is in the book is written within a live 1990s timeframe, I've had the benefit of adding a touch of nostalgia for both me and for you.

I've already mentioned that Paige turns 21 this year, Heather my youngest daughter 16 and Mrs T 50. We also celebrate 21 years of marriage (no it wasn't a shotgun wedding before you ask). However, as mentioned I also attended the funerals of two of my best buddies.

So, I am releasing *Things They'll Never See* within a very personal year for me.

I hope you enjoyed reading *Things They'll Never See* as much as I enjoyed writing it. I'll be connecting with you soon, thanks as always for your support.

Martin Tracey
Birmingham
August 2016

ABOUT THE AUTHOR

Martin Tracey is an author who likes to push the boundaries of reality. He lives in Birmingham and is happily married with 2 daughters.

87740361R00181

Made in the USA
Columbia, SC
26 January 2018